Melinda Hammond lives in a farmhouse on the edge of the Pennines. Her interests include theatre and music, and supporting her son's go-kart racing team — although she feels obliged to stay at home and keep the log fire burning during the winter months.

DANCE FOR A DIAMOND

It's 1815, and Antonia Venn describes
herself as a very average sort of female: a
poor little dab of a girl, and certainly
nothing to win the heart of a man of
fortune or fashion. So in a bid for
independence, and at a time when the
waltz was born, she decides to open a
dancing school in Bath, despite the
misgivings of her family. And it is here that
she takes on the beautiful Isabella
Burstock as a pupil. However, this
decision puts Antonia on a collision course
with the young heiress's autocratic
brother . . .

Books by Melinda Hammond
Published by The House of Ulverscroft:

SUMMER CHARADE
FORTUNE'S LADY
AUTUMN BRIDE
THE HIGHCLOUGH LADY
A LADY AT MIDNIGHT

MELINDA HAMMOND

DANCE FOR A DIAMOND

Complete and Unabridged

ULVERSCROFT
Leicester

First published in Great Britain in 2005 by
Robert Hale Limited
London

First Large Print Edition
published 2007
by arrangement with
Robert Hale Limited
London

British Library CIP Data

Hammond, Melinda
    Dance for a diamond.—Large print ed.—
Ulverscroft large print series: historical romance
1. Love stories
2. Large type books
I. Title
823.9′14 [F]

ISBN 978–1–84617–591–6

Published by
F. A. Thorpe (Publishing)
Anstey, Leicestershire
Set by Words & Graphics Ltd.
Anstey, Leicestershire
Printed and bound in Great Britain by
T. J. International Ltd., Padstow, Cornwall

This book is printed on acid-free paper

Author's Note

Out of a Europe torn by the Napoleonic Wars came one of the most popular dances of all time, the waltz. The early form of this dance began with a slow movement *la marche*, followed by the quicker *Santeuse* and ending with the *Jetté*, an energetic third movement. *Dance for a Diamond* follows this form.

First movement:
La Marche

Spring 1814

Prologue

It was to be the most glittering occasion of the year: Lord and Lady Bressingham's ball to celebrate the betrothal of their daughter, Lady Pamela to Viscount Moran. Not even the French king's forthcoming visit to London and the planned Peace Celebrations could detract from the dress ball that my lady envisaged. No invitation had been refused and Lady Bressingham could even report to the earl that the Prince Regent had promised to look in later in the evening. Alas for my lady's sanguine hopes — the Bressingham betrothal ball would indeed become the most talked of event of the year, but not in the way she wished.

At the impressive entrance to Bressingham Hall, the last of the carriages had rolled away and the bewigged and powdered footmen were moving indoors when a travelling carriage bowled towards the house, its dusty sides and sweating horses indicating that it had travelled some distance. The footmen turned wearily to greet the newcomer: the carriage drew up at the steps of the great house, the horses stamping and pawing the ground. A lackey ran to let down the steps of the coach and a tall gentleman descended from the carriage with some difficulty, leaning heavily upon his cane. The footmen looked at each other in perplexity as they recognized the gentleman now limping painfully up the steps. He wore the usual evening attire with a silk evening cloak thrown over his shoulders, but his gaunt features and grim demeanour did not sit well with the sumptuous surroundings. As he entered there was consternation amongst the servants: a quiet murmuring that echoed around the hall. With some relief they observed the earl's youngest son appear, making his way to the ballroom. As the young man crossed the landing he glanced idly at the staircase and stopped, staring at the figure slowly climbing the steps.

'What the devil — Oakford!' Lord Henry Bressingham ran down the steps until he drew level with the gentleman. He laid a hand on his shoulder, saying quietly, 'This is no place for you, my friend.'

The stranger paused, plucking a yellow rosebud from one of the garlands that decorated the staircase and tucking it into his buttonhole.

'What, when the flower of England is gathered here? No, no, I must pay my respects to the *Honourable* Pamela.'

'Let me help you — '

'The outstretched hand was shrugged off.

'Thank you, Harry. I can manage quite well alone.'

Lord Henry stepped back, shaking his head, then turned to walk slowly up the steps beside the black-browed figure.

'Laurence,' he said gently, 'pray, think what you are about! Pamela will be as mad as fire to see you here, damme if she won't! Come with me, my friend. I'll find us a good bottle of cognac to share . . . '

The dark eyes swept over him, amused contempt in their depths.

'Damn your cognac, Harry,' he swore softly.

With a shrug, the young lord continued in silence beside the latecomer, who finally struggled to the top of the stairs. His face was taut with pain, accentuating the white scar running along his jaw. He paused, breathing heavily, then, with a slow, determined step, he made his way to the ballroom.

★ ★ ★

The orchestra was playing the minuet at a lively pace, and the betrothed pair had been joined now by several other couples while the remaining guests stood around the edges of the room, watching the dancers and talking idly. With the entrance of Lord Henry and his companion a sudden hush fell over the guests. The countess, seeing who had entered, began to fan herself vigorously and looked round in vain for her husband, but the earl had taken himself off to the card-room, considering he had fulfilled his obligation by greeting their guests upon arrival.

The stranger stopped for a moment, glancing around him, then moved directly towards Lady Pamela and the viscount in the centre of the room, his stick thudding a slow beat on the wooden floor. The dancers became aware that something was amiss and stopped, dispersing into the crowd. Lady Pamela, enjoying the dance, was laughing at some remark of her partner's when her green eyes alighted on the dark figure approaching her. With a small shriek she stopped dancing, her hands flying to her blanched cheeks.

The music trailed away as one by one the musicians realized that a drama was unfolding before them. In the ensuing silence the only sound was the thud of the stick and the drag of the dark gentleman's step as he moved inexorably across the floor. Lord Moran stood silently beside his lady, a slight frown creasing his brow.

'Well, Oakford? What do you want here?'

The newcomer ignored him, his attention fixed upon the lady. His black hair, damp with the effort it had cost him to make his way so far, had fallen across his brow and his dark eyes were fever-bright as they rested on her.

'Good evening, Pamela. I trust I am not too late to give you my felicitations?' Lady Pamela stared at him.

'You!' she whispered. 'I thought you were — I thought — '

'You thought I was on my deathbed? Or perhaps the reports were not quite so grim. Did they say that I had lost the use of my legs? I am sorry to disappoint you, my dear, but I am very much alive, if a little — incapacitated — at present.' He laughed bitterly. 'Your delight at my arrival is overwhelming.'

'We are naturally relieved to know that you are recovering so well,' put in the viscount. 'I am sure that, had Lady Bressingham known of it, you would have received an invitation for this evening — '

'Pretty words, sir, but spare me the pleasantries, I want none of them.'

'Then pray, sir, what *do* you want?'

Sir Laurence thrust his right hand inside his evening coat and there was a sudden hiss around the room. The ladies drew back and the gentlemen reached to their sides, although the fashion of wearing dress swords was long passed.

Lord Moran stepped forward slightly, as if to shield his lady with his substantial frame, but when Sir Laurence withdrew his hand it bore nothing more dangerous than a gold locket threaded on a worn velvet ribbon. He tossed it at the viscount, who caught it upon his chest.

'My betrothal gift to you, Moran. *I* have no more use for it.' Sir Laurence shifted his hard gaze to the Lady Pamela, standing mute and pale before him. 'That locket with its portrait of you gave me the will to live during those black days in the Peninsula, madam.' His voice softened. 'Why did you not tell me, Pamela? You could have written. Why leave me to learn of this through a damned notice in the *Gazette*?'

Lord Henry, standing silently beside Sir Laurence, touched his arm. 'That's enough, my friend. Remember where you are.'

Lord Moran thrust out his chin belligerently.

'Your conduct is unacceptable here, sir. If it were not for your condition, I would have no hesitation in calling you to book for this outrage.'

'If it were not for my *condition*, as you call

it, *I* should be standing in your place now!'

'Do not think it,' put in Lady Pamela, two spots of high colour flaming her cheeks. 'What, with the Oakford estates mortgaged to the hilt?' She laughed shrilly. 'How can you compare that with Moran's vast wealth? No, sir, I would *never* consider your suit!'

Lady Bressingham's fan moved even faster: that Pamela should mention anything so vulgar as money! A tense silence hung over the ballroom; all eyes were on the late-comer, his face now ashen as Lady Pamela's words hit home. At length he spoke, his words clipped, as though each one cost him an effort.

'Thank you — you have told me all I need to know. I wish you joy of her, Moran. Oh don't look so worried, Harry, I am leaving — you won't have to throw me out.'

He turned to Lady Pamela and held up his left hand to display the diamond ring on his little finger. 'This was for you, madam — a small fortune that could have been put to better use on my estates.'

He moved his hand so that the light glinted and flashed on the large solitaire. Lady Pamela's cat-like eyes glowed with desire; a small sigh escaped her lips and involuntarily she reached out, but the gentleman snatched his hand away with a savage laugh. 'Never again will I dance to any woman's tune!'

He turned to leave, then stopped and looked back at the viscount. 'If I were you I would commission a fresh portrait for that locket, Moran. One that shows the lady's true colours.'

Lord Moran's fleshy face reddened and he stepped forward, only to be held back by Lady Pamela, who threw herself upon his chest to restrain him. A murmur ran around the room but no one moved as Sir Laurence made his way slowly out of the room. By the time he was descending the stairs, the orchestra was striking up again and he made his way alone out into the night.

★ ★ ★

Shortly after midnight the dusty travelling carriage pulled into a quiet street off St James's Square and set down its occupant at a discreet door, where a burly footman allowed the gentleman to enter after only the briefest hesitation. Relinquishing his hat and cloak to a liveried servant, Sir Laurence limped slowly upstairs to the grand salon.

Candles glowed richly against the red and gold furnishings and a gentle hum of conversation filled the room. Gorgeously dressed women, their skins painted white, were gathered in small groups with the few gentlemen already present. Upon the new-comer's entrance, one of the women came forward to greet him. She had a majestic figure and was some years older than her companions, with a pair of lively dark eyes that swept over him, assessing him in a moment.

'Sir Laurence Oakford: welcome to my humble house.'

He raised his brows. 'You know me?'

'But of course.' She smiled slightly. 'It is my business to know everyone in Town, sir, especially gentlemen like yourself, who can be relied upon to be generous.'

She beckoned to a waiter to approach and Sir Laurence accepted a glass of champagne. Madame lifted her own glass to return his sardonic salute. She watched him over the rim of her glass, noting the cold glitter of his black eyes, the tightened jaw-line and suppressed anger.

'You are looking for a little — entertain-ment, sir? Something to help you forget the world for a short while?'

'Something of that nature.'

She moved closer, until he could smell the cloying perfume, see the grains of white powder caked on her breast.

'Only tell me your pleasure, sir. I have a

selection of beauties for you to choose from, all practised in the art of pleasing . . . mayhap your taste runs to the oriental . . . ' With a small grimace the gentleman stepped back, shaking his head. He rubbed his eyes.

'No — that is — I'm not at all sure why I came here — '

'Oh don't go!' She spoke swiftly, laying a white hand upon his arm. 'Pray, sir, come and sit down for a few moments, at least take another glass of wine.' She led him through a curtained archway into another, smaller salon where someone was playing a lively tune on the pianoforte and a number of females in thin muslin gowns danced to the music. She guided him to a chair. 'There, sir, is that not a pretty picture? Why not rest a while and watch their disport. No one will disturb you and it is possible one of my girls might take your fancy . . . ' She drifted away, leaving the gentleman to sip his champagne and watch the figures dancing and laughing in the candlelight. For the most part they ignored his presence, although occasionally one or other of them would look towards him. One figure, he noticed, was intent only upon the dance — a slender form in a pale gown the colour of spring leaves. She moved gracefully in time to the music, her feet flying effortlessly over the floor as she swirled and weaved amongst the other dancers. He found himself relaxing as he watched her, the images and music calming him. When Madame looked into the room some time later he was leaning back in his chair, watching the dancers with half-closed eyes. He beckoned to her.

'Madame — that one, the girl in the green muslin. She moves so much better than the others.'

'Ah, little Ann. She is one of my newest girls, Sir Laurence. A virgin, fresh as a country rose — perhaps you would like to know her better?'

A mood of recklessness had overtaken him. Sir Laurence tossed off the rest of the wine from his glass and nodded. At a word from Madame the dancers parted, giggling and whispering as the figure in the pale-green figured muslin stepped forward. She stopped at the table, her gaze flickering nervously over the gentleman before resting upon the older woman, who smiled benignly.

'This gentleman would like to sup with you, my dear. Show him into the blue chamber, everything is ready.'

The green figure curtsied, keeping her eyes lowered.

'As you wish, Madame.' Her voice was low and surprisingly cultured.

Sir Laurence rose and followed her through a narrow corridor and into a small room. It was decorated in blue and gold, with heavy brocade curtains drawn across the window. A cheerful fire enhanced the candlelight and to one side of the fireplace was a velvet-covered daybed scattered with cushions, a silk wrap thrown carelessly over the back. A cold collation was set out on a side table and in a small alcove stood a washstand and several fresh white towels. Madame, he mused cynically, had thought of everything.

'A glass of wine, sir?' The quiet voice brought his attention back to his companion. He could see now that she was older than he had first thought. Her girlish figure and air of fragility were deceptive.

'Come here.'

She stepped towards him and he cupped her face with his hands. He could feel the tension in her. The grey eyes raised to his were dark with apprehension. With a sudden frown he dragged his thumb across her lips, smearing the carmine on to her cheek where it rested like blood in an open wound. He released her and pointed to the washstand.

He said harshly, 'Go and wash your face.'

Silently she obeyed him, and when she next turned towards him the thick mask of paint

14

had been removed to reveal a flawless ivory skin.

'That's better. You have a perfect complexion — you have no need to hide it.'

'It is Madame's rule.'

He had removed his coat and thrown it over a side chair and he stood before her now, the white satin waistcoat unbuttoned to reveal the snow-white lace of his shirt. He pulled her towards him and began to unfasten the tiny pearl buttons that ran down the front of her gown. He felt a frisson of pleasure as his fingers brushed the firm swell of her breast.

'You are shaking. Do I frighten you?'

'It . . . it is the first time I have ever . . . done this, sir.'

He slipped the gown from her shoulders. The flimsy muslin sank silently to the floor and she stood before him uncomfortably, wearing only her shift.

'Faith — was Madame telling the truth? Are you indeed a virgin?' She did not answer but blushed rosily. He put his hands on her bare shoulders. 'Look at me — *look at me!*' He could feel her trembling beneath his fingers but the grey eyes returned his gaze without flinching. With a sigh he released her and threw himself on to the daybed. 'I'm damnably drunk, but it has never been my policy to seduce innocent young maidens, and unless you are a superlative actress, that is exactly what you are.'

She stared at him anxiously.

'I'm . . . I am sorry, sir — I . . . '

He picked up the silk wrap and tossed it to her.

'Here, put that on, you will feel more comfortable. Then you may pour me some wine — and bring a glass for yourself. You can talk to me.'

'What — what do you wish me to tell you?' She handed him a glass.

'To begin with, what you are doing here! Sit down — here, beside me. I promise I won't bite you.'

She perched herself on the very edge of the daybed and sipped at her wine.

'I — I came to London to take up a post as a dancing teacher — '

'A teacher, you?' he interrupted her, frowning. 'What is your birth?'

'Better than that of my late employer, sir,' she answered bitterly. 'I am gently born, but — circumstances made it necessary for me to earn my living and I answered an advertisement. I was engaged to teach music and dancing to the daughters of — of a merchant in Cheapside. It should have been a very good post, the salary was considerable and I hoped to save a little each month . . . '

'So what happened?'

'I thought everything was going so well, the children liked me, but . . . then . . . the eldest son came home from abroad.'

'Ah — I see.'

'Sir?'

'The young man fell in love with you.'

'Love did not enter into it.'

'He seduced you.'

'He tried to do so, certainly.' She looked up, her chin tilted challengingly towards him. 'I — I know how a man's baser instincts can overcome him, sir — *that* I could forgive — but when . . . when he realized I was not to be persuaded, he told his mama that I had . . . had seduced *him*.' She looked away, her fingers clenching around the stem of her glass until the knuckles showed white. 'It was a wicked lie, but of course they would not believe me. There was no question of being paid the three months' salary that was owing to me. I was turned out of the house immediately with scarcely time to pack a bag. How can men be so base?'

He was watching her from half-closed eyes.

'Do not think it is only *my* sex that inflicts such pain, child.'

She looked at him, frowning at the bitterness in his voice.

17

'If you have been wronged, sir, I am sorry for it.'

He shrugged. 'So too am I. When did you come to this house?'

'Last night. I was thrown on to the streets yesterday morning and my attempts to find honest employment came to nothing. I had no references, no money — '

'Having seen you dance, perhaps you should try the Haymarket.'

'I did — even though I know the dancers there are not quite respectable I made enquiries, but the manager is away. They said to come back in a week. I thought then I might find work as a kitchen maid until I could earn enough money to leave London.' She paused, frowning, 'No one would listen. The women told me to go away and the men . . . ' She shuddered. 'Just when I thought I would be forced to shelter in some doorway for the night, Madame chanced by.'

'And she brought you here.'

'Yes.'

'Very affecting.'

'You do not believe me.'

'Should I do so?'

She shrugged. 'It is the truth, but it makes very little difference to my situation.'

'My dear girl, don't you realize that you are ruined now just as surely as if you had given in to your seducer?'

She hung her head, saying in a very small voice, 'I was too frightened to remain on the street.'

'Oh my God.' He put his hand to his head. 'I have heard this tale a hundred times — heaven knows why I should choose to believe *you*. Child, have you no relatives who could take you in?'

'There is an aunt, near Marlborough, but until I have saved enough for the fare I will not write to her — I would not have her discover my situation here.'

'No, I can understand that.' He sat up. 'Are you hungry?'

'No.'

'Well I am, and we should not let Madame's hospitality go to waste. Come, sit with me.' He limped across to the table and pulled out a chair for her. 'Come along. Why do you stare?'

'Your leg, sir, is it causing you pain?' She flushed under his glowering look. 'I am sorry. It is not for me to question you.' She moved to the table and sat down. 'You have been very kind, sir, but I think you have problems of your own.'

He gave a bark of mirthless laughter and refilled his glass.

'Perhaps you would like me to leave — I-I

could send in one of the others . . . '

'No! No, I want no other company. God knows why I came here at all — only that I did not want to go home yet.' He helped himself to a selection of cold meats and insisted that she should eat. 'What are you going to do?'

She put a small piece of chicken on her plate.

'What do you mean, sir?'

'What plans have you?'

'For the moment, none.'

'Because you have no money.'

'Correct.'

'And you think this way you will earn some?'

'I hope to do so.' She risked a smile and a quick glance at him. 'Although I do not seem to be making a very good start.'

He laughed. 'Perhaps you have other talents.'

She smiled suddenly, a full, radiant smile that lit up her face.

'Yes, I dance! My dream is to set up my own dancing school, then I need be dependent upon no man.' She looked at him. 'You think it is a foolish idea?'

'Not at all,' he said politely. 'But what about marriage?'

'What of it?'

'I thought it was every young woman's ambition. I have a sister who seems to think of nothing else.'

She pushed away her plate. 'For me it is out of the question. You said yourself, sir, that I am ruined.'

She cut off a piece of cheese and nibbled at it, watching him. The glow of the candles softened the harsh contours of his face but did not disguise the lines of strain about the eyes. She noticed for the first time the thin scar along his jaw. A rapier, perhaps, or sword . . .

'Well, ma'am?'

His cold tone did not disconcert her.

'I wonder how you came by the scar on your face. The Peninsula, perhaps? You are a soldier?'

He ran a finger along the mark.

'Yes. A French sword. But its owner was not so fortunate. I killed him.'

She shuddered slightly. 'I am sure it was necessary.'

'Unfortunately, war makes such things necessary.'

'But the war is over. Bonaparte is safe confined on Elba and that is all behind you now.'

'Aye. Though with this damned leg wound I could not fight as I would!'

21

'You are alive, sir. You must be thankful for that.'

'Ha! I wish to God they had left me to die at Burgos.'

She laid down her knife, shaking her head at him.

'Shame on you, sir. How dare you say so? You think yourself ill-used because you have been wounded, and that not even sufficient injury to call you 'cripple'! Yet there are many widows in this country who would be glad to see their men with such slight disfigurement — aye, and many orphans, too, who will no longer see their papas!' She stopped, aware that he was scowling. She said stiffly, 'I beg your pardon sir — I speak out of turn.'

'Since I arrived back in England no one has dared speak thus to me.'

'Perhaps they do not wish to add to your pain.'

'Instead they have allowed me to wallow in self-pity. Yet you, a stranger — ' He threw back his head, listening to the voices from the passage, a man's deep voice was followed by a shriek of laughter. Abruptly he stood up and limped across to the bell-pull. Its summons was answered almost immediately by a liveried servant. 'Order my carriage.'

She looked up. 'You are going?'

'Yes — and so too are you. Get dressed, and fetch your things. We are leaving here.' His brows snapped together as he observed the look in her eyes. 'Good God, *I* have no designs on you! I will give you your fare and set you on the night mail to Bath — how will that suit you?'

'You would do that, for me? But — but why? When I have failed so miserably to . . . to . . . '

He smiled grimly.

'*Because* you have failed so miserably! Now quickly, we must make haste if you are to catch the mail.'

Ten minutes later, Sir Laurence walked through the hall with the young lady on his arm. She was wearing a sober brown pelisse and a plain, high-poke bonnet covered her soft brown curls, while in one hand she clutched a small cloth bag. Madame opened her eyes very wide at the sight of the couple and looked a question at the gentleman, who shook his head at her.

'I regret, madam, that I feel you will never succeed with this young person. She has no looks, no figure and nothing to fix the attention of any man.' He drew out a small leather purse, which he handed to the astonished woman. 'She also has friends who could make life very difficult for you. I think you would be advised to forget that she was ever here.'

He swept the young woman out of the house and into the waiting carriage before the startled dame could find her voice.

'Oh dear. Will she be very angry, do you think?'

'Not when she has counted the guineas in that purse. Do you care?'

'Not for Madame, but — is it true?' she asked in a small voice.

'What?'

'That I am so . . . unattractive.'

He laughed and there was genuine amusement in his voice as he answered her.

'Of course not — you are well enough, but it would not do to tell Madame so.' He took the yellow rosebud from his coat and held it out to her. 'With a little polish and a more becoming dress you would be quite taking. Satisfied?'

She nodded, smiling faintly and leaned back with a sigh of contentment against the luxurious padded seat. The carriage bowled through the dark streets, past shadowy buildings with the occasional lighted window until the pace slowed and they swung into the yard of a busy coaching inn. The gentleman leaned out of the window and directed a series of questions to one of the ostlers, who tugged at his forelock and offered the information that yonder was the Bath Mail and it would be setting off within the hour. Bidding his companion remain in the carriage, Sir Laurence climbed out and went across to speak to the driver. A few minutes later he returned, holding out his hand for her to alight.

'I have purchased your ticket to Bath.' He pressed more coins into her hand as he led her across to the mail-coach. 'This should be enough to hire you a gig or some such thing to get you to your relatives, with a little extra for refreshment on the journey. You should be safe at home with them by tomorrow night.'

'Thank you, sir.' She dropped the coins into her reticule. 'If you will give me your direction I will ensure you are repaid.'

His finger pressed against her lips.

'I want no thanks for this. Tomorrow I fear I shall have the very devil of a headache and will doubtless remember nothing, so you had best forget it, too.'

Her hands clasped his and she stared up at him, as if trying to memorize every feature.

'I shall *never* forget you. I had prayed that some sort of angel would rescue me.'

He bent his head to kiss her, holding her to him. She did not resist and for a brief moment he considered putting her back into his carriage and taking her with him. He might make her his mistress: after all it would be better than the situation in which he had found her. As the thoughts ran through his head he met the glance turned so trustingly upon him and he pushed her away.

'Get thee gone, child, before my good intentions desert me. Wait! Here, take this.' He drew the solitaire from his little finger and held it out to her.

'Oh — but — no sir. I could not!'

'Yes.' He placed it in her palm and wrapped her fingers about it. 'It was purchased for a most unworthy recipient; if you were to throw it in the river it would still be put to better use than the one I had intended.'

She put her hand up to stroke his cheek, running her finger along the fine scar on his jaw.

'She has hurt you very much, I think, sir.'

'Aye. I've learned a hard lesson, and I won't make the same error again. Now go, child. Take your seat.'

He bundled her almost roughly into the mail-coach and from the small window she watched as he limped across the lighted yard towards his waiting carriage, the evening cloak flapping about his shoulders like the wings of some dark angel.

Second movement: Sauteuse

January–May 1815

1

' . . . And this, madam, is the withdrawing room.' The land agent ushered the two ladies into the apartment. 'You can see that it is excellently proportioned and if one throws back the connecting doors,' he said, suiting the action to the words, 'there is space enough for — oh, thirty couples to stand up together.'

'Nearer twenty, surely,' murmured the younger of the two ladies, a good-natured smile robbing her words of offence.

'It is a fine opportunity, madam,' continued the agent. 'Queen Square is perhaps not quite so popular these days, but such a property is rarely available at so advantageous a rent, especially fully furnished *and* on the north side. In this instance, you see, the owner is an elderly gentleman who is now wholly confined to his country estate.'

'And he is willing to allow a twelve-month lease on the house?'

'Indeed he is, miss. Once the papers are signed the property could be yours within the month.'

The young lady laughed and executed a

neat little dance step.

'It is perfect for my needs. I shall take it!'

The land agent bowed, his brows raised in faint surprise as he glanced at the young lady's companion.

'Oh, it is no good looking at me, young man!' she declared, in a voice of long-suffering. 'Miss Venn is mistress of her own fortune, spend it how she will. Whatever I may say on the matter is of no consequence!'

'But you will surely agree, Aunt, that it is ideal.'

'Yes, I am sure it is, my dear, but . . . ' She broke off, fluttering her hands nervously.

She looked at the agent. 'Perhaps, Mr Pound, you would be so good as to give me a few moments alone with my niece . . . '

The agent bowed again and retired, leaving the two ladies facing each other. Mrs Haseley's kindly face wore a look of acute anxiety as she gazed at her niece. Miss Antonia Venn was in no way disconcerted, but returned the look steadily, a slight, mischievous smile pulling at the corners of her mouth.

'I am truly sorry if you do not like it, Aunt,' she said, in a low, musical voice, 'but I have quite made up my mind.'

'I know it and I am quite *wretched*!' cried

Mrs Haseley, pulling out her handkerchief to dab at her eyes. 'If only I had not come with you!'

'That would have made no difference, dearest.'

'No!' replied the aggrieved matron. 'I have no doubt you would have come house-hunting alone — and how would *that* have looked!' Mrs Haseley stared resentfully at her niece. 'You were always a difficult child, Antonia. Oh, not disobedient or ill-mannered, but you were always headstrong and quietly determined to go your own way! When your father sent you to Miss Rosehill's Seminary, I thought it might do you some good, but — '

'And it *did*, Aunt. It gave me every accomplishment — which is why I am now able to embark upon this course of action.'

'One thing it did *not* give you is sense, and if your father were alive now — '

'If Papa was alive, I am sure he would be the first to say that I should make my own way in the world, and not be a burden to you or my Uncle Haseley.'

'But you are not a burden, my love. We had thought that your brief spell in London had cured you of this taste for independence. Indeed, if it had not been for that unexpected legacy from your mama I believe you would even now be reconciled to living quietly at home with us.'

'I know, my dear aunt, but such a windfall could not be ignored — and Papa would certainly approve of this, I know.'

'Yes, you are probably right,' admitted Mrs Haseley bitterly, 'for if ever there was a man with shatter-brained notions it was your father — but we should not speak ill of the dead,' she finished, realizing this was not helping her cause.

'Quite right, ma'am.'

Mrs Haseley regarded her imploringly. 'Pray, Antonia, only consider — '

'Dearest Aunt, I *have* considered.'

'Yes, but — a dancing school!'

Antonia laughed. 'Really, Aunt, you make it sound most improper, but I assure you, it will be a very *select* dancing school.'

'And who will be your pupils, pray?'

'That I do not know, yet — I suppose I must place an advertisement.'

'What? My dear child it is not to be thought of. Why, it is most likely that you will be approached by — by common traders!'

'And if I am? If they wish their daughters to learn the finer points of dance and deportment, why should they not come to me? There are great fortunes to be had in trade, I believe.' She saw her aunt's dismayed countenance and reached out to grasp her fluttering hands. 'No, I pray you, Aunt, do not distress yourself. Mine will be a most genteel establishment.' She put a temporary end to the discussion by recalling the agent, who agreed to draw up a lease immediately.

★   ★   ★

A little over a month after her first visit to Queen Square, Antonia took up residence in her new home and a chill February evening found her sitting before a cheerful fire in the small sitting-room, reading aloud to Mrs Haseley from the local news-sheet.

' . . .   Private lessons in dance and deportment, essential skills for every lady. Discreet tuition in social accomplishment by an experienced teacher.'

'But you are not experienced,' objected Mrs Haseley.

'I taught the younger girls at the academy, as well as my few months in London, so it is not completely false. It reads quite well, do you not agree? And I have written to several of the local seminaries, offering my services. I wonder, how soon do you think I might expect a reply?'

'Never, I hope.'

Antonia laughed. 'Oh, Aunt, pray do not be

so uncharitable. I have invested everything I have in this venture and it is very important to me.'

'Your uncle and I would prefer you to invest everything in a good sound marriage!'

'My poor aunt — I am a dreadful disappointment, am I not? But it was very good of you to come to Bath with me, I only hope my Uncle Haseley will not be too uncomfortable without you.'

'I could not let you come to Bath unprotected, and I will stay until that silly little woman turns up.'

'You mean Beatrice Chittering, ma'am,' said Antonia, her eyes dancing. 'I had a letter from her this very morning, promising to join me here just as soon as ever she can today; she even thought she might be here before the mail! Poor thing, from her letter she appears quite desperately grateful for my offer.'

'That I can well believe,' agreed her kind-hearted aunt. 'It must be very frightening to grow old with no family to support you and only meagre savings to live upon.'

'And yet you urged me to become a governess,' Antonia reminded her.

Mrs Haseley shook her head, setting her faded curls bouncing merrily.

'Only as an alternative to setting yourself

up here. You know you need not do either of these things.'

Before Antonia could reply, there was a knock on the door and an elderly butler entered to announce Miss Chittering's arrival. This was followed shortly by the entrance of the lady herself, a small figure of indeterminate age and colouring, dressed entirely in grey. She fluttered up to Antonia, her hands outstretched before her.

'Oh Antonia, my dear, dear child! You cannot know how good it is to see you again. Oh, and Mrs Haseley, good evening to you, ma'am. What a long time it is since we last met — it must be six years at least — no, eight. I remember it was when dear Antonia went off to school and she was sixteen then, was she not? Antonia, my love, did you receive my note? Oh good. I set out directly I had written it, you see, and was fortunate enough to find there was a coach within the hour to take me to Bristol. I am so sorry I could not give you a more accurate time for my arrival but you know how it is when one is obliged to travel on the common stage — at least you *won't* know it, my dear, and I hope you will never be reduced to such straits, because — but there, it is done and I am arrived safely.'

'Yes, yes, I can see that you are, Beatrice,

and you are very welcome.' Antonia tugged at the bell-rope. 'Your room is all ready for you so I will ask Mrs Widdecombe, my house-keeper, to show you upstairs so that you may put off your outdoor things and when you come down, you can tell us all about your journey.'

'Thank you, yes, you are so kind.' Miss Chittering fluttered again, her cheeks pink with pleasure. 'I am sure I don't know what I have done to deserve such kind treatment — '

'You have always been a most loyal friend to me,' Antonia interrupted her, as a maidservant opened the door, 'Ah, Jenny — pray ask Mrs Widdecombe to show Miss Chittering to her room and then perhaps you would bring in the tea tray.'

When Miss Chittering had finally left the room, Antonia and her aunt exchanged glances.

'My poor child, she will drive you distracted before the month is out!'

'I confess I had forgotten how much she rattles on, but she is such a kind-hearted soul and so loyal. I have no doubt we shall get along famously — and her experience with young people will be a great asset.'

'Well, I still cannot think that it will work. In fact,' uttered Mrs Haseley in dire accents, 'I am more convinced than ever that you have squandered your fortune!'

★ ★ ★

Antonia laid aside her pen and sat back with a sigh of satisfaction: even the April sun streaming into the little sitting-room echoed her happy mood. A scratching at the door heralded the arrival of Miss Chittering, who stood, hesitating, in the doorway.

'Antonia, dearest, do I disturb you? I have just come to ask if you have any commissions for me — we have no more pupils this afternoon and I thought I might take the opportunity to buy some lace to trim the bonnet I purchased last week; you know the one, my dear, the straw with the sage-green ties that we saw in Milsom Street. You may recall that I was not sure about it when I bought it, but now I have looked at it closely I know I cannot wear it without a little lace trim.'

Antonia rose.

'If you will give me just five minutes, Beatrice, I will come with you. I would like a little air before dinner. I have just reckoned my accounts for the past two months and I am pleased to say that business is better than I had hoped. The number of pupils increases steadily and although we may never make a fortune, I believe we shall soon be earning enough to pay our way.'

'My dear, I am so pleased for you. You have worked so hard these past few months to make this a success.'

'No more than you, Beatrice, my dear,' returned Antonia warmly. 'You play so well for my lessons and your kindness immediately sets the new pupils at their ease. I do not know where I would be without you.'

Miss Chittering turned quite pink with pleasure at these words and she proceeded to lose herself in a confusion of unfinished phrases until Antonia took pity on her, kissed her hot cheek and ran off to fetch her coat and bonnet.

They set out from Queen Square in the best of spirits and even Miss Chittering's constant chatter could not dampen Antonia's happy mood. She had long ago learned the secret of ignoring the older woman's continuous stream of inconsequential talk, allowing her mind to wander as it wished. Miss Chittering completed her errands but the warm sunshine persuaded them to extend their walk. They strolled on towards the Abbey, Antonia mentally composing her next letter to her aunt and uncle. She allowed herself a mischievous inward smile as she imagined her uncle's displeasure at the news of her success. It would suit him better, she knew, for the whole venture to fail. She would then be obliged to return to Wiltshire and admit she had been wrong. She could acquit him of any malice, but Antonia was well aware that her independent actions outraged his sense of propriety — indeed, if he had known how close she had come to disaster last spring, she would have found it very difficult to argue against him. Uncle Haseley was a stolid English country gentleman: he had disapproved of her father's reckless lifestyle, which was in stark contrast to his own placid existence, but while Antonia could not condone the actions of a parent that had left her reliant upon the charity of her relations, neither could she quite stifle the pang of envy for the independent life her father had known, free from the petty restrictions that now bounded his daughter.

★ ★ ★

When they returned to Queen Square they were met in the hall by the butler, who said, with a slight bow, 'You have a visitor, miss. A young lady. She has been waiting here for some time — I have shown her into the small sitting-room.'

'A visitor, Dawkin? Do we know her?'

He coughed, his countenance even more

wooden than usual.

'As to that I could not say, madam. She would not give her name and I did not recognize her — she is heavily veiled. However,' he added, by way of reassurance, 'her dress is that of a person of *very* comfortable means, and her manner is most ladylike.'

Antonia's eyes twinkled.

'A mystery! Come, Beatrice, let us immediately make the acquaintance of our visitor.'

She led the way into the small sitting-room where a young lady in a fine sprig muslin gown was sitting by the window. She had put off her wide-brimmed bonnet and veil and was idly flicking through the pages of a ladies' magazine. As Antonia entered she put down the periodical and rose to her feet, regarding Antonia with a look that was appraising and at the same time slightly apprehensive. Antonia met the gaze with a friendly smile. The child was about sixteen — seventeen at most, she guessed — and the sprig muslin with its rich blue velvet spencer had been fashioned by a modiste of the first stare. A pair of sparkling violet eyes, fringed with thick dark lashes enlivened a heart-shaped countenance that was framed by black hair which, released from the confining bonnet, curled riotously around her head. The visitor spoke first in a pretty, musical voice with just a hint of shyness.

'Oh — excuse me — are you Miss Venn?'

'Yes, I am Antonia Venn. How may I help you?'

The young lady clasped her hands together before her, and said, breathlessly, 'I wish to have dancing lessons!'

Antonia smiled.

'Well, this *is* a dancing school, Miss — I do not think you have told me your name?'

A roguish dimple appeared and the young lady's eyes began to dance.

'No — oh pray do not be offended but I have come here quite secretly. You see, Mama would never consent to bring me and when Rosamund — Miss Claremont, Sir Rigby Claremont's daughter — ' she added, observing Antonia's puzzled look, 'when she told me of your lessons I just had to find out for myself, because I want to know all the latest dance steps when I go to London next season and even though Laurence says I will pick it up, Mama understands that I shall be at *such* a disadvantage if I cannot dance.'

'That is all very well, miss,' put in Miss Chittering, gently disapproving, 'but if your mama does not know you are here I really do not think — '

'Perhaps we should have tea while all this is explained to me,' Antonia interrupted her. 'Beatrice, do go and find Dawkin and arrange for some tea, if you please.' She smiled at her visitor. 'I am sorry if I seem very slow, but I fear I do not quite understand. Will you not sit down and start again, from the beginning?'

'Oh yes, I beg your pardon,' the young lady said, blushing, and resumed her seat while Miss Chittering went off in search of refreshment.

'Now,' said Antonia when they were alone, 'let me see what I have understood so far. First of all, you want me to teach you to dance.'

'Yes, if you please. At least, I *can* dance, of course, but only country dances and I need to learn everything before my come-out next season. You see, Mama and I have lived very secluded in Nottinghamshire and I have had no opportunity to pick up any of the steps. Many of my friends have older brothers or sisters who can tell them just how to go on, but Laurence does not dance now and I am so afraid that when I go to Town everyone will think I am a poor country miss. Signor Magnini was with us for such a short time and Laurence refuses to let Mama engage another dancing master, so you see that I am quite *desperate*!'

'Yes, I can understand that, but tell me — who is Signor Magnini?'

'Oh I am so sorry, Mama is forever saying that my tongue runs on wheels! Signor Magnini was the dancing master that Mama engaged for me. He was quite the most magnificent teacher I have had — and there have been several, you know.'

Antonia's lips twitched. 'I can well believe that!'

'Well, you see, in general Laurence is the very best of brothers, but upon occasion he can be so — so *despotic*! I sometimes think that if he was perhaps one-and-twenty instead of one-and-thirty he might be more understanding. He dismissed one of my instructors just because he wrote some verses for me. They were not very good, perhaps, but quite pretty and it was *such* a compliment, do you not think?'

Antonia nodded gravely but maintained a strict silence, only her eyes showing how much she was enjoying her visitor's artless chatter.

'Then there was Mr Avery, who was engaged as a tutor for me — Mama told me he was a brilliant scholar but *I* cannot see it. When he was supposed to be teaching me he would stare at me silently for long periods, and he could never speak to me without stuttering. He wrote me a letter, telling me that he wanted to keep me in an ivory tower and worship at my feet — it was very touching and I really cannot think it kind of Laurence to turn him off so abruptly. Of course, I have finished all my schooling now and only need to learn to dance, which was the reason Mama engaged Signor Magnini, a very amiable Italian gentleman who said he could teach me all the dances I would need for my come-out.'

'And — er — what happened to Signor Magnini?'

'He wanted to take me to Italy with him, to visit all the grand palaces there. Quite out of the question, of course, but it would have been an excellent opportunity to broaden my knowledge of that country, do you not agree? Laurence is forever extolling the virtues of education, which makes his treatment of the poor *signor* even more unjust.'

'Oh? What did he do?'

'He gave the poor man just twenty minutes to pack up and leave the house! And when Signor Magnini tried to defend himself, Laurence threatened him with violence if he did not go. That was last November and since then I have had no one to teach me, because Laurence has consigned all dancing masters to the devil.'

'Very unfeeling of him,' murmured Antonia, 'but if your brother is so set against you dancing, I really do not think I can help you.'

'But he is not really my brother. You see, Mama was widowed when Laurence was a boy and she married again, so he is only a half brother, and I must learn to dance, Miss Venn! When I go to London I will *not* sit at the side like a ninny, while all the other debutantes are enjoying themselves. I want to enter Society with every accomplishment.'

Regarding the stormy face of her visitor, Antonia could not think of a suitable reply and was thankful that Miss Chittering returned at that moment, followed by Dawkin with the tea tray. Miss Chittering, catching only the last part of the young lady's outburst, beamed at her.

'A very proper sentiment, child and one that does you credit. Thank you, Dawkin, put the tray down here, if you please and I will prepare tea for Miss Venn and her guest.'

Antonia waited until the butler had retired before resuming the conversation.

'Let me see if I have the right of it — your parents are against you learning to dance?'

'Oh no. Mama is quite as anxious as I am that I should learn all the latest dances and Papa died a good twelve months past, so he does not count.'

45

Miss Chittering, who was in the act of sipping her tea, choked at this calm dismissal of a parent, but the young lady continued unabashed.

'You see, it is only Laurence who has forbidden any more dancing masters in the house, but Mama has it fixed in her head that he is against *all* dancing lessons. Of course, when Mama first brought me to Bath I thought that I should dislike it excessively, but then I met Rosie Claremont and naturally when she told me about your school, I knew it would be just the thing. I realized there could be no objection, but Mama says she will not go against Laurence's wishes. I have even written to him asking for his consent, but he is away on some dreary estate business and has not bothered to answer, so there is nothing else for it but to come to you myself.'

'But, my dear child, you must see that we cannot go against the wishes of your family,' said Miss Chittering gently.

'But if Miss Venn were to write to Mama, explaining to her that this is a most respectable establishment — you see, Rosamund has told me that it is, so there cannot be the least objection to my coming here.'

Antonia set down her empty cup.

'But I can hardly write to your Mama if you do not tell me her name,' she said reasonably.

'Then you will help me?'

'That I cannot promise until I know who you are.'

The young lady stared at her, then gave a slight nod. 'Very well. I am Isabella Burstock — my mother is Lady Burstock,' she added, as if this explained everything.

Antonia shook her head. 'We live very retired here and have no knowledge of your family, my dear.'

Miss Burstock fixed her dark eyes on Antonia. 'But you will write to Mama?'

Antonia hesitated. 'I am afraid not. I think it would be most presumptuous of me to write to Lady Burstock. However,' she added quickly, aware that her visitor was about to protest, 'I shall give you my visiting card and if your Mama would like to call upon *me* to satisfy herself that you would come to no harm in this house, I should be most happy to welcome her.'

'Oh, but — '

'Miss Venn is right, my dear,' put in Miss Chittering. 'It would be most improper for her to write to your mama and it would do nothing to advance your cause. Much better to explain it all to your mama, and invite her to see for herself that we are perfectly respectable.'

Miss Burstock was much struck by this point of view and refrained from further argument. Instead she asked Antonia a number of questions about her dancing classes before rising to take her leave. Antonia insisted that her own maid should escort her home. Miss Burstock was naturally reluctant to trouble her new acquaintance, but Antonia was adamant that propriety should be observed and returned chuckling to the sitting-room once she had seen her guest safely on her way.

'I pity her mother, if she has sole charge of such a spirited child.'

'There was mention of a brother, I think?'

'Yes. I know one should not set too much store by Miss Burstock's chatter but he does sound a little tyrannical, lays down the law upon a matter and then takes no further interest. Just the sort of behaviour to set him at loggerheads with his lively sister.'

'Ah, poor child.'

'Nothing of the kind,' Antonia retorted. 'I have no doubt that the child is very used to getting her own way — and I shall not be at all surprised to receive a visit from the mother before the week is out.'

* ★ *

In the event even Antonia was not prepared
for Miss Burstock's powers of persuasion
when, the following day, Dawkin interrupted
a dancing lesson to announce the arrival of
two visitors. Antonia was instructing a group
of young ladies from a local seminary in the
finer points of the country dance and she
broke off to glance at the card Dawkin
presented to her.

'Our young visitor from yesterday, with her
mama,' she murmured, as Miss Chittering
came from the pianoforte.

'Lady Burstock, and so soon! If you wish to
go now, Antonia dearest, I will continue this
lesson for you.'

'Thank you, yes, I think I ought not to keep
her ladyship waiting. Go through the dance
again, if you please, and see if you can
persuade the little redhead to turn her feet
out.'

Outside the sitting-room where Dawkin
had shown her visitors, Antonia paused to
check her appearance in a looking glass:
glancing critically at her dress, she hoped the
pale-blue muslin with a snowy kerchief filling
the low neckline presented a suitably demure
picture. A few strands of hair had escaped the
glossy topknot and she patted them back into

place before entering the room. The first glimpse of her visitors caused Antonia to check momentarily. The likeness between mother and daughter was immediately apparent, the same violet eyes and luxurious hair, but Lady Burstock was taller, her features were more aquiline and the dark curls showing beneath the black bonnet were finely streaked with silver. The black silk gown proclaimed the widow and a fine black shawl was drawn across her shoulders, emphasizing her pale complexion.

As she paused in the doorway, Antonia found herself being scrutinized by those keen, dark eyes, but there was no hostility in the look and after the briefest hesitation, Antonia curtsied and moved forward, greeting her visitor with her usual friendly smile.

'Lady Burstock — how do you do. I am Antonia Venn.'

'Good morning, Miss Venn. You have already met my daughter, I understand, so there can be no need for me to tell you why I am here.'

Antonia smiled at Miss Burstock, who stood beside her mama, her eyes shining expectantly.

'No indeed, ma'am, although I confess I did not expect you quite so soon. Won't you sit down?'

Lady Burstock moved to an armchair and sank down gracefully. She gave a faint smile.

'When Isabella has an idea fixed in her head she can be extremely tiresome.'

'I understand Miss Burstock wishes to dance.'

My lady nodded. 'She has had dancing masters in the past but . . . it has not worked out.'

Remembering Miss Burstock's artless chatter, Antonia repressed a smile and patiently waited for her visitor to continue.

'I shall be taking Isabella to London at the end of the year. We have been in mourning for her dear papa for a little over twelve months now and although Isabella is wearing colours again, I have not yet put off my widow's weeds. I hope that by the winter it will not be considered improper for Isabella to be presented at Court.' My lady folded her hands in her lap and said slowly, 'Events since Lord Burstock's sudden demise have left me feeling very low, and I have come to Bath to take the waters. It was not my original intention to bring Isabella with me.'

'Laurence wanted me to stay with him in the country, but that would be so *dull* — nothing but fields and trees for miles and miles. I told Mama I would run away if she left me there.'

'That will do, Isabella.' Lady Burstock frowned at her outburst. 'I admit it was suggested that you should spend a few months with your brother, but I have no doubt that you will prefer to be here with me.' She turned to Antonia. 'I think it important that young girls are not turned out upon Society without some experience of the world. We have any number of friends here and Isabella may find her way about a little in readiness for her London come-out. It is of course imperative that she is *au fait* with all the latest dances — Lady Jersey is an old friend of mine and naturally she will provide Isabella with vouchers for Almack's.'

'Naturally.'

'I have promised Isabella that she shall not be lacking in any of the accomplishments when she is presented, and I consider there will be time enough for her to polish her performance in the ballroom when we return to Burstock Hall at the end of the summer, but you will understand that the young are very impatient and she does not wish to wait so long.'

'I do not want a few hurried lessons, Mama, when all my friends are already proficient!'

Lady Burstock ignored this interruption and looked at Antonia, her dark eyes keenly searching, in spite of her languid manner.

'I have heard of your academy, Miss Venn, but — forgive me! Are you not a little young to be the mistress of such an establishment?'

'I am four-and-twenty, ma'am, and with no fortune of my own I must needs make my living as I can,' was the frank reply.

'And you consider your knowledge of dancing sufficiently wide to enable you to teach?'

'Dancing was always a passion of mine at school, and I was fortunate enough to have an excellent instructor — a Frenchman who had fled the Terror and was obliged to teach to live. He was, however, an inspired dancer — I believe we were all a little in love with him.'

Lady Burstock exchanged glances with her daughter.

'I believe it happens quite frequently,' she murmured.

'Also, I spent two seasons in London.' Antonia paused briefly. 'I too have danced at Almack's,' she added, a glint in her eye.

'Really? Who brought you out?'

'My aunt, Mrs Haseley.'

'What — Amelia Haseley?' cried my lady, sitting bolt upright. 'Why, we were at school together — she was Amelia Venn then of course. I should have realized when I heard your name — you must be poor Philip's daughter.' Lady Burstock's gaze became a little abstracted, as though she was looking into the past. 'A sad rake, of course, but one could not help liking him — so charming and generous.'

'So I believe, ma'am.' Antonia's dry reply was not lost upon Lady Burstock.

'It would have been better for you if he had been a little less open-handed with his friends and more considerate to his family, would it not, Miss Venn? But all that is in the past. Let us concentrate upon the matter in hand. Isabella is very taken with your establishment, Miss Venn, possibly because her new friend Rosamund Claremont speaks so highly of you. What dances do you teach?'

'The allemande, minuet, cotillion and the boulanger of course — as well as all the country line dances and one or two in the square — little used now I know, but useful practice.'

'And the new turning dance?'

'The waltz? I learned the dance some years ago, but I confess I have only ever danced it with my cousins. It was considered too forward for Almack's when I was there.'

'Since the Czar danced the waltz with Lady Jersey last year it has become the rage and I suppose Isabella must learn it.' She stopped, struck by a sudden thought. 'What do you do for male partners?'

Antonia smiled. 'My pupils have to take turns at playing the man, Lady Burstock. If it is a private lesson then I take the role while Miss Chittering plays the piano — you may rest assured the only male your daughter will meet on these premises is Dawkin, my butler.'

'So you see, Mama, it is quite unexceptional,' Miss Burstock put in eagerly.

Lady Burstock hesitated.

'Perhaps, ma'am, you would like your daughter to take one or two lessons with Miss Claremont's group,' Antonia suggested. 'It is a small class, scarcely more than a half-dozen young ladies and it is so much more congenial to be with friends, is it not?'

'True. Well, I will allow Isabella to attend here, but I should like to observe a lesson or two for myself, to judge the benefits to my daughter.'

'You would be very welcome to stay, ma'am.'

'And may I come twice a week, Mama? With Rosamund?'

'Perhaps.'

Taking this for an assent, Isabella beamed.

'Thank you, Mama. And you will not need to escort me every time, if I am with Rosamund. I asked Sir Rigby days ago if he had any objection to my coming along with Rosie and he was very charming about it. He even offered to escort us both.'

'That is very kind of Sir Rigby, my love, but I have already decided that I shall come with you for your first few lessons and after that, well, we shall see. Come, Isabella. We have taken up enough of Miss Venn's time.' Lady Burstock rose. 'Goodbye, Miss Venn. Please pass on my warmest regards to your aunt and assure her that I should be very pleased to see her, should she come to Bath.'

The ladies took their leave and Antonia made her way back to the ballroom, where the lesson was over and her pupils were changing their silk pumps for more robust walking shoes. Miss Chittering was eager to talk, but propriety kept her silent until the girls had filed out into the street under the watchful eye of their instructress.

'Well? What is she like? What did she say?'

Antonia smiled. 'We have another pupil, Beatrice.'

'Oh, I am so pleased for you my dear! And such a prestigious family, I understand. It will set the seal on our little academy.'

'Will it really?' replied Miss Venn, laughing. 'Then we must thank Aunt Haseley in some measure for this, it appears she and Lady

Burstock are old schoolfriends. My lady
warmed towards me visibly when she learned
of my relations. I will go directly and write to
my aunt, to inform her of her part in my
success.'

2

True to her word, Lady Burstock accompanied her daughter to the first dancing lesson. They arrived at Queen Square some minutes before the rest of the pupils and were shown into the empty ballroom. It was a handsome apartment with tall windows overlooking the square, sparsely furnished and the large double doors were thrown open to allow the maximum space for dancing.

'You have a fine ballroom here,' Lady Burstock commented when Antonia entered a few moments later.

'Thank you, my lady. I am very happy with it — and we can accommodate more than twenty couples together, with room to spare.'

'Goodness me, do you have so many pupils at one time?'

'No, ma'am, usually less than half that number, but I plan to bring some of the groups together occasionally, to give them an idea of a large assembly.'

Isabella, who was sitting at the side of the room changing her shoes, looked up.

'At Burstock Hall two Christmases past we

had over two hundred guests, did we not, Mama?'

'Yes indeed, although I hasten to add they were not all dancing at one time.' She gave a sad little smile. 'That was the last ball dear Lord Burstock ever attended. He died two weeks later, a weak heart, you know.'

'I am very sorry, Lady Burstock.'

There was a brief silence. The widow gazed out of the window, but Antonia guessed that her thoughts were far away from Queen Square and she was loath to interrupt the reverie. Finally my lady gave her head a tiny shake.

'What an excellent view of the square you command here, Miss Venn — and here is Sir Rigby escorting his daughter to the door. Ah, he is coming in.' She turned away from the window. 'You are acquainted with Sir Rigby, Miss Venn?'

'We have met, ma'am.'

'Isabella has struck up a friendship with Miss Claremont. I am acquainted with Sir Rigby of course, although I confess that I find his conversation a little — overpowering.'

Antonia's eyes twinkled. 'Yes indeed, ma'am. But you will note that on this occasion he has left his daughter at the door, so we need fear no delay in the lesson.'

Miss Claremont's entrance put an end to

conversation. Miss Chittering appeared and was introduced to Lady Burstock, by which time most of the other pupils had arrived and were ready for their lesson. Lady Burstock took a seat by the door, promising not to interrupt. Antonia could not help feeling just a little nervous — from Miss Burstock's conversation she guessed that the finest dancing masters in the country had been employed to teach her and she wondered how her own performance would compare. She tried to concentrate on her pupils, instructing Miss Chittering to play a merry gigue to start the lesson. Very soon she had forgotten her visitor as she guided the young ladies through the movements of a minuet and galliard before allowing them to giggle their way through what should have been a stately pavanne. To close the lesson, Miss Chittering rattled off a lively gavotte, leaving the young ladies laughing and out of breath as they prepared to leave. They made their way downstairs to the hall where their maidservants or governesses were waiting to escort them home.

★   ★   ★

'Well, I am sure that Miss Burstock enjoyed herself,' remarked Antonia, returning to the ballroom, 'I can only hope that her mama approved of my methods.'

'Not a doubt of it,' declared Miss Chittering. 'She looked to be enjoying the lesson quite as much as the girls. I am confident Miss Burstock will be a regular pupil from now on.'

Miss Chittering was proved correct, for Miss Burstock arrived punctually with her mama the following week and at the end of the lesson Lady Burstock announced that she was perfectly happy for Isabella to continue her lessons and to attend with Miss Claremont twice a week. She was rewarded with a beaming smile from her daughter, who promised to be the model of propriety. Witnessing this scene, Antonia could not suppress a smile, and meeting the widow's glance she surprised an answering gleam in those dark eyes. She felt herself warming towards the lady as she realized that the rather austere appearance hid a ready sense of humour. This was borne out over the following weeks, when Lady Burstock often came to fetch her daughter from lessons and always found time for a few moments' conversation with Antonia.

As April progressed the dancing school became busier than ever. Antonia was engaged in tackling her accounts in the morning-room when Dawkin brought in a letter. Antonia eagerly broke the seal and scanned the pages while Miss Chittering, who had been engaged in hemming a fine handkerchief, looked up enquiringly.

'It is from Aunt Haseley. She writes that she is overjoyed to learn of our success — and she says even my uncle has uttered a grudging compliment.'

'I am very pleased to hear it. I know they would much prefer you to live with them, but even dear Mr Haseley must be a little proud of your success. Does your aunt say when she next means to visit Bath?'

Antonia shook her head.

'She is much preoccupied with my cousin Charles at present. She writes that he is still pestering his father to allow him to join the army. My uncle has refused to countenance the idea and says he must apply himself to his studies.'

'Oh poor young man!' declared Miss Chittering, 'I truly feel for him, although naturally I can understand his mama's anxiety.'

'Charles was always a favourite with you, was he not, Beatrice?

'I remember dear Charles very well. He had such a sweet nature one could never be cross with him for long.'

'You certainly could not, Beatrice! His mama now fears she has indulged him too much and that he is become headstrong. She writes of her worry that he may do something foolish such as run away and enlist, especially with this latest news from the Continent. If Bonaparte is raising an army in France it will surely mean another war.'

'I know nothing of that — I scarcely look at anything other than the court pages of the newspaper, but your poor aunt, she must be very anxious.'

'Well, Charles was always far too ready to act without considering, but I cannot think he would be such a gudgeon as to give up his studies and follow the drum. No, I do hope he will put the idea aside, at least until he has completed his time at Oxford. After that I don't doubt he will marry and that will give his thoughts another turn — Beatrice, why do you look so cast down? What have I said to upset you?'

'Thinking of Charles marrying has made me think how much I should like to see you married,' said Miss Chittering with a sigh. 'I know you will be angry with me for saying so, but marriage would be an end to all your worries, Antonia.'

Antonia put down the letter and stared at her companion.

'Beatrice, how can you be so disloyal to me, especially when the dancing school is going so well.'

Miss Chittering glanced down at the papers on the table.

'Yes, but we are only just paying our way, dear, are we not? I confess I know very little about business, but I have tallied all the money we have received, and made a list of all the bills we have to pay, as you instructed me, and there is very little left . . . I know you will say that we are doing very well, and when I think of how some of the poor souls live here — take poor Miss Cowan — my acquaintance from the Pump Room; living with her widowed sister in South Parade — a most amiable woman with a cheerful word for everyone, but I hear she has very little income and no family to fall back upon. Life can be very uncomfortable for a lady cast penniless upon the world.'

'Indeed, I know it,' agreed Miss Venn with feeling. 'But that is where we are so very fortunate, Beatrice. We have some funds in reserve. I know it is taking a little time to establish ourselves, but we are over the worst now; we have made an encouraging start, so I see no reason why we should not make a success of the business. And you can have no notion how satisfying it is to be an independent woman!'

* ★ ★

'My dear, should we not commence?' Miss Chittering glanced at the clock ticking gently on a side-table.

Antonia was standing by one of the long windows of the ballroom, looking out into the square.

'I think we must. It is unusual for Miss Burstock to be so late for her lesson.'

'I do hope nothing is amiss — oh dear, perhaps there has been an accident!'

Antonia shook her head impatiently.

'I doubt that — it is probably something very simple. I am sure she will tell us the next time we see her. Come, Beatrice, let us make a start. Everyone else is here . . . '

They were halfway through the first minuet when Antonia heard the faint clamour of the bell in the hallway below. She guessed it was Miss Burstock and continued to call out the steps to the dancers, expecting to see Isabella at the door at any moment, apologies for her tardiness tumbling from her lips. No late-comer appeared, but sounds of a commotion could be heard above the music — raised voices that caused Miss Chittering to break off her accompaniment and the pupils to stop in confusion.

Antonia hurried to the door and went

out on to the landing, followed by the young ladies who ignored Miss Chittering's feeble protests that they should not leave the room. Gazing down from the landing, Antonia was surprised to see the calm, classical elegance of her hallway disturbed by the dominating presence of a gentleman in a dusty travelling coat towering menacingly over Miss Burstock, whose wrist he held in a vice-like grip, much to that young lady's indignation.

★　★　★

Miss Venn summed up the situation in a moment. She turned and ushered her pupils back into the ballroom, instructing Miss Chittering to continue with the lesson. Firmly closing the door upon them, she hurried down the stairs to the hall, where the gentleman was still holding Isabella, impervious to her protests.

As she approached, Antonia glanced at the gentleman and her eyes widened slightly, but with scarcely a check she said pleasantly, 'Good afternoon, Miss Burstock — I wonder if I may be of service?'

'Miss Burstock will not be taking her usual lesson today,' came the gentleman's harsh reply.

'You have no right to rule my life!'

'You are certainly not fit to do so!'

Antonia coughed. 'Perhaps you would like to step into the sitting-room and discuss the matter,' she suggested.

'Thank you, but that will not be necessary!' replied the gentleman shortly. 'We are leaving immediately.'

'You cannot make me come with you!' retorted Isabella.

'Oh can't I? I do not have a carriage outside, but if necessary, my girl, I will take you home across my shoulder!'

Observing Miss Burstock's heightened colour, Antonia stepped forward, saying firmly, 'Now that is quite enough, both of you. I really do not think the hall is a proper place for an argument, do you? Pray come into the sitting-room and give my servants no further food for gossip!' She stepped across the hall and opened the door, 'Come!'

After a slight hesitation, the gentleman moved towards her, dragging Miss Burstock with him. He crossed the hall with a halting step and entered the sitting-room with Isabella as his reluctant companion. Following them into the room, Antonia shut the door firmly upon the interested stares of the footmen.

Antonia surveyed her unwilling guests. The gentleman's powerful frame was out of place against the soft colours of the room, which now seemed woefully small and the furnishings far too frail for the energy emanating from her visitor. He was tall, well above average height and the many capes of his coat emphasized the broad shoulders. She noted that his hair, almost covered by the stylish beaver, was as black as Isabella's but his features were more harshly drawn and a scar ran along one side of his jaw. From his blazing black eyes and thinned lips Antonia surmised that he was extremely angry.

'This is my brother, Sir Laurence Oakford,' muttered Isabella, feeling that some explanation was required.

'Thank you, I had already guessed as much.'

The fierce gaze swept over her. Not to be intimidated in her own house Antonia returned his stare defiantly.

'Not only her brother, her guardian. Pray fetch your mistress that I may explain why I am here.'

Miss Venn's brows rose a little.

'*I* am the mistress here, sir,'

He looked at her, taking in every detail as his eyes raked her from head to toe.

'Impossible!'

'Indeed, Laurence, this *is* Miss Venn.'

He looked at his sister, then turned again to stare at Antonia.

'Good God!' A faint colour tinged his cheeks. He said abruptly, 'I beg your pardon ma'am. Isabella had said — that is, I had expected someone — older.'

'Quite possibly, but that does not give you the right to cause such a disturbance in my house.'

'For that I apologize,' he said curtly, 'but in this my sister must take her share of the blame. I had not been in Bath above an hour before I found that she had left the house and come here expressly against my wishes. She must learn that I will not tolerate disobedience.'

Antonia looked at Miss Burstock, who pouted.

'It is true, but it is so *unfair* to forbid me to come without giving Mama any time to explain — '

'That is quite enough!' Sir Laurence cut her short. 'You knew from the outset that I would not allow this.'

'But Mama agreed!'

'I have no doubt your mother succumbed to your cajoling, 'Bella, but *I* shall not do so.'

'Mama gave her consent — Miss Venn will tell you so. And I have been so *good*, just as I promised.'

Antonia suppressed a smile, but with Isabella's imploring gaze upon her she felt obliged to speak.

'Perhaps it would have been wiser to stay at home, dear, at least until the matter had been discussed.'

'But there will *be* no discussion!' cried Isabella vehemently. 'Laurence will refuse his permission and I shall not be allowed to come here again!' She dissolved into tears.

'But, child, you cannot know that — '

Sir Laurence raised his hand.

'Madam I pray you will not enter into this argument. It is a family matter.'

Antonia stiffened.

'I have no intention of arguing, sir.' She looked at Isabella. 'I am sorry, my dear, but you must know that I cannot act against your guardian's wishes.' She raised her cool grey eyes to the gentleman. 'As for you, sir, I think there is no more to say on the matter. I regret the course of action you have taken — I think a little reflection might have shown you another course. However, having made your decision I can quite see that you wish to remove Miss Burstock immediately.' She paused, then added thoughtfully, 'Of course, the task of dragging your disconsolate sister through the streets of Bath is not one that *I* would relish, but doubtless you will not let yourself be troubled by the gossip-mongers. I will bid you good-day.' She reached for the bell-rope but his voice stayed her hand.

'One moment, if you please.' He fixed his eyes upon his sister. A sigh escaped him, but whether it was fatigue or exasperation Antonia could not tell. 'You are quite right, I do *not* wish to drag a watering-pot home behind me. Since we are here, Bella, you may as well join in the lesson — *if* Miss Venn permits.'

Surprised by this sudden change of heart, Antonia could only nod.

He continued to address Miss Burstock. 'If it is true that your conduct here has been exemplary, it would be harsh to deny you this pleasure — God knows there is little enough for you to do here. Well, go on, child.'

Isabella had been staring at her brother in amazement, hardly daring to believe his words. Tears still sparkled on the ends of her lashes, but she now dashed these away.

'Do you mean — I can take my lessons as before?'

'Yes, yes — now go.'

With a radiant smile she almost ran out of the room, leaving her brother looking after her, shaking his head.

'From desolation to joy in the twinkling of an eye.'

71

Antonia tugged at the bell-pull.

'You will doubtless send a servant to meet Miss Burstock. The lesson concludes at four o'clock.'

'You are offended.'

'Not at all,' she said politely.

'If it is my attire that upsets you, then I apologize for entering your house in all my dirt. I arrived in Bath less than an hour ago and I had not changed when I discovered Bella's intention and followed her here directly. I have been on the road for several hours.'

She was unmoved.

'Common civility would normally oblige me to offer you some refreshment, sir, but under the circumstances — '

Sir Laurence lowered himself into an armchair.

'Thank you — a glass of Madeira would be most welcome.'

She stared at him, but he met her look blandly. Dawkin entered the room at that moment and she briefly toyed with the idea of asking him to escort her visitor from the house. However, his behaviour so far gave no indication that he would go willingly, and observing Dawkin's aged frame, she guessed her butler would not relish an unseemly struggle. The gentleman spoke again.

'If you have no wine, perhaps a glass of brandy . . . ?'

'No, no — Madeira for Sir Laurence, if you please, Dawkin — and bring me a glass of ratafia.'

'Perhaps you would like me to send word to Miss Chittering?' suggested Dawkin in a carefully indifferent voice.

'Miss Chittering is taking the lesson, Dawkin. Now do go away and fetch refreshment for my guest.' As the butler left the room Antonia looked up to find Sir Laurence watching her, amusement in his face. She said coolly, 'I too have my guardians, sir.'

'I thought you might ask him to throw me out.'

'I am not at all sure that he could do so,' she answered frankly.

'I am certain he could not!' He fixed his hard gaze upon her face. 'You look familiar. Have we met before?'

She put up her chin and hoped her expression was one of disdain.

'I am certain we have never been introduced, sir.' Antonia held her breath and after continuing to stare at her for another minute, he shrugged.

'You look pale and out of countenance Miss Venn. Do you dislike my plain speaking?'

'I do not dislike it, sir, merely it is not what I expected.'

He leaned back in the chair, his eyes glinting as they rested on her face.

'Oh? And just what did you expect?'

'A gentleman, sir, with at least the appearance of manners!' she retorted, nettled. 'Not a boorish bully who tries to start a brawl in my hallway.'

He grinned. 'Bravo, Miss Venn. It was very wrong of me to invade your house in such a way, forgive me.'

Antonia found she was not immune to the humble note in his voice. She inclined her head in acknowledgement of the apology, but said nothing.

'Do you wish me to promise that I will not take advantage of your being alone, thus, with me?'

Antonia's ready sense of humour overcame her anger.

'Having offered you refreshment, sir, it would seem inhospitable to withdraw now.'

He laughed. 'Very true! I am relieved you are not going to leave me. I want to know more about you.' He saw the guarded look in her eyes and added quickly, 'As Isabella's guardian, it behoves me to learn something of this establishment.'

His hostess moved to a chair on the far side

of the room and sat down.

'You will perhaps wish to know what I can teach your sister, Sir Laurence. I like to give all my pupils knowledge of the older dances, the pavanne and the galliard — and of course the courante. Then there is the *rigaudon* — very good for allowing the young ladies to expend a little energy. I also like them to try the sarabande and the passacaglia, then coming up to date we have the minuet and gavotte, the bourré, the allamande and of course the polonaise . . . '

'Yes, yes I am sure you could name me a dozen more dances, if I cared to listen, but I don't. I've no doubt my mother has already assured herself of your fitness to teach Isabella. No, I want to know how you come to be in Bath, running a dancing school.'

She shifted uncomfortably and found herself unable to look at him.

'It — it has always been an ambition of mine.'

Sir Laurence was no longer lounging in his chair. He was sitting upright and very still, regarding her intently.

'We *have* met before — ' A slow grin dawned. 'Hell and damnation!'

Antonia felt a hot blush suffuse her cheek. She did not attempt to dissemble.

'I had hoped you would not remember. You

were rather drunk that evening, I fear.'

'Damnably!' He fell silent, frowning. At last he said, 'Did I advise you to open a dancing school?'

'No, sir.'

He rose and took a turn about the room, frowning blackly. Antonia clasped her hands before her. She said slowly, 'I have no cause to remember our meeting with anything but gratitude, sir.'

'The devil you do! I have but the haziest recollection. I remember taking you out of that brothel and putting you on the mail-coach.'

She winced. 'Knowing of — of our past meeting and my circumstances, sir, you have it in your power to ruin me. No one else knows of that . . . incident. You will appreciate that I was not tempted to tell any of my acquaintance.'

'Nor I — all I wanted to do was to forget the whole damned evening!' He frowned. 'I used to know a Philip Venn in Town a few years ago.'

'My father.'

'I knew he had a family somewhere . . . '

'I am his only child.'

'And you have been reduced to this.'

'Reduced?' The lady's eyes flashed, 'I was *reduced* to living as my uncle's pensioner. My aunt and uncle were very good, but I could never forget that I was living on their charity. Here at least I have my independence and I infinitely prefer that.'

'Yes, I am sure you do. My apologies, Miss Venn.'

There was a silence as Dawkin reappeared with the refreshments, which he dispensed with a rigid propriety that expressed his disapproval eloquently. Unmoved by these silent reproaches, Antonia glanced at her guest, concerned that he might detect some incivility in the butler's manner, but she saw only amusement in his eyes. At length Dawkin departed at his most stately, closing the door behind him with a decided snap.

'I fear we offend his sensibilities,' murmured the gentleman, sipping his Madeira.

She nodded. 'I know it! Poor Dawkin, I only hope he will not leave us: he adds such distinction to the establishment.'

'Has he been with your family a long time?'

'Goodness, no. He comes with the house — that is, he was butler here when I took over the lease and he agreed to stay on.' Her eyes twinkled. 'He is a *great* asset.'

'No doubt.' He raised his glass. 'I wish you success with your business, Miss Venn.'

'Thank you — I — no doubt you would

prefer Isabella to find another dancing teacher . . . '

'No, why should you think that? After my initial refusal today, I was ready to concede the point, until I discovered the chit had already left the house. But no, ma'am, I have no objections, except, perhaps to your youth . . . '

She put up her chin. 'I am full four-and-twenty, sir.'

'In your dotage, in fact.'

She bit her lip. 'Scarcely that, but to be serious, Sir Laurence, I am very pleased with the success of my dancing academy and I shall tell you the same thing I said to Lady Burstock, you are welcome to attend any of my lessons and judge my abilities for yourself.'

'Thank you, Miss Venn. I shall take up your invitation, perhaps, at a later stage.' He finished his wine and set the glass down. 'I must take my leave, to stay longer might do serious damage to both our reputations. I have already sent her maid home so I shall send the carriage for Isabella at four. Your servant, ma'am.'

Before Antonia could think of a reply he was gone, hurrying out of the room with his halting stride and almost colliding with Dawkin, who was hovering just outside the door.

Miss Venn made her way to the ballroom where Miss Chittering was playing a country dance for the young ladies, but when this ended the pupils were granted a short respite.

'Well, my dear Antonia, has he gone?' asked Miss Chittering, when the music ended.

'Yes. A strange man — '

'Was he very cross, Miss Venn?' Isabella came up to her. 'I do hope he was not rude to you. Laurence is the very best of brothers, but I fear I angered him deeply today.'

'No, child, he was not at all uncivil. In fact,' — Antonia hesitated, a faint smile playing at the corners of her mouth — 'I quite enjoyed the meeting.'

'I confess I do not like to think of you confronting the gentleman,' put in Miss Chittering solemnly, 'but I could not leave the girls, and I felt sure that you would be safe enough, with Dawkin and the servants present.'

Antonia wondered what her companion would say if she knew that she had spent full twenty minutes alone with her guest, but she decided it would be wiser to say nothing. Instead she turned her attention to the remainder of the lesson, which she conducted with even more energy than usual. A tiny voice inside whispered 'coward', but she pushed this aside, not wishing to question too deeply why she did not want to discuss Sir Laurence's visit. She could only be thankful when the clock struck four and the first of the carriages arrived at the door. Miss Claremont and Isabella were the last to leave and when Sir Rigby arrived to collect his daughter, he came in breathless after climbing the stairs. He was carrying a large bunch of spring flowers, which he gallantly presented to Antonia.

'For you, Miss Venn, though they can't hold a candle to your own bloom, eh girls?'

Rosamund blushed fierily at her papa's remarks, but Antonia was obliged to frown at Isabella, who was trying to stifle a giggle. She accepted the flowers gracefully and turned aside the fulsome compliments with a laughing rejoinder as she escorted Rosamund and her father to the door. Returning to the ballroom a moment later she shook her head at Isabella.

'Wicked girl! How dare you laugh at the poor man.'

'But you were laughing too!' returned that young lady, unabashed. 'I could tell by the way your eyes were twinkling — just as they are doing now.'

'No, no, Miss Burstock, I am sure Miss Venn would not be so rude as to laugh at any gentleman,' said Miss Chittering, mildly reproving. 'I think it is very gallant of Sir Rigby to bring you flowers, dear Antonia. He is a widower, I understand . . . '

'Now Beatrice, you must not start match-making.'

'Of course not, my dear, but I admit it would be comforting to see you settled.'

'But not to Sir Rigby,' declared Isabella. 'He would bore you to distraction within the month, Miss Venn.'

'My dear child, I really do not think you should speak so disrespectfully of the gentleman!'

'Oh I would not say so to anyone else, Miss Chittering, but Miss Venn knows I mean no harm and it is such a relief to be able to talk to someone who knows when you are joking, so that one does not need to explain everything! She is so unlike anyone else I know, except perhaps Laurence, when he is not in one of his provoking moods.'

Antonia laughed. 'I *think* you are complimenting me, but I cannot be sure.'

The announcement that Sir Laurence Oakford had arrived to collect his sister curtailed the young lady's answer. She turned in surprise as he came in.

'Laurence! I thought you were sending the carriage for me.'

'That was my intention, but it is such a pleasant afternoon I thought we might walk back together — that is if you have any energy left from your dancing.'

'Silly; of course I have. Are you in a dreadful hurry? I have yet to change my shoes.'

'You may take your time.' His eyes rested on the flowers laid carefully upon a chair. 'Miss Venn has an admirer,' declared his sister roguishly, reading the question in his eyes.

'Nonsense!' Antonia replied, flushing slightly. 'It was merely a friendly gesture.'

'What, when he compared their beauty so unfavourably with your own?' Isabella teased her.

'Hush, child, you are putting me to blush.'

'You know you enjoyed the joke as much as I. Oh Miss Venn, it is so good to have a friend one can laugh with.'

Antonia was aware of Sir Laurence's eyes upon her, but she was relieved to see only amusement in his glance. He took out his snuffbox.

'And just who is this admirer, may one enquire?'

'One may not,' retorted Antonia firmly. 'And I would be obliged if you did not quiz Isabella on the subject. It would be most improper.'

'Oh do not worry, Miss Venn, I will not breathe a word!' Miss Burstock assured her.

'Indeed, ma'am, you may consider the matter forgotten.' added Sir Laurence gravely. 'Now, Isabella, if you are ready, let us be on our way.'

Miss Chittering had observed this interchange in uncharacteristic silence, but as soon as the door was closed upon the visitors she came up to Antonia, shaking her head.

'I cannot think it proper for Miss Burstock to be making fun of Sir Rigby in such a way. And you really should not be encouraging her to do so, Antonia.'

'I know it, but she meant no harm, Beatrice, and I am sure it will all be forgotten by the next lesson.'

★ ★ ★

Despite her calm assurances, Antonia was relieved when Miss Burstock's next visit passed off without a mention of the subject. The lesson finished promptly at four o'clock and, glancing out of the window, Antonia noticed the elegant Burstock carriage waiting at her door. Miss Burstock was descending the stairs with Miss Claremont, trying to persuade Rosamund to send away her maid and ride home in the barouche. However, this charming scheme was foiled by the appearance of Sir Rigby, in the very best of spirits. He entered the hall, greeting all the young ladies with a smile and a little bow and pinching the cheeks of the prettiest as they passed him.

'Ah, Rosie m'dear — I was out for a stroll and thought to m'self that I might as well call in for you — and Miss Isabella, looking as pretty as ever, eh, m'dear?'

Isabella giggled but was saved the necessity of replying by Sir Rigby immediately switching his attention to Antonia and Miss Chittering, who were descending the stairs with the very last of their pupils.

'Good afternoon to you ladies. I find you both in health, I trust? Good, good — and I have a little surprise for you, Miss Venn. I have procured vouchers for the concert at the New Rooms on Friday next, is that not good news?' Observing her blank look he continued, 'I know your love of music, dear lady, and when I heard of the concert I thought how much you would like to go — and I hope you will give me the honour of escorting you.'

Isabella's keen gaze flickered over the gentleman and Antonia quickly escorted her to her carriage before coming back into the hall to make her reply.

'That is very kind of you, Sir Rigby — '

'Now is that not fortuitous, Antonia?' Miss Chittering interrupted her. 'You were only saying yesterday how much you would like to attend.'

'Yes I *did* say that, Beatrice, but what I failed to tell you was that I have already made sure of places for us both.' She turned to Sir Rigby. 'I thank you most kindly, sir, but you see that I must decline your offer.'

Sir Rigby's florid face clouded.

'Oh, of course, Miss Venn, of course. Pray do not allow yourself to be down-hearted, ma'am, it was only a passing thought, but if you have already made other arrangements . . . Come then, Rosie, everyone has departed and it is time we too were off. Miss Venn, Miss Chittering — your servant.' He bowed himself out and Dawkin closed the door upon the last of the visitors.

'Well, what a pity that you already have vouchers for the concert, my dear, when Sir Rigby is so ready to escort you,' sighed Miss Chittering.

'It is not a pity at all, Beatrice. I could not accept Sir Rigby's invitation — surely you can see that.'

'But my dear — he is a widower and the most *pleasant* gentleman . . . '

'Oh Beatrice — he is an incorrigible flirt, as everyone in Bath knows. How would it be if I were to accept? Imagine the gossip. However, I certainly have no wish to offend him, which is why I said that I had tickets.'

'But when did you arrange this, Antonia dear? You said nothing to me.'

'No, because I have made it all up! Of course I quite see that we *must* go to the concert now, so I charge you, Beatrice, with the duty of procuring two vouchers for us. You may go tomorrow and see what you can achieve, but we must ensure that Sir Rigby does not learn of our deception.'

For once Miss Chittering was speechless, torn between disapproval of Antonia's treatment of the gentleman and horror at the task she had been set. In Miss Chittering's world it was gentlemen who made such arrangements. Realizing something of these thoughts, Antonia relented a little, saying as she made her way to the sitting-room, 'Poor Beatrice. Pray do not look so anxious — you may ask Dawkin to get the tickets for you — I am sure he will be most discreet.'

3

Escorting his mother to the Assembly Rooms on Friday evening, Sir Laurence surveyed the crowds with misgiving and muttered that he had not realized half the population of Bath were music lovers. Lady Burstock tapped his arm with her fan.

'Hush, Laurence, pray do not be disagreeable. Look, there is Miss Venn and her companion. And see how Lady Nattersby snubs her. Insufferable creature, both her daughters take lessons with Miss Venn, I know, yet she does not even acknowledge her with a civil nod. Come along, we will go over immediately and speak to the poor young woman.'

'Mama, she is merely Bella's dance teacher, surely we do not need . . . '

Lady Burstock took his arm and led him purposefully across the room.

'She is the niece of my very good friend, Laurence and as such she deserves every attention. Ah, good evening, Miss Venn, Miss Chittering. The concert is very well attended, is it not?'

'Yes indeed, ma'am,' replied Antonia. 'I

only hope we may all find seats.'

'Your escort will attend to that, I am sure,' put in Sir Laurence, recalling Isabella's artless chatter.

Antonia looked puzzled. 'Escort, sir?'

'You are no doubt referring to Mr and Mrs Partridge,' remarked Miss Chittering, fluttering, 'We *were* talking to them a few moments ago, but it was only a chance meeting sir. We are not of their party, although they are the most amiable couple imaginable.'

Lady Burstock smiled at Antonia. 'And your aunt, Mrs Haseley, have you heard from her recently, is she well?'

'Yes, my lady, she is very well, and plans to visit Bath again before too long.'

'Good. Pray tell her when you next write that I am most anxious to see her. Come, Laurence, we must not keep the ladies any longer. You must find me a chair, my dear.' With another bow she moved away, leaving Miss Chittering visibly swelling with pleasure.

'Well! How kind, what an honour! How truly good-natured of her ladyship to come over and speak to us.'

'Yes, it was very civil of her,' responded Antonia coolly. 'Do you know, I think that Mr and Mrs Partridge have indeed reserved seats for us? Look, Beatrice, they are signalling to us to join them.'

'Antonia, how can you be so dismissive? Lady Burstock deliberately sought you out. She has the most pleasing manners, not a bit high — and her son, so polite, so considerate.'

'Did you think so?' Antonia raised her brows. 'I thought he looked most disapproving. I daresay he would not have spoken had his mama not brought him over.' She continued to move through the crowd with Miss Chittering close behind her until they had reached Mr Partridge, a large, florid-faced gentleman in an old-fashioned bag-wig who stood beaming down at them.

'My dear ladies, such a crush. I suspect you have not yet found a place to sit — no, I thought as much. The tiered settees are already full but my dear wife is keeping two seats for you, you see, on the far side, if you would care to join us.'

'Oh, so kind,' murmured Miss Chittering as she sat down beside Mrs Partridge, who listened with good-natured patience as Miss Chittering poured out her gratitude for such unlooked-for hospitality.

The noise and chatter in the rooms died away quickly as the musicians finished tuning up and prepared to begin their recital. There was a last minute disturbance as another party arrived and chairs were brought in for them. Antonia noticed Sir Rigby amongst the late-comers, rearranging the seats to his own satisfaction with a supreme disregard for the glares of both audience and the musicians, who were waiting to commence.

'Perhaps it was providential that we did not join Sir Rigby's party,' whispered Miss Chittering, watching the proceedings with mild disapproval. 'I cannot think that you would want to have everyone staring at you so — even though they will be ideally placed to slip out of the rooms at the interval.'

'That would certainly be an advantage,' agreed Miss Venn, 'but surely you would much rather be here.'

'Oh yes, of course, not a doubt of it. It is always so much more comfortable to be amongst people one can talk to. Not that Sir Rigby is ever uncivil — in fact he is always most charming, but one cannot help but notice that gentlemen are not interested in the trivial matters that we find so engrossing, do you not agree, Mrs Partridge? Oh — what was that, Antonia? Oh yes, I see. They are about to play. And what is to be their first piece — something of Mr Handel's I believe . . . what? Oh yes, of course, we must be silent. But my fan — where is my fan? Ah yes, here it is on the floor! How silly of me to drop it, but it won't take me a minute to — there, I have it. Now I can be comfortable.'

★ ★ ★

It was not to be expected that Miss Chittering's enforced silence would continue into the interval, but with the music still running in her head Antonia found herself loath to talk. She excused herself, gracefully declined Mr Partridge's offer to fetch her something to drink and declared her intention of going outside in search of a little fresh air. Despite the open windows and the rapid movement of every lady's fan during the recital, the room had grown very warm and Antonia was relieved to be able to move at last. In the anteroom the doors had been thrown wide in an effort to coax a little air through the building. Turning her back on the crowded refreshment room she walked towards the main entrance where the heat was a little less oppressive. The footmen standing on each side of the doorway regarded her impassively and she smiled to herself, imagining how eager they must be for the concert to begin again so that they could relax once more.

'Miss Venn — is there anything wrong, can I be of assistance?'

She turned to find Sir Laurence at her elbow.

'No, thank you, sir. I came out for a little air.'

'I am commissioned to fetch a glass of lemonade for my mother — perhaps I could bring one for you . . .'

'Th-thank you, but it is not necessary.' Thrown off balance by his unexpected kindness, she realized her words sounded churlish and tried to make amends. 'I think I am more in need of a little cool air. It is so warm and crowded, and I prefer to keep my own thoughts than to be chattering' — she broke off, her hand flying to her mouth. 'Oh dear — that sounds as though I want *you* to go away!'

'And do you?'

'No — of course not! I would not be so impolite.'

He was watching her closely, a faint smile curving his lips.

'Bella was correct, your eyes *do* smile!'

She blushed. 'She told you that? What nonsense.'

'No, it is true — and very becoming.' He glanced round. 'There is less of a crush in the refreshment room now and I must procure the lemonade for my mother — can I not persuade you to accompany me?'

Antonia declined gracefully and with a bow he walked off to the octagon. What a strange man he was, she reflected, his manners a little too abrupt to be generally pleasing, and when he paid her a compliment, it was uttered in the same matter-of-fact tone that left her wondering if she had heard him correctly. At length she made her way back to her seat where Miss Chittering was looking out for her.

'My dear, you were so long, I was beginning to worry about you. Mrs Partridge and I have been chatting here the whole time. If only you had allowed Mr Partridge to fetch you a glass of lemonade you could have been sitting here comfortably with us.'

'I went to the door for a little fresh air, Beatrice, and I assure you I was not a bit uncomfortable.'

Miss Chittering regarded her closely.

'Are you sure, my dear? You are looking very flushed and your eyes are over-bright. I trust you are not running a fever.'

'I am confident I am not!' laughed Antonia, fully aware of the reason for her heightened colour. Inwardly she upbraided herself for behaving like one of her young pupils, starry-eyed because a gentleman had taken notice of her.

* * *

Antonia was relieved when the musicians struck up again and a William Boyce symphony put an end to any further conversation. The air within the crowded concert room grew ever warmer, so that it was a relief when the last notes died away and the audience was free to make its way out into the night. Miss Chittering, who had been dozing through the final movement, woke up in time to join in the applause that greeted the end of the concert.

'Well, was that not delightful, Antonia dear? And to have such good seats. I was never more pleased to see Mr and Mrs Partridge — so kind.'

That gentleman puffed out his cheeks.

'As I have said before, Miss Chittering, it was a mere trifle. My good lady and I live but a step away in Russell Street, but perhaps I can be of service in finding you a chair?'

Antonia assured Mr Partridge that they would manage and the kindly couple took their leave. Antonia waited while her companion collected her fan, which had slipped again to the floor, then the two ladies made their way to the anteroom.

'Now, is there a cab or a chair to be had, my dear Antonia?' murmured Miss Chittering as they came out into the street. 'Heavens, it is such a crush.'

'I think we will walk, Beatrice. It is not far to Queen Square and we have been sitting all evening. I really long to be moving.'

'Miss Venn, may I take you up?' a voice called from the darkness of a nearby carriage.

'Thank you, Lady Burstock.' Antonia stepped up to the vehicle. 'We have but a short way to go and I am sure we would be the better for a little exercise.'

'Then my son shall escort you. Jump down, Laurence. I will not allow Miss Venn to walk through the streets of Bath at night and unattended.'

The look of exasperation on Sir Laurence's face as he opened the carriage door was not lost on Antonia and she quickly declined his services.

'Thank you, but I am not unattended, my lady. Miss Chittering is with me — '

She was cut short by a rich, deep voice at her elbow.

'Well, 'pon my soul — Lady Burstock — your servant, ma'am. I think you were persuading Miss Venn she must be escorted. Pray allow me to be of service to you.' Sir Rigby made her a flourishing bow and pro____ his arm, but was prevented from mo____ closer by the top of Sir Laurence's cane pressing against his chest.

'Bad luck, Claremont. I'm afraid you are

too late. Miss Venn already has an escort.' The corners of Sir Laurence's mouth lifted at the disappointment evident in Sir Rigby's countenance. 'Perhaps you would care to offer your arm to Miss Chittering.'

'Oh no, no, that is not at all necessary. Pray do not put yourself out on my account Sir Rigby,' she cried, agitated by such attention, but Sir Rigby was not one to shirk his duty.

'It would be an honour, ma'am!' he declared, rising nobly to the occasion.

Sir Laurence pulled Antonia's unresisting hand on to his arm.

'Then it is settled. Mama, I shall be with you shortly.'

The little group set off for Queen Square, Sir Laurence guiding his charge away from the carriages and chairs crowding into Alfred Street. When they had left the bustle of the Assembly Rooms behind, Antonia glanced up at her escort.

'Ungallant, sir,' she murmured.

'Not at all, Miss Venn. I am merely carrying out my mother's wishes.'

'You did it to spite Sir Rigby,' she accused him. 'I think you were not at all inclined to escort us, until Sir Rigby came along.'

Sir Laurence laughed. He glanced back at Sir Rigby, following with Miss Chittering on his arm.

'Well, admit it is the truth.'

'Sir Rigby's intervention certainly added a little — zest — to the event, but my mother is right. You should not walk unattended at night, Miss Venn. It is most foolhardy.'

'There are any number of people abroad, sir.'

'But not all of them respectable.'

'Then perhaps it would be safer if you found me a chair.'

'Yes, but not nearly so interesting, for either of us.'

She was surprised into a chuckle.

'You are a strange man, Sir Laurence.'

'Why, because I make you laugh?'

'No . . . because I know you disapprove of me and yet this is the second time in one evening that you have behaved most chivalrously.'

'Disapprove of you? Nonsense,' he said gruffly, a flush mounting his cheeks.

'Yes, you do. You know it is so,' came the frank reply. 'In your perfect world ladies should always be meek and — and *biddable*.'

'Hah! Then you know little of my sister.'

'But Miss Isabella is an heiress and a beauty. With such advantages she will most likely marry well and continue to enjoy her full life. For the rest, you think gently bred females should keep to their place, even if that place is genteel poverty.'

''Pon my soul, you think to know me well, Miss Venn!'

'It is not only you, sir,' she told him kindly. 'Society in general mistrusts a woman making her own living — unless it is by catching a rich husband, which is always acceptable.'

'But not to you?'

'Oh, I am not against matrimony, sir, but only where it is accompanied by true affection and regard for one's partner.'

'I remember your father was considered a charming man,' he said. 'Perhaps you are searching for his equal.'

This made her laugh.

'God defend me from such as my father! I am sorry, Sir Laurence, have I shocked you? If you knew my father at all you will know that he was an inveterate gambler, generous to a fault and with a happy nature that allowed him to give not one thought to the future. A very lovable character but *not* a good husband! He gambled away his fortune and all my mother's portion that was not tied up in Funds, leaving me with the choice of remaining as my uncle's pensioner or making my way in the world.'

'And do you resent that?'

She paused. 'I try not to do so, but I find it very difficult to forgive him. He was rarely at home, you see, and, as I grew older, I realized how difficult it was for Mama to try to keep household and look after us both while Papa spent his days in London, losing what little fortune he had left. When Mama died Papa was more than happy for my Aunt Haseley to take me in. He has never spoken of it directly, but I am almost certain that my uncle paid for much of my education — in fact, he once said that we should be grateful the fever carried off Papa while the dibs were in tune, so at least he could pay for his own funeral.'

'I am sorry.'

Antonia's step faltered and she felt herself flushing in the darkness.

'There is no need to be — and it is I who should apologize to you for rattling on. I do not generally prattle so.'

He squeezed her hand, lying snug against his arm.

'Then I am flattered by your confidences.'

Antonia was uncomfortably aware that she had said far more than she had intended and in an attempt to regain her composure she asked him if he had enjoyed the concert.

'Why yes, much more than I had expected, in fact.'

'I understand the concerts at the Assembly Rooms are considered comparable with those of London, do you think so?'

'Very likely, although I cannot tell you, for I have never attended a concert in Town.'

'Perhaps you prefer the theatre. I know during my time in Town I enjoyed it very much. I saw Kemble, of course, but I understand now that young Edmund Kean is all the rage. I missed his performances in the provinces and now of course he is quite settled in London. Ah well — I shall have to be content with the concerts Bath has to offer.'

'But I think you will find with all of them that it is not so much the content as the company that makes an evening enjoyable, Miss Venn.'

She wondered if he was paying her another compliment but quickly dismissed the thought — it would be conceited of her to read too much into his every utterance. She was thankful that they were now within sight of Queen Square, where an anxious Dawkin had been looking out for his mistress and opened the door upon her approach. Antonia turned on the steps and held out her hand.

'Thank you, sir, for your escort, even though I mistrust your motives.'

'Thank *you*, Miss Venn, for that salutary lesson on the ills of our society.'

She chuckled. 'Have I offended you? I am

sorry! I merely wanted to make you understand why I find it necessary to earn my living in this world.'

'I understand perfectly, Miss Venn and I am pleased to think I have been of such use to you.'

She would have questioned his remark but Sir Rigby was beside her, having handed his charge up the steps and he was waiting to take his leave of her.

★ ★ ★

Miss Chittering scarcely waited for Dawkin to shut the door behind them before she spoke.

'Well! What perfect manners. To escort us both — I vow I do not know when I have met with such courtesy before. And Sir Rigby, so kind, so gallant — all because of you, of course, my dear Antonia. I am sure they both have a very high regard for you.'

'Nonsense.' Antonia unbuttoned her pelisse and handed it to the waiting servant. 'It is due to Lady Burstock's kindness, since she insisted that her son escort us home.'

'But that does not explain why Sir Rigby should put himself out. He had nothing but praise for you during the journey home.'

'Then you must have had a very sorry time

of it. Now, before you say anything more, Beatrice, I can see that Dawkin has something to tell us. Well, Dawkin, what is it?'

'Begging your pardon, miss, you have a visitor — in the morning-room.'

'A visitor, at this time of night? Whoever can it be?' cried Miss Chittering, her eyes widening.

Dawkin coughed. 'The — ah — person did not wish me to make any announcement, ma'am.'

Antonia's eyes twinkled. 'Now here's a mystery!' She crossed the hall with Miss Chittering in close attendance. 'Is it Aunt Haseley, I wonder? It is the sort of joke she would enjoy.' She opened the door to the morning-room and stopped, a delighted smile spreading over her features. 'Charles!'

A fair-haired young man had been dozing in a chair but at her voice he jumped to his feet, grinning broadly.

'The very same, Cos! How are you, my dear?' He crossed the room in a stride and embraced her, planting a kiss on her flushed cheek.

'I am very well, but you — should you not be at Oxford?'

'Well, you see . . . Miss Chittering, how delightful to see you again. Come now, ma'am, there is no need to stand in the doorway like that, come in, do.'

'How do you do, Master Charles?' Miss Chittering fluttered towards a chair. 'How good of you to remember me — you were but a boy when I left your mama's house and now you are grown into such a fine young man. But, forgive me — has the term ended, is it the vacation already?'

'No, no — I'm afraid I was in a bit of a scrape. There was a slight problem with a pig in the dean's study.' He grinned at Antonia. 'A wager, Cos, that went awry. I won't go into detail but the outcome is that I have been sent down for a while and — well, I thought I'd come to Bath and pay you a visit.'

His cousin looked at him, her eyes twinkling. 'Afraid to go home, Charlie?'

He grinned, a faint flush mounting his cheeks. 'Devil a bit, Cos! Though I have to say I'd as lief not see Papa for a few weeks yet. I have written to him, of course, explaining the situation — had to, the old bag-wig said *he* was going to write, so naturally I had to make sure Papa knew my side of the story.'

'Naturally.'

'No, my main reason for coming to Bath was to see this famous dancing school for myself. Mama has kept me informed of it in her letters. I understand it is doing very well.'

'Your cousin's establishment is a great success, Master Charles. Some of the highest families in Bath bring their daughters here.'

'Thank you, Beatrice, you will give Charles a very exaggerated view of how we go on here,' laughed Antonia. 'It is true that we have sufficient pupils now to make the school pay for itself, but I have every expectation that numbers will fall off a little as summer approaches, so it is important to keep all the goodwill that we have built up.'

'If that is a warning to me, you may be sure that I will not be in your way.'

'You will be very much in my way,' she retorted. 'This is a very respectable dancing academy, Charles, and I dare not risk any hint of impropriety.'

'Oh my dear,' exclaimed Miss Chittering, looking shocked, 'I do not think Master Charles would — that is, surely . . . ' She tailed off, looking most uncomfortable.

'I will be the soul of discretion, I promise.'

Antonia looked at him doubtfully.

'You must stay out of sight during lessons and when the young ladies are entering and leaving the house. I do not want any of my pupils falling in love with you.'

'Dash it all, Cos, schoolgirls ain't in my line,' he assured her, 'but I will certainly make myself scarce if that is what you wish.'

'I am sure Antonia did not mean to be rude, Master Charles, but it is our reputation, you see, with so many young ladies in our charge . . . '

'I perfectly understand,' he told her with his charming smile. 'You may be sure that I would do nothing to jeopardize Antonia's venture, I promise you.'

'Perhaps, Beatrice, you would go and find Mrs Widdecombe and assure yourself that a room has been prepared for Charles.'

'Oh yes, of course, Antonia dear. Our housekeeper is a good, kind creature, but I will check that she has aired the sheets properly. And your baggage, Master Charles, I've no doubt Dawkin has taken care of that, but one can never be too careful . . . ' Still talking, the good lady hurried out of the room leaving Antonia to turn her direct gaze upon her cousin.

'You have not lost your power to charm, I see. Poor Beatrice is already under your spell. But I am in earnest, Charlie, when I say that you must be discreet. This dancing school is my livelihood; it is not a game. I will not let you endanger it.'

'I give you my word.' He pinched her cheek. 'Trust me, Antonia, I would do nothing to harm you, you know that.'

She eyed him thoughtfully. 'Not intentionally, perhaps, but — Charles, please try to keep out of mischief while you are in Bath.'

She had to content herself with his assurances and she could not deny that she was pleased to see her young cousin. His sunny good humour and quick wit would be a welcome addition to their evenings and she was forced to confess to herself that she had been finding Miss Chittering's idle chatter each night a little hard to bear.

★　★　★

Whilst Antonia was anxious for her handsome young cousin to avoid the dancing classes, she had no intention of denying his existence. She happily accepted his escort on a visit to the lending library a few days after his arrival. She had no classes that morning and stepped out with her cousin in a sunny mood that matched the warmth of the late spring day. There were any number of introductions to be made: it was generally known that Antonia Venn's lineage was impeccable and despite her odd behaviour in setting up her own establishment, the matrons of Bath were only too eager to become acquainted with her personable young cousin. Always happy to please,

Charles was at his most charming and Antonia could not help but admire the way he responded to the ladies' questions with just the right mixture of deference and liveliness that won their approval. She was moved to comment on it as they made their way back through Milsom Street, having exchanged her library books and executed the few errands that Miss Chittering had requested.

'I am very much afraid, Charles, that you are becoming a regular Bond Street beau.'

'I am sure I know not what you mean, Antonia. I have been politeness itself today.'

'You have been charming the ladies very prettily, I vow. I should not be surprised if you do not receive a dozen invitations after this performance.'

'Then tell me if I may accept them.'

'That is for you to decide, it is no matter of mine.'

'But you have been so vigilant in keeping me away from your pupils.'

'Ah, but that only applies to Queen Square, where I cannot afford to have anything other than the very highest standards of behaviour. However, if any of the fond mamas we have met today wish to invite you to their own parties, that is a very different matter.'

'Sounds like a fudge to me,' muttered Mr

Haseley, 'and if you are talking of Bond Street beaux, the gentleman bearing down upon us now is one such and you will agree we are nothing alike!'

'That gentleman is the father of one of my most amiable pupils,' murmured Antonia as Sir Rigby came hurrying towards them, greeting Antonia with a low bow that set his corsets creaking.

''Servant, Miss Venn. This is indeed a pleasure. I have just come from Queen Square, where I was told you were not at home and now Fate has granted me this meeting! Just the sight of you has brightened my morning.' He paused, casting a questioning glance at her companion.

'Good morning, Sir Rigby. May I present to you my cousin, Charles Haseley?'

'Your servant, sir.' Sir Rigby favoured the young man with a small nod and an appraising look. 'New to Bath, eh? D'you make a long stay?'

'Yes, it is my first time here, Sir Rigby, but I cannot tell you the length of my visit — a few weeks, perhaps, until my cousin has had enough of me.'

Antonia was faintly amused to note that her cousin's charming manner, which succeeded so well with the ladies, did not have the same effect upon Sir Rigby. He gave the younger man a knowing look.

'Hmmph! Been rusticated, have you? Oh, no need to colour up, my boy, we've all done it, although it was more years ago than I care to remember.' His attention returned to Antonia. 'I am glad I have seen you. I have left a little token in Queen Square for you, nothing much, merely a few spring blossoms, but I hope you like 'em.' With a courtly bow to Antonia and her companion he took his leave, to continue his stately progress through the streets.

'You should be on your guard with that one, Cos!' remarked Mr Haseley, as they resumed their walk.

'His compliments are a little . . . effusive, I admit, but not beyond what is acceptable.'

'Well I don't trust him.'

'Do you think he has designs upon my virtue?'

'You may joke, Antonia, but you had best beware of that old roué.'

'You recognize the type, perhaps?' she asked innocently.

'Dash it all, Cos!' he replied with his disarming grin. 'I appreciate a pretty face, but I ain't in the petticoat line! No, but this Sir Rigby of yours looks like a very shady character to me — and when I think how you have been warning me about your precious reputation — '

'Very true! But his daughter is a pupil and I cannot stop the gentleman calling at my house, so it would appear that I will have to rely upon Miss Chittering to protect my good name. She is so respectable I do not think there can be the least objection there.'

Mr Haseley did not laugh with her.

'Do stop funning, Antonia, I pray you, and be serious. You have set yourself up here without a — a patron or any male protector: some men will think you fair game for a little flirtation, or worse. And pray do not fly back at me. I know you are no longer a schoolgirl and that you consider yourself to be up to snuff, but I have been allowed far more freedom than you, Cos, and I know there are any number of fellows — fashionable men, too and from the very best families — who would take your situation as a positive encouragement.'

Realizing that he was very much in earnest, Antonia forbore to tease him. She squeezed his arm.

'I am very grateful for your concern, Charlie, *truly* I am. I promise you I shall take care. And I shall make sure we go out together regularly while you are with me, so that everyone can see that I am not unprotected.'

Charles was not convinced, so Antonia set about turning his thoughts in another direction. She asked him about Oxford and encouraged him to talk about his life there. His constant references to gaming hells and cards raised a faint alarm in her breast and she asked him bluntly if he was in debt.

'Of course not! At least, no more than any of my friends. You have to realize, Cos, how expensive it is at Oxford, if I am not to live like a recluse. Papa's allowance is very generous, of course,' he added hastily, 'but one cannot be expected to be studying all the time, you know, and then there is one's tailor to pay.' He sighed. 'The thing is, Antonia, I don't really want to be there at all. I'm not one of your bookish coves, wishing to spend all my time poring over some ancient manuscript. I want action! Bonaparte is loose in Europe again and I would much rather be confronting him than reading a dreary book.' He glanced down at her anxious face. 'Oh don't worry, I have already promised Mama that I will not take the King's shilling. Papa has agreed that when I have finished my studies he will consider buying me a commission, but that is more than twelve months' hence. I suppose I must be content with that, but it could well be too late by then. Antonia, do you not *see*? If Bonaparte is not stopped soon he will overrun the whole of Europe, then turn his sights upon us. And when he sends his soldiers over here, promises or no, I shall enlist!'

'I am sure your parents would understand such circumstances, my dear, however, it has not yet come to that.'

'Yes, well, I would so much rather be doing something to help — after all,' he added despondently, 'most likely by the time I leave Oxford it will all be over and I shall not see any action at all.'

Realizing that assurances of his family's relief at this prospect would not find favour, Antonia uttered a few soothing but non-committal sentences and could only hope that her restless young cousin would not allow his yearning for adventure to land him in trouble.

4

Mr Haseley looked at his watch. It was four o'clock and he guessed that the majority of the dancing lessons would be over and he could safely return to his cousin's house without meeting any of her pupils. He reached Queen Square and was almost at his destination before he noticed the carriage at the door. He hesitated. Was it a tardy pupil, or perhaps a visitor for Antonia? Realizing he could not turn away now he strode on, reaching the steps just as a vision in pink and white muslin appeared in the doorway.

The young lady had paused on the threshold to pull on her gloves and for some moments was unaware of the young man gazing up at her. Charles had stopped, entranced by the picture before him. His glance swept from the dark ringlets peeping out beneath the wide brim of her straw bonnet, over the heart-shaped face with its generous mouth and moved on to the dainty figure shown to advantage by the close-fitting spencer of rose-pink velvet whose low neckline was modestly filled with lace. He was about to speak when the young lady raised her eyes from the task of buttoning her gloves. He found himself being surveyed by the largest, darkest eyes he had ever seen and the words died on his lips. Isabella Burstock had tarried a little longer than usual at her dancing to practise a particularly difficult step and the glow of exercise still shone in her face. Charles was transfixed, but as he continued to stare, he became aware of a decided twinkle in that dark gaze. He struggled to recover his manners. Raising his hat, he stepped aside with a bow, allowing the vision to descend the steps and climb quickly into the coach, but not before he had glimpsed an extremely pretty ankle.

The carriage set off immediately and, shaking himself out of his reverie, Mr Haseley ran up the steps and into the house where he found Miss Chittering alone in the morning-room.

'Was that perhaps Sir Rigby's coach I saw leaving the house as I arrived?' he asked casually.

Miss Chittering shook her head. 'Oh no, that was Lady Burstock's carriage, come to fetch Miss Isabella. She stayed a little later, today. She is a lovely child, but very spirited, you know. Once she has an idea in her head, there is no turning her from it. She was determined to perfect the boulanger, even though the carriage was at the door. Antonia was reluctant to continue, but as she said, it is as quick to show her the steps as to argue.'

'Perhaps she is too much indulged by her parents.'

'By no means — that is, her papa is dead, but Lady Burstock is very conscious of her duty and, indeed, Isabella is a very prettily behaved young lady, in general.' She paused. 'Perhaps your mama has mentioned Lady Burstock? I believe they were close friends at school — my lady always asks after her when she calls with her daughter.'

'Lady Burstock is here to take the waters, perhaps?'

'I believe so. I understand she had not been well since Lord Burstock's sad demise two winters since. Isabella tells me she visits the Pump Room every morning. Of course, the waters do not agree with everyone. I remember Mrs Partridge telling me only yesterday of an acquaintance who came to Bath and was laid quite *low* after just a week. And I know myself that I have never found the waters efficacious, although I am told one should persevere, but they taste quite horrid, you know, at least you *won't* know, will you Master Charles, but as I was telling Antonia only yesterday — '

Remembering his dinner engagement, Charles excused himself hastily and fled.

★   ★   ★

The next day Charles left the house early and made his way to the Pump Room. Matrons who knew him as Antonia's handsome young cousin greeted him with pleasure. He conversed with them engagingly, confided to them all that he had come in search of his mama's friend, Lady Burstock, confessing that he had never yet met the lady. His auditors laughed, tapped his arm playfully and promised to perform the necessary introduction, should she appear, which was by no means certain.

He then only had to wait for Lady Burstock to arrive, which she did in due course and the introductions were made. Charles found himself presented to an elegant woman, a taller, older version of the vision he had seen on the steps of Queen Square the day before. Charles noted that Lady Burstock's dark eyes had all the brilliance of her daughter's and there was a great deal of humour in her countenance as she regarded the young man before her.

'So you are Amelia's son. How do you do?' She smiled and held out one elegantly gloved

116

hand. 'I trust you left your mama in good health?'

'Yes — that is, she was very well when I last saw her,' stammered Charles.

'And is she planning to visit Bath soon? I would so much like to see her here.'

'Well, she has said nothing to me,' he responded truthfully.

Lady Burstock had fixed him with her smile, but now she looked past him and her smile grew as Isabella came up.

'My dear, have you completed your errands? Good. Come here, child, and let me present Mr Haseley to you. He is the son of my dearest schoolfriend — I am sure you have heard me mention Amelia Haseley?'

'Why yes, of course. How do you do, sir?' Isabella's dark eyes rested upon Charles, but she gave no sign that she recognized him.

'And where do you stay, Mr Haseley?'

'With my cousin, ma'am, in Queen Square, although you will never find me there during the day,' he added hastily.

'And do you attend the Assemblies here?' Isabella asked him. 'Mama is taking me tomorrow night.'

Charles felt his spirits rise: this must be an invitation! He was careful to keep his enthusiasm under control.

'Oh, well, I usually look in, if I have no

other engagements.'

Lady Burstock's smile deepened at his studied air of indifference.

'Then we will look out for you, Mr Haseley. Isabella is eager to show me that her time at your cousin's establishment has not been wasted.'

'I am sure it has not,' smiled Charles, allowing his gaze to rest upon that young lady's face. Isabella met his eyes for a brief moment before the dark lashes swept down again, but in that instant Charles saw the flash of triumph in her eyes, everything was working out just as she had planned it!

★ ★ ★

Antonia came down to breakfast two days later to find Charles awaiting her and she quizzed him on his early rising.

He flushed. 'Dash it, Cos, I'm not always a lazy-bones. By the by, I saw Lady Burstock at the Assembly Rooms last night, and she's invited us to dine with her tonight.'

'Lady Burstock? I did not know you were acquainted.'

'Well, she is a good friend of mama's so I thought it only right to introduce myself,' he said airily. 'But the invitation, Antonia, will you go?'

'How kind of her, but I cannot go.'

'She thinks very highly of you, Antonia, and has made a point of inviting you.'

'Did she consult her son on the matter?'

'I beg your pardon?'

'Oh nothing. I am very obliged to her, but it will not do.'

Charles picked up his knife and fork saying, 'Well, I think you are being far too nice. If Lady Burstock sees no objection, then why should you?'

'Because — because I do not want to be stared at like some freakshow. People do not understand why I prefer to earn my keep when I could be living idly with my aunt and uncle. No, Charles, I am sorry, I will not change my mind. I will write to Lady Burstock this afternoon, excusing myself, but you must not let it spoil *your* enjoyment.'

He grinned at her. 'I won't, don't worry about that. Oh, what o'clock is it? Great heavens, I must go.'

'But you have not finished breakfast! Charles — where are you going in such a hurry?'

'What? Oh-I-um — I am meeting friends in town. Must dash — oh, excuse me, Miss Chittering! Good morning — must dash. Goodbye!'

'Well, Master Charles is in a mighty hurry,'

declared Miss Chittering, straightening her cap as she came to the breakfast-table.

'Did he collide with you, Beatrice? What a harum-scarum boy he is. You should scold him soundly.'

Miss Chittering flushed and clucked her tongue, reminding Antonia very much of an agitated hen.

'Oh no, that is, I couldn't possibly — I am sure Master Charles did not intend to.'

Antonia's eyes twinkled.

'What you mean is that Charles has learned to turn you up sweet!'

'I mean nothing so vulgar,' declared Miss Chittering, affronted.

'No, of course you do not, and I apologize for suggesting it. Now I am sorry that I cannot stay with you for breakfast, Beatrice, but I want to write a letter before our first class this morning. Lady Burstock has invited me to dine with her this evening.'

'Lady Burstock!'

'Yes, is it not kind of her? Charles too has been invited, and I see no reason why he should not go, although naturally *I* must decline.'

'Oh — but — are you sure you cannot accept?'

'Quite sure. I would not be seen to be moving out of my station.'

'No indeed, my love. I always think a single lady has to be so careful these days not to incur censure. Although I daresay you are as well-born as any you might meet in Bath, but your profession will sit ill with some. But Charles is to go? Well, we must be thankful that he will come to no harm in that company. I doubt Lady Burstock will allow any card game more serious than a little whist. And we will not repine, Antonia. We shall be able to spend a very snug evening here together.'

At the thought of yet another *snug evening together* Miss Venn stifled a sigh and with a muttered 'excuse me!' she made her escape.

$$\star \quad \star \quad \star$$

Sir Laurence walked into the dining-room of Great Pulteney Street, carrying a large parcel.

'This has just arrived for you, Bella, so I brought it up.'

Miss Burstock had been quietly reading to her Mama while that lady reclined upon a sofa, but at her brother's words she dropped her book and jumped up with a cry.

'My dress! Oh Laurence — give it to me — give it to me.'

He held the parcel at arm's length above his head, defying her attempts to reach it.

'What, is it so important to you that you cast aside Mama's book and behave in such a hoydenish manner?' he demanded with mock severity.

Isabella drew a deep breath and forced herself to stand still, her hands clasped before her.

'Please, Laurence, *dear* Laurence. Give me my dress.'

'Take it, then, brat.' He tossed the parcel into her eager arms and walked over to greet Lady Burstock. 'Well, Mama, are you feeling at low ebb today?'

'By no means,' she replied, sitting up and presenting her cheek for his salute. 'But you will recall that we are having a little dinner party this evening and I am recruiting my strength.'

A little crow of delight brought their attention to Isabella, who was kneeling on the floor beside the open package, surrounded by silver tissue.

'Oh look, Mama, is it not exquisite?' She held up the gown, a flimsy creation in pale-yellow muslin, dotted with gold spangles. 'Look at the gold sash, Mama, and the flounces at the hem and sleeves, just as we directed.'

'As *you* directed, Isabella,' corrected her mama fondly. 'You will look delightful in it.'

'And may I wear it this evening?'

Sir Laurence raised an eyebrow: 'Oho — are you wishing to make an impression upon some young buck tonight?'

Isabella tossed her head. 'No such thing, but it is Mama's first party since we came to Bath and I want to look my best.'

'Then I am sorry I shall miss it. I am engaged to dine with Monkton at the White Hart tonight. He leaves for Brussels in the morning so I cannot cry off.'

'No indeed, my dear. You will be missed, of course, but there will be none of your particular friends. I have merely invited those of our acquaintance with young families of Bella's age and, who knows, with so many young people we may even have a little dancing after supper.'

Isabella laughed. 'Miss Venn would enjoy that!'

Sir Laurence looked at Lady Burstock. 'You have invited Miss Venn?'

'I met her cousin at the Assembly Rooms last night and issued an invitation to them both. I do hope she will come. I find her most refreshing.'

'Perhaps Laurence is now trying to think of an excuse to cry off from his engagement,' said Isabella shrewdly.

'Nothing of the sort.' He strode to the

door, 'I must go up and change, if I am not to be late. Monkton dines early tonight. I wish you a successful evening, Mama — and Isabella, behave yourself.'

★ ★ ★

'Good morning, Rosamund — Isabella. You are my only pupils today, so I hope you are prepared to work.'

Antonia entered the ballroom carrying a bundle of music which she deposited on the pianoforte.

'Oh Miss Venn! I do wish you had been with us last night,' declared Isabella, slipping on her dancing pumps. 'We had such a delightful evening.'

Antonia inclined her head a little. 'My cousin has already told me how much he enjoyed it.'

'Everyone was talking about the new turning dance — the waltz — do you know it?'

'Of course.'

'Oh pray, will you teach Rosie and me to dance it? Bertrand Ormerod wanted me to try it last night, but Mama refused lest the evening should turn into a romp.'

'Lady Burstock is very wise. It is still considered forward in some quarters and certainly not for young ladies who have yet to be presented. It will also be best if you both learn to perform it very well before trying it out in public.'

Isabella sighed ecstatically. 'Then you will teach us?'

'Perhaps, but later. First you must attend me for the usual dances — especially the rigaudon — you still need to perfect the steps for that!'

'Oh yes, yes, of course we will. And it is agreed that Rosie and I will walk back to Great Pulteney Street together, so there can be no objection if our lesson overruns a little.'

Antonia laughed at their happy excitement.

'Very well then. We will start with a gavotte. Rosamund, remember to arch your foot.'

What the class lacked in numbers the two young ladies certainly made up for in enthusiasm. They skipped their way through the dances with Antonia correcting or improving their steps while Miss Chittering played tirelessly. A lively gavotte and rigaudon were followed by the much more stately pavanne, but as the clock chimed the hour, Miss Burstock reminded Antonia of her promise.

'You said you would show us the turning dance, Miss Venn.'

'Very well, if Miss Chittering will play for

us. You will find suitable music there on the piano, Beatrice.'

'Rosie is off to the country in a se'ennight and she needs to know it,' confided Isabella, 'especially if Sir Rigby invites his London friends to stay.'

Antonia closed her lips firmly against a reply to Isabella's artless speech: if reports were correct, she thought it unlikely that Rosamund would be allowed to spend very much time with Sir Rigby's more colourful friends.

'Let us not waste any time chattering, girls. Now, Isabella, you can take the man's part to begin. You must stand, thus, and take Rosamund's hand, like so, with your other hand around her waist, there. Now let us walk though the steps before we ask Miss Chittering to play for us.'

Soon the ballroom was echoing with their laughter as the girls held each other and paced out the unfamiliar steps.

'There is no need to blush, Rosamund,' Antonia told her. 'It is a quite respectable dance. Once you have made your come-out it will be perfectly acceptable for you to take part, at a select gathering, of course. There can be no objection. Now, Isabella put your hand a little higher on Rosie's back, thus, and remember what I have taught you. One, two three, one two three . . . '

At a gesture from Antonia, Miss Chittering began to play and the girls began to move around the floor.

'No, no girls, that is *not* the way! Rosamund, you will never move gracefully if you continue to giggle so! And Isabella, if you are dancing the man's part you must lead your partner. It is up to you to guide Rosamund around the floor.'

'Perhaps they need an example.'

Startled, Antonia turned to find Sir Laurence standing by the door, watching them with an amused smile on his face. He was dressed for walking in a morning coat of blue superfine and pale, skin-tight pantaloons which disappeared into shining Hessians.

'I beg your pardon for the intrusion, Miss Venn, I heard the laughter and my curiosity overcame me.'

Miss Burstock skipped across the room to him.

'Laurence, *dear* brother, you are just what we need. You were telling Mama only this morning that your leg has healed sufficiently to allow you to do almost anything now, so will you waltz with me, please?'

Sir Laurence limped across the room, pulling off his gloves and laying them on a nearby chair, together with his hat and cane.

'Certainly not. But if Miss Venn will permit me, we will show you young ladies how it should be done.'

Antonia's brows rose. 'Can you dance in those boots, sir?'

'Oh I should think so. They are extremely pliant, you know. Well, ma'am?' He held out his hand.

'I — that is — I don't think . . . ' Antonia struggled for words, but Sir Laurence seemed to have taken control. He took her hand and led her unresisting to the centre of the room.

'Miss Chittering, if you please,' he commanded.

That lady, silenced for once, looked helplessly at Antonia, who nodded at her to begin.

'I should tell you, sir, that I have not danced this for some years,' Antonia warned him, as he put one arm across her back.

'Then you will be glad of the practice,' was the only reply.

They paced the first four steps slowly, side by side, then Sir Laurence skilfully turned his partner until they were facing one another, turning slowly as they moved around the room. Antonia strained to concentrate on the steps, all too aware of the strong arm around her waist and the firm warm clasp of his fingers on her hand. She also realized with some surprise that the dragging step disappeared once Sir Laurence began to dance. Then, without warning, he stopped.

'Miss Venn, Miss Venn!'

The music trailed away into silence.

'I beg your pardon, sir. I was concentrating on the steps.'

'I have no complaint about the steps, but I do object to having to address my remarks to the top of your head. Can you not look at me occasionally?'

She was aware of Isabella and Rosamund giggling together in the corner. 'I-um — I am sorry.'

'Very well, then let us try again. Isabella, you will note this, if you please. You are at Almack's, a young man of your acquaintance has led you on to the floor: you keep your head up, as Miss Venn is now doing and perhaps, if the gentleman is very fortunate, you may even favour him with a smile.' A small chuckle escaped his partner and Sir Laurence glanced down at her, his hard eyes glinting. 'That is much better. Now, let us begin again.'

Miss Chittering started to play and they began once more to circle the room slowly. As they moved away from the two young ladies, Sir Laurence spoke.

'I understand you did not attend my

mother's little party last night.'

'Oh? Were you not there?'

'Unfortunately I was engaged to dine elsewhere. Why did you not go?'

'I did not think it fitting — you of all people should understand that.'

'You are too severe upon yourself, madam. My mother would have welcomed your presence. She likes you very much.'

'Th-thank you,' she stammered, nonplussed.

They moved on to the sauteuse, the second section of the dance and were silent, concentrating. As they grew accustomed to each other their steps became even more perfectly matched. Antonia felt again the long-forgotten exhilaration of the dance: her eyes shone and her body swayed to the rhythm of the music. She twirled and twisted as Sir Laurence deftly led her around the room. When they reached the jetté, the final, liveliest part of the waltz they seemed to fly over the floor, turning and circling together as the music flowed about them, their eyes locked together, oblivious of spectators. They halted as the final bars of the waltz died away, Antonia gracefully raising her arms in an arc above her head, signalling the end of the dance. Sir Laurence did not relax his hold, standing with his hands circling her waist, nor did Antonia make any move to pull away. They continued to gaze at one another, as if they had both discovered some previously unacknowledged truth. Eventually the laughing applause from their audience brought them back to the present. With an effort Antonia looked away from her partner and gently disengaged herself from his grasp.

'There, now you have seen it. At your next lesson it will be your turn.' She was surprised how normal her voice sounded, when she felt such turmoil in her brain.

'But it is wonderful!' cried Isabella. 'Pray could we not try it now, just once?'

Antonia shook her head. 'I am sorry, my dears, but there really is no time.'

'Oh surely, just a few more minutes . . . '

Sir Laurence retrieved his hat and gloves from the chair.

'We have already encroached upon Miss Venn's time for far too long, Isabella.' He saw the disappointment in her face and added casually, 'And you have yet to ask me why I have called for you, when it was agreed you would make your own way home.' Miss Burstock's look of disappointment was replaced by one of curiosity and he continued, 'I understand there has been a delivery of ice to Carter's store in Milsom Street, where they are even now serving iced cream. I thought you and Miss Claremont might like to stop there on the way home.'

Isabella clapped her hands and gave a little crow of laughter.

'Oh yes, please, *dearest* of brothers! Come, Rosie, we must change.'

Antonia smiled. 'Alas, even the attraction of my dance class is eclipsed by the promise of ices.'

'The perfect refreshment for a warm day, Miss Venn, yet May is scarce begun. Bath can be very uncomfortable in the summer months. Do you plan to go away?'

She shook her head. 'I shall stay here for those pupils who remain in town.'

'You may find your rooms a little thin of company.'

She stifled a sigh. 'I know it, but I have committed everything to this venture and I cannot turn custom away, however small the return.'

He looked as if he would say more, but Isabella and her companion had by this time replaced their satin dance pumps with outdoor shoes and were urging him to hurry. With a wry smile he made his bow, picked up his hat and cane and ushered his charges out of the room.

'Well, I vow I have never met two such lively girls,' declared Miss Chittering, closing the pianoforte. 'They are most charming, of course, but I cannot think it right for them to press you into teaching them to waltz. It is such a — a *forward* dance. Oh I know you will say that it is perfectly respectable, especially since Lady Jersey introduced it to Almack's last year, but I certainly could not feel comfortable with a man's arm about me in such an intimate fashion. And when Sir Laurence insisted you should dance it with him I declare I was ready to drop. Of course, you are no longer a young girl in your first season but, my dear, did you not find it a trifle disconcerting? Antonia, my dear, it was a little — bold — was it not?'

Antonia was standing at the window, gazing down at the street and Miss Chittering had to repeat her question once again before Antonia responded.

'I am sorry, Beatrice, were you speaking?'

'Yes, my dear. I was saying how wrong it was for Sir Laurence to dance with you — it was a most uncomfortable situation for you.'

'Not at all. It was delightful to be partnered by such a good dancer.' She felt a fluttering in her stomach as she recalled circling the room in Sir Laurence's arms. Her cheeks grew hot. 'Excuse me, Beatrice, I promised to see Cook as soon as the lesson was finished — she will think I have forgotten her.'

Miss Chittering watched her young friend's retreating form and shook her head, smiling a little as she gathered up her music. Poor Antonia. How bravely she bore all the more disagreeable parts of her situation. Miss Chittering was fully alive to the dangers and difficulties of running a dancing academy: one was at the mercy of one's clients. It seemed very unfair that Antonia could not accept a gift such as the very fine painting that Sir Rigby had wanted to bestow upon her, yet she must endure the company of such men as Sir Laurence Oakford who, in Miss Chittering's opinion, had none of the polish and address of Sir Rigby. Yet Antonia suffered it all with such good grace.

★ ★ ★

Sir Laurence entered the morning-room to find Lady Burstock at her writing desk. Upon his entry she laid down her pen and turned a smiling face towards him.

'Well, my dear?'

'Well, Mama! Isabella is gone upstairs to remove her outdoor clothes and will be with you directly.'

Lady Burstock gave a sigh of relief. 'That is good news. And she did not fly into the boughs when you fetched her?'

'Not in the least! In fact she was very pleased to see me. We should have returned sooner but we stopped for ices in Milsom Street and then we delivered Miss Claremont to her home.'

'Thank you, Laurence. It was very kind of you to give up your time.'

'It is no trouble, Mama.' He stooped to drop a kiss on her forehead. 'Isabella was very happy with my escort and is even now preparing to come riding with me. I see no sign of her wishing to be elsewhere.'

'You think I am mistaken, Laurence? I wish it may be so, but I know her moods so well and lately she has been far too quiet and docile for my liking. I am convinced she has met some young man. She walked with her maid in Sydney Gardens yesterday and did not return until it was nearly dinnertime. I know these signs, Laurence, believe me.'

'I do believe you, Mama. Isabella is a minx, never more so than when she appears to be behaving herself impeccably. You have no hint who the gentleman might be?'

'No, none. I hoped I might learn something more at dinner last night, but no, all the young men seemed quite besotted, of course, but as for Bella herself — I did think perhaps it might be young Ormerod, but although she spent quite a deal of time with him, I saw nothing in her manner to suggest anything more than a flirtation. So it must be another, someone who was not invited and *that* makes me think that he must be wholly ineligible. Oh Laurence, I do not want to forbid her to leave the house without me, but what else can I do?'

'Pray do not fret yourself, Mama. I think perhaps it might be best to leave Bath for a while. The summer months can be very uncomfortable here, you know.'

'Oh my dear. I do not think Isabella would wish to return to Burstock.'

'Isabella will do as she is bid,' he muttered grimly. 'I do not propose returning to the country, however. I thought perhaps you might like to spend some time at Brighton. There would be sufficient entertainment there to keep Bella amused and you would benefit from the sea air, Mama, instead of white-hot Bath. What say you?'

Lady Burstock considered the idea, then nodded.

'I think it is an admirable plan. We must set to work to find a house . . . '

'It may be that I have already solved that problem. You will recall I dined with Monkton yesterday. He told me his own Brighton residence will be empty for the summer — a substantial house, I understand, on Marine Parade. He has told me he would be delighted for you to take it. If you wish I will settle the details with the agent this week and we can be gone from Bath before the end of the month.'

'It would be a solution. But will you accompany us, Laurence?'

'Yes, for part of the time at least. I confess to another reason why the idea appeals to me. It is but a few hours' drive from London, so when there is news of this wretched war it can be with me the same day.

'I have a great many friends over there now, waiting to meet Boney. I may not be able to be with them, but I want to hear the news as soon as it arrives.'

'Would you prefer to remove to London?'

'By no means. You would be fagged to death there, Mama, and Isabella would be nothing but a nuisance, wanting to attend every rout and party. No, I can ride up to Town from Brighton and leave instructions for any news to be brought to me express.'

'You think an engagement will be soon?'

'Aye — Heaven help us if Bonaparte should march on our men too soon, before we have had time to meet up with the allies. By God, I wish I could be there,' he declared, his iron self-control giving way for an instant, 'if it were not for this curst leg!'

Lady Burstock said nothing, but it pained her to see the anguish in his eyes. She could only guess at his suffering as he thought of his lost career. She rose swiftly from her chair and went to him, folding his clenched hands between her own soft fingers.

'Pray, Laurence, do not torture yourself. You must be patient. The doctors are confident you will be completely healed in time.'

His dark eyes burned.

'But that will be too late. The battle will be won or lost and I shall not be there!'

She gazed up into his stormy face, so like his dear father. Most people said he had inherited his mother's looks, yet occasionally she saw that other beloved parent in him, in a sudden wry smile or impatient gesture. It was there now in his hard, angry eyes, the tightening of the jaw that enhanced the thin white scar. She reached up one hand to touch his cheek.

'It is not your destiny to be there, Laurence,' she said tenderly. 'You have said yourself often and often that Wellington is the best man to take command and that we must trust to him — and to your gallant comrades.'

She felt the tension in him ease slightly. He fought back his frustration.

'Of course, Mama. You are right. My place

now is here, with you and Bella. Wellington will manage very well, with or without me. So now, let us consider Brighton. Is it settled that you would like to go there? When shall we tell Bella?'

'Not yet. Let us make sure everything is in order first. She may be a little reluctant to leave Bath and I would not wish to endure her sulks any longer than necessary.'

He nodded.

'We will find a solution to that, Mama. But for now we must both be vigilant, to keep Isabella out of mischief.'

5

Antonia laid down her pen and rubbed her eyes. She felt very tired: perhaps it was the humid weather that made her feel so low, or the falling number of pupils. That was to be expected, of course, as families moved out of town for the summer, but she really would need to plan very carefully if she was not to outrun her budget. There was a light scratching at the door and Miss Chittering peeped in.

'Antonia, my dear, do I disturb you? Ah — you are working at your books, I see, so I will not keep you. I met Miss Cowan in the town yesterday and promised to give her my recipe for calves' livers braised in milk. Her poor sister is not so well again and I think this may be just the thing for her, so I determined to take it to her today. That is, my dear, if you can spare me? It occurred to me that I could return your book to the circulating library since I shall be passing that way.'

Antonia rose. 'Thank you, I will fetch it. I shall be glad of the break, since I cannot get these wretched figures to balance.'

'What is it, my dear, your accounts again?

Let me see: it is so often one of those little figures at the side that is omitted . . . I will look at it when I return, if you would like . . .'

'I have a better idea, Beatrice, if you are amenable,' declared Antonia. 'You can look at the books for me while I take the recipe to Miss Cowan. That is, unless you especially want to see her today?'

'No, no, I have already arranged to visit Miss Cowan and her sister later in the week, but I did so want her to have this recipe today, because she was so particularly interested in it and thought it might help her poor sister. And I would willingly look at the accounts, my dear, for nothing pleases me better than to have those little columns of figures just so. But are you sure you wish to go out? It is so close, and there is a threat of rain, I think.'

'I am very sure I want to go out,' laughed Antonia. 'I think it is the very thing to help me throw off this blue mood that has come over me today.'

Leaving Miss Chittering poring happily over the ledgers, Antonia fetched her spencer, put on her walking shoes and set off alone. Beatrice had given her Miss Cowan's direction in South Parade and she walked briskly away from Queen Square, only allowing her pace to slacken when she reached the shops of New Bond Street and High Street.

★ ★ ★

She was glad to be out of the house, and alone. Much as she hated to admit it, Antonia was finding her new life just a little irksome. Dear Beatrice was invaluable in the classroom, but Antonia found the evenings spent solely in her company interminably long and her inconsequential chatter often provoked a headache. Antonia longed to discuss the spring riots in London and the continuing unrest in the country, or the problems in Europe, but her companion considered such matters to be unsuitable topics for a lady, although she was eager enough to discuss Princess Charlotte's marriage plans or the Prince Regent's latest extravagance. Antonia shook herself mentally: she would not complain, all that was needed was a little more activity.

With sudden decision she turned into Stall Street and entered the Pump Rooms to study the noticeboards: there must be more concerts to attend. She noted the forthcoming visit of a famous Italian soprano, a lecture on rheumatism and its several cures and a recital by Mr Lovelace upon the 'Sticcardo Pastorale and various other glass instruments'. By the time she had made this short detour and returned her book to the circulating library, it was past noon and she hurried along to South Parade, where she found Miss Cowan so grateful for her visit that she could not follow her first intention of handing over the recipe at the door. Miss Cowan insisted that she should step inside and share a dish of tea.

'There is nothing my poor sister likes better than to receive visitors,' she declared, leading the way upstairs. 'It does her so much good to see new faces, for I am sure she must be tired of mine.'

Antonia made no reply as she followed her hostess to the small parlour on the first floor. The room smelled of camphor and it was very warm, for all the windows remained resolutely closed to protect Mrs Norton from any chance draught.

'And you will be our second visitor today,' Miss Cowan announced proudly. 'Even now my sister is entertaining a gentleman, is that not so, Martha my dear?'

As Antonia stepped further into the room she smiled at Mrs Norton, sitting beside the empty fireplace, wrapped in shawls. She had been a fine-looking woman, now made gaunt by ill-health, but despite her infirmity her countenance was welcoming and her eyes bright and intelligent.

'Don't crow, Sarah, or Miss Venn will think us stuffed full of our own importance. Come in, my dear, there is plenty of room for everyone.'

The booted leg of the invalid's gentleman visitor was just visible from the armchair in front of her, although the rest of the figure was hidden by the high back of the chair. Upon Miss Cowan's announcement, the gentleman rose and Antonia's eyes widened to see Sir Laurence standing before her.

'I-I came only to bring a recipe from Miss Chittering,' she stammered. 'Pray do not let me interrupt — '

'Your arrival is most welcome, I assure you,' declared Mrs Norton, smiling, 'Pray come in and sit yourself down.'

'Sir Laurence served in the Peninsula with my poor brother-in-law,' Miss Cowan explained. 'Whenever he is in Bath he always makes a point of coming to see how we go on. So very kind.'

'Not as kind as I would wish to be,' he said with a faint smile. 'How do you do, Miss Venn. Have you come to join us for tea?' He guided her to a chair beside his own while Miss Cowan disappeared to fetch the tea tray.

'I feel as if I am imposing on you,' smiled Antonia.

'Not at all,' declared Mrs Norton, 'I am sure Sir Laurence would rather be entertained by a charming young lady than a couple of old crones.'

'Nonsense, ma'am,' laughed Antonia. '*I* have no doubt that you can entertain Sir Laurence very well without my help.'

'Nevertheless, you are a very welcome addition to our party,' insisted the older woman. 'And how is that charming young cousin of yours? I had the pleasure of meeting him when I managed a short trip to the Pump Room a few days ago. A very personable young gentleman — I don't doubt he has all your pupils in a swoon.'

Antonia was immediately aware of Sir Laurence's hard eyes upon her, but she answered easily. 'Charles has been most careful to keep well away from my impressionable young ladies. Indeed, he has been so busy of late that even I scarcely see him.'

'I do not believe I have met the young gentleman,' ventured Sir Laurence.

'Have you not, sir? I believe he is acquainted with Lady Burstock. He is down from Oxford at the present and is making a short stay with me before going home — putting off the evil hour of confessing his misdemeanours to his parents, I suspect,' she added with a laugh.

Miss Cowan's entry with the tea tray caused a lively diversion and the conversation soon turned to military matters.

'So Bonaparte is on the loose again,' remarked Mrs Norton, sipping her tea, 'I thought we had him secure on Elba.'

'Not secure enough,' returned Sir Laurence gravely. 'I believe he is marching through France even now, gathering an army about him.'

'But can he be contained, do you think?' asked Antonia.

'Oh pray do not mention that man!' cried Miss Cowan, shuddering. 'I live in constant fear that he will overrun us, then there will be riots and revolution and we shall all be murdered in our beds.'

'There are already riots in the cities, Sarah, as you would know if you would bother to read the newspaper,' retorted her sister drily. 'If the government cannot do something to bring down the price of bread there will be no need for Bonaparte to send his soldiers over here.'

'I am sure it will not come to that,' said Antonia calmly, observing Miss Cowan's fearful countenance.

'Of course it won't,' added Mrs Norton.

'Why, Wellington is at this very moment in Brussels, ready to counter any attack by the French. Is that not so, Sir Laurence?'

'Indeed he is, ma'am, and those of us who fought under him in the Peninsula know how good a general he is.'

'But he has never faced Bonaparte directly, has he?'

'That is true, Miss Venn. Yet by the same token, Bonaparte has never fought against Old Hookey.'

'Ah, how well I remember my dear departed Norton calling him that,' sighed the widow. 'He always said he would back Old Hookey against a dozen French generals. No doubt you would prefer to be with your regiment at this time, Sir Laurence?'

'I would, of course, but I have estates here that need my attention and I can only wait and pray, like so many others. Besides, with my leg not yet healed I would be a liability even before the battle started. My comrades would soon be wishing me at Jericho.' He smiled, yet Antonia guessed from the tense lines of his jaw how much his disability irked him. She searched for some words of comfort.

'I have no doubt Lady Burstock is glad of your support at this time.'

Antonia flushed beneath Sir Laurence's

mocking glance, aware of how inadequate the words were. She bore little part in the conversation, being content to sip her tea and listen. Never had she seen Sir Laurence so relaxed: there was no sign of the haughty gentleman, no cruel snubs or cold looks. Mrs Norton might be for the most part housebound but her knowledge of the outside world surprised Antonia who, when asked for her opinion on a point, had to admit to ignorance.

'You are so well informed, Mrs Norton; I envy you your knowledge.'

'It is no great thing, my dear. I read widely and Sir Laurence has arranged for the London papers to come here directly — such an extravagance but he will not change it! And I correspond regularly with my friends in London. I may not be able to get out as much as I would like, but I try to know what is going on in the world.'

★ ★ ★

The afternoon was well advanced when Antonia rose to take her leave. Miss Cowan begged her to take more tea, but she was adamant.

'Thank you, but indeed I must not. I had not intended to be from home so long, Miss

148

Chittering will be growing anxious.'

'I too must be going,' said Sir Laurence. 'You are sure, ma'am, that there is nothing I can do for you?'

Mrs Norton shook her head, holding out her thin hand to her guest.

'No, indeed, Sir Laurence, as you can see we rub along quite comfortably here and want for nothing except a little company, which you are kind enough to supply.'

Miss Cowan escorted Antonia and Sir Laurence to the front door, thanking them both profusely for their visit.

'It makes all the difference you see, to have company. Martha's spirits are very low at times. But the doctor you recommended is very good, sir, and I am confident we will be out and about again in a few more days. Oh and I almost forgot to thank you for the fruit, Sir Laurence. Bless you, sir, we lived like royalty for a week. Plums and peaches from his very own hot-houses, Miss Venn,' explained Miss Cowan proudly. 'Fetched up especially for us. Thank you, Sir Laurence, and you Miss Venn, for your visit.'

'You are a most generous benefactor, sir,' smiled Antonia, as the door closed behind them and they turned away from the house.

'Not a bit of it. Captain Norton attended me when I was wounded at Burgos

— without his help it is unlikely that I should have returned to England alive. He had me strapped to a wagon during the long retreat to Portugal and shared his rations with me. When I was shipped home I promised to carry a letter to his wife and since then I have done my best to keep in touch.' He paused, then added in a matter-of-fact voice, 'Norton was killed at Vittoria. It was some months before I heard. I would do more for his widow financially, if I could, but she will not allow it.'

'Martha Norton is a proud woman, sir. She is not ungrateful for your help, but she values her independence.'

'As you do.'

The sudden turn in the conversation surprised Antonia, but it also served to remind her of her situation.

'As I do,' she nodded. They had reached the corner of South Parade and Antonia stopped. 'And I will thus bid you goodbye, Sir Laurence. My way lies to the far side of the Abbey and Pump Rooms. Yours, I believe, is via Pulteney Bridge.'

With what she hoped was a polite smile and a nod of dismissal she continued on her way. Sir Laurence fell into step beside her.

'Where is your maid, Miss Venn?'

Antonia raised her brows. 'I did not

consider it necessary to be accompanied on this occasion — nor do I need to explain my actions.'

'Meaning, I suppose, that it is none of my business.'

'Exactly. Forgive my plain speaking, but pray, go your own way, Sir Laurence, and allow me to go mine.'

'But this *is* my way, Miss Venn. Would you have me walk behind you, or in front, as if we were strangers?'

'I wish to heaven we were,' she muttered. Aloud, she said, 'You owe me no undue attention, Sir Laurence. Our acquaintance is very slight — to make anything more of it would be to court trouble.'

'Oh? Why is that?' he asked her conversationally.

'Because — because tongues would wag, sir. I am your sister's dancing mistress. People would say — would say that I — ' She broke off in confusion.

'They would say that you were setting your cap at me?' he finished for her. 'Or perhaps that my designs on you were something less than honourable.'

'Neither would be acceptable to me, sir!'

'Then perhaps you see why it is necessary to have your maid with you at all times.'

'Would my maid's presence make any

difference in this instance?'

He grinned. 'Possibly, but I think not.'

She laughed. 'Sir Laurence you are incorrigible! But to be serious, I cannot agree with you. One should not require an attendant to walk through the streets of Bath in the middle of the day. Why, the notion is quite Gothic.'

'Then I too must be quite Gothic,' he responded, 'since it does not suit my notions of propriety. I would not allow my sister to behave thus.'

'But the case is quite different. And I am not your sister.'

'I thank God for that.'

She stopped. 'Then there is no need for you to escort me. And if you are about to argue that our paths lead the same way,' she continued, as he was about to speak, 'pray, sir, *take another route!*'

Any answer that Sir Laurence might have made was interrupted by a sudden crash of thunder, followed immediately by large drops of rain that spattered on the flagstones. With a smothered exclamation, Antonia caught up her gown and dashed to the nearest shop doorway. Sir Laurence followed her, but she could not condemn him for seeking shelter from the heavy rain that was falling like a curtain in front of her and turning the dusty road into a river of mud.

They stood in companionable silence. Antonia closed her eyes, breathing in the scent rising from the dusty streets.

'I love rain storms at this time of year. That lovely rich earthy smell from the dry ground and everything is so — so fresh afterwards. It reminds me of the country.'

'Do you miss it?'

'Occasionally. More so as the days grow hotter. I suppose it is something to which I must accustom myself.'

'Do I detect a wistful note in your voice — are you regretting your decision to come to Bath?'

No, only — oh if I am honest I should say that I — you see, I thought that my independence would bring freedom, but I find I am as much hedged about as ever. My method of independence means I am unable to go to Assemblies and dance, which is the thing I would most like to do. And at the concert the other night — oh, I tried to ignore them, and Beatrice certainly did not notice, but the looks of disapproval I received for merely daring to appear — had I been a demi-rep I should have received no worse a reception.' Her hands flew to her mouth and she looked up guiltily. 'Oh, I should not have said that. I beg your pardon.'

'No, no, you may say what you like to me, I take no offence.'

'My wretched tongue! And all because some of the matrons stared down their high-bred noses at me, it set me in a passion. It is not so bad, after all. And when I think of poor Mrs Norton and her sister, I am ashamed of myself. I have so much, you see.' She stopped: Sir Laurence had raised his glass and fixed her with his hard gaze that had been known to unnerve weaker mortals. Miss Venn merely raised her brows in an enquiry.

'Sir?'

'Strange, that I should suddenly remember more of our first meeting.'

Antonia felt her cheeks grow hot. 'I had hoped you would not.'

She froze as his fingers stroked her cheek. 'You have nothing to be ashamed of, madam. As for myself — '

'Pray, sir, say no more.'

Antonia felt the tears prickling her eyelids. She was very aware of him standing beside her and knew an impulse to lean her head against his shoulder, so conveniently close and inviting. Her mouth felt dry, perhaps she had misunderstood him. She dared to look up. There was no mistaking the glow of desire burning in his dark eyes. She knew a moment of panic.

'It — it has stopped raining, Sir Laurence. We — we should continue, I think.'

As suddenly as it had started the rain cleared and within moments the hot sun was drying off the walkway. Antonia stepped out from the doorway. She did not look at Sir Laurence, and did not know whether she was pleased or alarmed when he fell into step beside her. She began to talk, trying to hide the sudden disturbance in her breast.

'At least here in Bath the streets are never waterlogged. When I lived with my aunt in Wiltshire we would not dare to venture out after such a storm without stout walking shoes. Papa was used to say it was one of the reasons he hated the country. He much preferred London, although from the stories he told me I cannot think it so very entertaining. I remember once he said that he and his friends laid bets on raindrops: which one would be the first to reach the bottom of the window. Utter folly of course, but gentlemen seem only too susceptible to such nonsense when they have nothing better to occupy their time.'

'Not all gentlemen, Miss Venn.'

'I can tell by your tone that *you* do not approve.'

'No.'

'And very likely you did not approve of Papa.'

'I was never one of his set. I was very young, you see, and new to London. Also, I was army-mad and could not understand their obsession with drinking, gaming and . . . '

'And women?'

'I am sorry, I did not mean to — '

'Think nothing of it, Sir Laurence. I cut my eye-teeth too long ago to worry about a few home-truths. As a matter of fact, I did not like my father overmuch. Have I shocked you? He could be very charming, I believe, and very generous to his friends but he was so rarely at home, you see, so we were never very close. Poor Mama had to cope alone with keeping household and looking after me. The money dwindled until we could not even afford a governess for me, although dear Miss Chittering could not be persuaded to leave and she stayed on for the merest pittance, which was so foolish of her, because she really should have been putting something aside for her old age.'

'Is that why she is with you now — to salve your conscience?'

'Of course not. Well, not entirely. I *do* feel responsible for her, but I needed someone to help me run my dancing school and she is an excellent pianist, and very good with the younger pupils.'

They walked on in silence for a few moments, then Sir Laurence asked abruptly, 'And are you truly happy with your life here?'

Antonia stopped. 'What a strange creature you are! How can you ask such a question?'

'Because I wish to know.' He turned to look down at her, a smile playing at the corners of his mouth. '*Are* you happy?'

'It is the life I have chosen for myself.'

'That does not answer my question.'

She began to walk on. 'Very few of us can have everything we want, Sir Laurence. I am very . . . satisfied with my lot.'

'Well you should not be,' he retorted. 'I had much rather you did not have to teach silly young girls like my sister to dance.'

'Well, I cannot change that,' she flashed, nettled.

'No, but *I* can.' He caught her arm, compelling her to stop. 'This is not the role I see for you. I would have you dancing till dawn, riding in an elegant carriage — your only worry should be which gown to wear, not how you will contrive to pay your creditors!'

She closed her eyes, disappointment flooding through her. By her own actions she had laid herself open to this. Charles had warned her — his words echoed through her head! What would he offer her, a little house somewhere where he could visit her discreetly? Suddenly she could not bear to hear it.

'Oh please, don't say any more.'

Sir Laurence heard the distress in her voice and he released her.

'What is it, Antonia, what have I said?'

Nothing — oh goodness — listen.' Hastily she wiped away a tear, trying to speak lightly. 'That is the church clock, striking the hour. I must get back. I promised Beatrice I would not be late.'

He accepted her rebuff with the faintest shrug of his shoulders and fell into step again beside her.

'I am sorry; I spoke too soon.'

'Pray let us forget that you have spoken at all.'

'By all means, but will you tell me what I have said that has upset you?'

She hesitated, then said in a low voice, 'I have invested everything I have into my school, Sir Laurence. I did so because it offered me a dignified, independent living. I am not beholden to anyone — nor do I wish to be, now or in the future.'

'Not beholden!' He stopped and after a small silence he said, 'Very well, madam. My apologies. Will you still accept my escort to Queen Square?'

It flashed through her mind that if she refused, she might never see him again. She put her fingers on his arm in silent acquiescence, refusing to think too deeply about why it should matter so much to her.

If she had been worried that the rest of their journey would prove uncomfortable, Sir Laurence soon allayed her fears. A few questions on the most unexceptional topics set her at her ease and by the time they reached her door she could almost believe his outburst had never occurred. Entering the house, Antonia felt unusually depressed and wanted nothing more than to spend a few moments in quiet reflection, but Miss Chittering was waiting for her.

'Antonia, my dear. I have been looking out for you. Come into the sitting-room — there is a most pleasant surprise for you.'

She tried to smile. 'Have you managed to balance my accounts, Beatrice? How clever of you.'

'Yes, yes, it was only a slip in one column that made it impossible to balance. But you know having totted up all our outgoings, my dear, I can see that we are not in such good shape as one would like. And several of our pupils will be leaving Bath for the summer, which will deplete our numbers even more.'

Antonia, aware of the servants hovering in the hall, frowned at her companion.

'What is it, my dear? Oh — yes — quite. But that is not what I meant to say to you, Antonia! There is such a surprise for you in the sitting-room! Come, my dear — come along!'

Stifling a sigh, Antonia followed her companion into the small sitting-room where a huge bouquet of roses had been placed on her desk.

'Sir Rigby brought them himself an hour since. I invited him to wait for you, but he would not, saying he would leave these to speak for him.'

'Oh.'

'I can see you are astonished, my dear. Is it not a very romantic gesture?'

'A very foolish one!' came the sharp reply. 'Pray have them returned to Sir Rigby at once. I cannot accept such a token.'

'But, my dear, such a compliment to you. And I am sure his intentions are most honourable.'

'And I am sure they are not!' retorted Miss Venn. She sighed. 'My dear Beatrice, gentlemen do not marry dancing teachers.'

Miss Chittering's faded cheek grew very pink.

'Oh — oh my goodness! Surely, surely you do not think — '

'Yes, I *do*. Now, please, Beatrice, have them returned immediately.'

'Oh course, my love, at once. But I cannot believe it, not of Sir Rigby.'

'Why not — he is a man, is he not?' said Antonia, quitting the room. 'And at this very moment I detest *all* men!'

6

With so few pupils Antonia found herself increasingly bored. Anxiety over her financial situation played on her mind but also there was the ever-present spectre of Sir Laurence to whom she felt increasingly attracted. Despite her rebuttal of his advances he still came regularly to collect his sister from her dance lessons and always contrived to spend a few moments in conversation. This was for Antonia a mixed blessing. No matter how many times she told herself that she was being nonsensical and that Sir Laurence was showing her nothing more than common civility, she could not prevent her heart from skipping a beat when she saw him waiting in the hall for Isabella. She scolded herself for succumbing to what she knew was a most dangerous passion, yet she told herself that it could do no harm, as long as she kept it secret. Nothing could come of it, she knew very well, but she found herself looking forward to the mornings when Miss Burstock took her lessons, waking to a delicious sensation of pleasurable expectancy. She came down to breakfast on one such morning to find Miss Chittering bewailing the lack of pupils to her cousin.

'Some days we have not one pupil. I know that Antonia has considered allowing daughters of tradesmen to take lessons with us but so far, thank goodness, she has decided against it.'

'And I shall continue to do so, at least for the present. Good morning, Beatrice — Charles. We have at present a very select clientele and I do not wish to offend them.'

'Especially not the head of a certain modish family eh, Antonia?' said Charles. 'Beatrice and I were just having a comfortable coze about your beau.'

Antonia felt the flush of embarrassment rise to her cheeks.

'I-I beg your pardon?' she stammered.

'Oh no, no. Antonia, I never meant — Charles, how can you be such a tease?' cried Miss Chittering, much flustered.

'But it is true,' he expostulated. 'You were even now telling me that a certain gentleman haunts the house at the end of lesson time and will not leave without sight of my cousin.'

'What nonsense,' declared Antonia, trying to look unconcerned.

'Not at all,' cried Charles, enjoying himself hugely. 'Beatrice assures me that it is all too true. I am tempted to stay at home today just to see this beau and to ask him to explain his intentions towards you.'

Although she was very much aware of the telltale flush in her cheeks, Antonia smiled at this.

'You absurd boy! He might well run you through for your impertinence.'

'Ho, as if I didn't know better than to accept a challenge from so old a gentleman.'

'Old!' cried Antonia, startled, 'He is not old — how can you say so?'

Charles looked across the room at Miss Chittering and winked.

'You see, Beatrice, I was right, it is a Case! Only someone deeply in love could say Sir Rigby is not old.'

Antonia, in the process of drinking her tea, almost dropped the cup.

'Sir Rigby?'

'Pray do not upset yourself, Cos,' cried Charles gaily. 'We will not betray your secret.'

'I think your foolishness has gone far enough,' retorted Antonia. 'If you dare to mention this again I will box your ears.'

'Fear not, Cousin. I shall be the soul of discretion.' Having finished his breakfast, Charles rose from the table. 'Just let me know when you set the day and I shall be very happy to be a witness, or shall you just elope?'

He flicked her curls as he passed, chuckling. Despite herself, Antonia smiled. She had scarcely noticed Sir Rigby's presence at the end of the dancing classes, but it was a lesson to her to be careful in future.

'He is a scamp!' declared Miss Chittering fondly. 'But we shall miss his nonsense when he leaves us.'

Antonia looked up. 'Oh? Charles, are you leaving us?'

'Well, I cannot stay forever, Cos, even though I have found Bath so delightful.'

'And do you go back to Oxford, or home?'

'Oh to Wiltshire, I think, although I have by no means made up my mind,' he said vaguely.

'We shall most certainly miss him,' sighed Miss Chittering, as Mr Haseley left the room.

'Yes, although I confess I shall also be a little relieved,' returned Antonia, buttering a slice of bread, 'I know very little of his business while he has been under my roof. He has been at pains to remain out of sight of my students, but I cannot help wondering just what such a lively young man can have found to amuse him in Bath.'

The chimes of the little ormulu clock on the mantelpiece put an end to such speculation. She left her breakfast and hurried away to prepare for the forthcoming lesson.

Miss Burstock and Miss Claremont were the only pupils that morning and at the end of the lesson Antonia rewarded their endeavours with a little waltzing before escorting them downstairs. She was aware of a small pang of disappointment to find only Sir Rigby waiting in the hall, but she scolded herself silently: it was unreasonable to expect Sir Laurence to fetch his sister from every lesson.

Sir Rigby greeted her warmly, bemoaned her decision to return his flowers and paid her several fulsome compliments. She responded with her usual cool politeness, casting an admonishing glance towards Miss Burstock, who was having difficulty stifling a giggle. Having exhausted the pleasantries, he began to bid Antonia farewell.

'Has Rosie told you this will be her last lesson?'

'She has, Sir Rigby. I shall be very sad to lose her, but I trust it will not be for ever.'

'Goodness me, no. We are taking a few weeks in the country, then there is Ascot of course, though with all the talk of war I daresay I shall not enjoy it as much as I should. Then I shall go on to Brighton to enjoy the benefits of the sea air.'

'And there is London at the end of the

summer, Papa, for my come out,' his daughter reminded him shyly.

Sir Rigby beamed at her. 'Of course there is, my sweet. But we shall be back here with our friends before then.' He gave her such a knowing look that Antonia felt the blood rushing to her face. She gently removed her fingers from his grasp.

'I believe you are escorting Isabella to her door, Sir Rigby. How very kind of you.'

'Yes, but so unnecessary,' cried Miss Burstock. 'My maid is here, so surely there can be no harm in my walking home alone.' She read disapproval in Antonia's eyes and added, 'Pray do not think me ungrateful, Sir Rigby, but to take Rosie and yourself so far out of your way . . . '

'Nonsense, child. It will be a positive pleasure to escort two such beauties through Bath. Now, come along, my dears, we had best be off. Good day to you, Miss Venn, until we meet again, eh?'

With no pupils at all the following day, Antonia rose early and set off on a brisk walk, hoping to dispel the restlessness that hung about her. She returned later to learn that Miss Chittering was waiting for her in the sitting-room, with Lady Burstock. Miss Venn took this particular news very calmly. In truth she suspected the visit was to tell her that

Lady Burstock was taking Isabella out of Bath for the summer and she resigned herself to losing yet another pupil. She ran up to her room to take off her coat and bonnet and tidy her hair before making her way to the small sitting-room. Despite her foreboding, the scene before her when she opened the door made her smile inwardly. Miss Chittering was entertaining her guest with a constant flow of chatter. Lady Burstock's face was fixed in an expression of polite interest but Antonia thought she detected a faint look of relief as she entered the room.

'Ah, here is Miss Venn now. Antonia, my dear, such an honour — Lady Burstock has called here especially to see you and I was mortified to find you had left the house. 'Depend upon it', I said, 'she is taking a walk and will be back directly'. Lady Burstock has been waiting patiently for you for *almost an hour*, my dear!'

'My apologies, ma'am, had I known you were here I would have cut short my walk. How kind of you to wait.'

'Pray do not upset yourself, Miss Venn, there has been no lack of hospitality, I assure you. Indeed, it is I who should apologize, for not giving you notice of my visit.'

'Well, and now that you are here, Antonia, I hope you will both excuse me if I leave you.

There are several tasks that need my attention and in any case I am sure Lady Burstock has had more than enough of my idle chit-chat. So if you will excuse me, Antonia — my lady.'

As Miss Chittering bustled out of the room Antonia glanced towards Lady Burstock, an apologetic smile hovering on her lips.

'I hope you do not regret your decision to wait for me, Lady Burstock.'

'Not at all. Miss Chittering has kept me well entertained.' She observed Antonia's sceptical glance and laughed. 'Very well, I admit I was very glad to see you, Miss Venn. Your companion is a dear creature, I am sure, but she is a little . . . garrulous.'

'Yes indeed! But she is a treasure when dealing with the pupils — she is so patient and good-natured, I really could not manage without her.'

'Quite. But could she manage without *you*, do you think?'

'I beg your pardon?'

'Miss Venn, pray forgive my impertinence but — may I ask if your classes are very busy at present?'

Antonia hesitated, then said frankly, 'No, my lady, in fact we have very few pupils here at the moment. With the summer approaching everyone seems to be leaving town. However, most have promised to return at the end of the year, and I am assured it is no reflection upon my teaching.'

'I am sure it is not.'

'Lady Burstock, if you are in any way dissatisfied with your daughter's progress — '

'No, no, I have no worries at all on that head, Miss Venn. Quite the opposite, in fact, which brings me to the reason for my visit.' She paused. 'Miss Venn, I will come straight to the point. I have a proposal to put to you, which I hope you will allow me to explain in full. We will be removing to Brighton in the next few weeks and I would like you come with us, as companion to Isabella. Pray do not be offended,' she begged, seeing the look of astonishment on Antonia's face. 'I would not for the world offer any kind of snub to you, but I am at my wit's end, you see. I have the gravest suspicion that Bella has embarked upon a-a liaison with some unsuitable person here in Bath; she is so set against leaving. However, I had hoped to be able to tell her that you would be accompanying us, for I know that she holds you in great esteem.'

'Lady Burstock, I am quite sure — '

'Pray, let me continue.' Lady Burstock smiled faintly. 'It is very difficult for me to admit this: Isabella has been spoiled from birth, you see. She was her father's darling, his only child, and I confess that she has been over-indulged. It is a credit to her sweet nature that she is not completely selfish. I am most sincerely attached to her and although I know that I can command her obedience, I had much rather she came to Brighton willingly. When her brother told her of our proposed move she was very much against it. Laurence — he is not the most patient of men, Miss Venn, and I am afraid he was a little harsh with his sister. Bella has a great deal of respect for you, Miss Venn, and I know that your presence would make the prospect of Brighton far more appealing to her. From a business point of view, I would of course pay you for your time, but it would be no sinecure. My health is not good and I cannot always accompany my daughter to the parties and outings that she craves. To have a sensible, trustworthy companion who could take my place would be such a comfort to me.'

'I-I do not know how to answer you, ma'am. I am sensible of the honour you do me — indeed, I am flattered that you should consider me suitable for such a responsible role, but . . . I do not know what to say.' She rose and walked to the window, trying to collect her thoughts. 'Does — does Sir Laurence approve of your proposal?'

'Of course. We have discussed it most fully.

If my son were to be fixed in Brighton it would perhaps be a different matter, but Laurence will be an infrequent visitor and it therefore becomes much more necessary for me to have someone who can help me look after Isabella. You need not answer immediately. Think it over. Perhaps you might like to discuss it with Miss Chittering. If she is willing to continue with the dancing classes during your absence, the remuneration you receive might well make up for the lack of pupils during the summer months.'

'There is that, of course. I cannot deny that it is a tempting offer, Lady Burstock.' Antonia pressed her hands to her temples. 'It is all so sudden, I really do need time to consider this very carefully.'

'If you would do that I should be most grateful.' She rose. 'I have not yet mentioned this proposal to Isabella, nor have I told her quite when we are removing from Bath. However, I must make plans and need an answer quite soon; would three days be sufficient? There are so many arrangements to be put in hand.'

'Three days!' Antonia drew a deep breath. 'Yes, Lady Burstock. I will let you know my decision by then.'

'Thank you.' Lady Burstock held out her hand. 'Goodbye, Miss Venn. I do hope you will give serious consideration to my offer; I would very much value your company.'

'Th-thank you.' Antonia took the out-stretched fingers. 'I shall give the matter my attention, ma'am, and reply within the three days, I promise you.'

★ ★ ★

Long after Lady Burstock had taken her leave, Antonia remained in the sitting-room, pacing the floor as she went over in her mind everything Lady Burstock had said. She was standing by the window, staring into space when there came a light scratching at the door.

'Antonia dear, Dawkin told me Lady Burstock left some time ago.' Miss Chittering advanced into the room, staring at her anxiously. 'My dear, are you quite well? You are looking very pale.'

'There is nothing wrong, exactly, Beatrice. I have been going over and over Lady Burstock's visit and the more I think of it, the less I know what I should do. Pray, Beatrice, sit down with me and we will discuss it.'

Miss Chittering settled herself comfortably on her chair.

'Very well, my dear. What is it you wish to say?'

Antonia fell silent again, her fingers idly pleating and smoothing the skirts of her gown.

'Lady Burstock is taking Isabella to Brighton for the summer.'

'Just as we expected,' nodded Miss Chittering sagely. 'Heaven knows how many more will be leaving us before the month is out. Well, my dear, we must trim our costs and pray that things pick up again in the autumn.'

'Beatrice, she has invited me to go with them.' Antonia's words brought a sudden hush to the room. Miss Chittering fell silent, her eyes widening in surprise and more than a hint of dismay. Antonia continued, 'Her ladyship wishes me to act as a companion to Isabella during the summer — for a fee of course.'

'Then you must close the school.'

'But we need not.' Antonia leaned forward eagerly. 'We have so few pupils on our books, I-I wonder if you would care to take the classes yourself?'

'I? Take the dancing?' Miss Chittering raised her hands to her cheeks and stared at Antonia. 'Oh-oh goodness, my dear, however could you think it?'

'Easily! You taught me my first steps, do you remember, Beatrice? With the exception of the waltz you are as adept as I am at all the dances.' Antonia's grey eyes twinkled. 'I do believe you could also teach the turning dance if you set your mind to it. Oh Beatrice, please consider — there are no more than half-a-dozen pupils with us now, but I should be loath to close the school for the summer. I-I thought that, perhaps, if you felt you could run the school while I went to Brighton with Lady Burstock and Isabella, we could recoup some of our losses and balance the books for the summer.' Looking at her companion's startled face she sighed. 'I am sorry, Beatrice. It is too much to ask of you.'

'No, no, my dear! Only — it is all so sudden.' Miss Chittering clasped her hands in her lap, her brow furrowed in thought. 'The lease is taken on this house until the end of the year, so we should save very little by closing the school and there would still be bills to be paid. She rose and crossed the room slowly while Antonia could only sit and watch in silence. At last she stopped and looked at Antonia, a smile spreading across her face. 'We will do it, Antonia dear. We must have someone to play the pianoforte, of course, but I think I might know just the person . . . and it will only be for a few months, after all, and the extra revenue will be very useful.' She wrinkled her nose. 'How dreadful to think that we should turn so mercenary. Really, we are no better than common traders.'

'It will be money honestly earned, Beatrice, and I am not ashamed of *that*!' declared Antonia stoutly. 'But . . . you are sure you wish to do this?'

'Yes,' came the emphatic reply. 'I know as well as you that our funds are running very low, and after all your kindness to me, inviting me to join you here and making me feel useful again, it is the least I can do to show my gratitude.'

Antonia flew out of her chair and hugged her.

'Dear Beatrice! Pray do not cry, there is not the least need to feel grateful to me. Indeed it is *I* who should be thanking you, for I could not have made such a success of this without your help. You play so beautifully for my classes, the younger children adore you — just as I did when I was a child. And now to all these attributes you have added accountancy.'

'Oh stop, stop!' Miss Chittering begged her, between laughter and tears. 'You will turn my head with such nonsense.'

'It is nothing more than the truth. Come, we will discuss it further over dinner and if we find no fatal flaws in our plans, then tomorrow I will write to Lady Burstock to accept her kind offer.'

★   ★   ★

Antonia's letter arrived in Great Pulteney Street just as the ladies of the house were setting out for the Pump Room. Lady Burstock was therefore able to pass on the good news to Isabella as they walked over Pulteney Bridge. Her daughter's reaction was much as she expected. She was surprised and gratified, but her open countenance could not completely disguise her suspicion.

'Do you think Miss Venn's presence will mar your enjoyment, Bella?'

'Oh no, no! I could think of no one better to be my companion, but — I cannot think it necessary.'

'My child, I am only too aware that my precarious health makes me a poor companion for you. When we are in Brighton a gentle stroll will be sufficient exercise for me, but you will want to go shopping, or to the Assemblies and I have no doubt that Antonia Venn will share your enjoyment of such pleasures, while I can rest secure in the knowledge that she is looking after you.'

'But I do not need looking after.'

Her mama smiled. 'Of course not, my love,

but Society demands a chaperon for you, if you are not to be considered fast. If you prefer, I will write to your aunt Grendlesham. She may like to spend the summer with us . . . '

'No, please!' cried Isabella in alarm; then she saw the twinkle in her mother's eyes and heaved a sigh of relief. 'Oh you are teasing me. Pray dearest Mama, promise me that you will not invite my aunt under any circumstances. She is so old, and not at all amusing.'

'Well, I confess that I, too, would prefer to have Miss Venn with us. I am sorry to say this of your sainted papa's only sister, but she is forever fancying herself to have some new illness; *not* an ideal person to take charge of you.'

'She would drive us all into a melancholy within the first week,' Isabella giggled. 'But to be serious, Mama, Maria can accompany me when you are unable to do so.'

'For the occasional walk in the park, certainly, but not to act as a duenna for outings and parties, my dear, and I am sure there will be many such occasions.' They had reached the Pump Room and Lady Burstock stopped and turned to face her daughter. 'You are so strongly opposed to going to Brighton, my love, that I thought by inviting Antonia Venn I could make the prospect a little more attractive.'

'Oh Mama, I do understand and I am very grateful, truly.' Isabella's eyes were bright with tears. 'If you think the sea air will benefit your health then, of course, we must go.'

'Thank you, Bella. It will not be so bad for you, believe me. Now, let us go in and see who is taking the waters today.'

★ ★ ★

It was not long before Isabella spotted Mr Haseley entering the Pump Room. She had procured a glass of the famous waters for her mama and, as soon as Lady Burstock was comfortably settled with an acquaintance, Isabella moved away to greet the gentleman.

'Have you heard?' she asked without preamble.

'That my cousin is going with you to Brighton? Yes — though I'm dashed if I understand it.'

'She is coming to spy on me.'

'No; Antonia would never agree to such a thing.'

'Oh no, I do not mean that she would deliberately do so,' she replied quickly, 'but with Maria and your cousin to escort me everywhere, I shall not have a moment to myself. Not that it will matter, since you will not be there. They will have succeeded in separating us,' she ended gloomily.

'Nonsense! We will think of something. I will come to Brighton.'

'But should you not be getting back to your studies?'

'Who could think of studying when one's happiness is at stake?'

Isabella sighed at this grandiose statement. 'Oh Charles, how wonderful you are.'

'Devil a bit!' he retorted, flushing. 'But perhaps, if we were to tell Antonia . . . '

'No, no, she could never understand. Pray do not breathe a word.'

'Oh very well, but I do not like this havey-cavey business, Bella. It is bad enough stealing the odd hour with you in the park, but — dash it all, I want to marry you.'

'I know, my love, but if Mama and Laurence found out, they would be sure to refuse and to demand that we never see each other again.'

'Well, if they don't know about me, why are they taking you to Brighton?'

'I think it is truly because of Mama's health. She has not recovered fully from her influenza last winter, you see. Oh, Mama is watching us, Charles. I must go.'

'When will I see you again?'

'I do not know. I do not think it can be

before Thursday, at the Assembly. Laurence insists upon meeting me from every dance class now; I am constantly watched.'

'Poor darling. Until Thursday then.'

She was gone almost before he had finished speaking and Charles watched her threading her way through the crowd to join Lady Burstock. There seemed nothing more to stay for but he knew he must make a push to talk to a few more people before leaving the Pump Room. If the Bath tabbies should notice that he came only to speak to Isabella, it would only be a matter of time before word reached Lady Burstock, then they would be in the suds.

★ ★ ★

'Antonia, my dear, can you spare me a moment? I need to ask you about a little matter before you go.'

Antonia wondered, not for the first time, if she had been wise to leave Beatrice in charge of the dancing school. She came to Antonia at least a dozen times each day to ask her opinion on some little problem. Should she take on new pupils if anyone enquired; should she keep the keys to the wine cupboard, or leave them with Dawkin; should she order new music to practise for the autumn?

Looking into her companion's anxious face, Antonia closed her lips on a sharp retort.

'Do you know, Beatrice, I think I can leave all this to your own judgement. When I am in Brighton, you know, you will have to make a few decisions of your own.'

'Oh I know that, my dear, and I do hope I will not let you down, but if I can resolve these nagging little questions first, then perhaps we will not go *too* far astray when you are gone.'

Charles, coming into the sitting-room at the end of this speech, grinned at his cousin.

'I am sure Antonia has full confidence in you. Is that not so, Cos?'

'Oh course. But you will not be here to see it, Charles.'

'No, no. I have promised you I will quit here before you leave.'

'Are you going back to Oxford, Master Charles?' enquired Miss Chittering.

'I have yet to decide. It scarcely seems worth it now, with term so far advanced. I might go home for a few days. I have had a letter from m'father, which I must answer, in writing or in person. I suppose you told him I was in Bath, Antonia.'

'I think I may have said so in my letter to your mama. I am sorry, Charlie, but I cannot be happy about you being here so long without telling them.'

'Oh well, I suppose if you had not written, Mama has so many acquaintances here one of them would soon have done so. Do you want me to carry any message to Wiltshire for you?'

Antonia laughed but shook her head.

'Thank you, Charles, but you are far too unreliable. You may meet some friends on the way and decide to set off for Ascot or some such thing. No, I will send my letter to Amelia by the normal route, thank you.'

'And will you let me have your direction in Brighton?' he asked carelessly. 'After all, I might need to get in touch with you.'

'Of course, if you wish it.' She looked a little puzzled, but Dawkin's entry with the mail at that moment distracted her attention. Charles muttered an excuse and took himself off, leaving Antonia to spend the day going through the accounts with Miss Chittering.

There was only one more dancing lesson for Isabella before setting off for Brighton. Antonia expected her young pupil to be full of the delightful treats in store, but she seemed rather subdued, a point Antonia put to Sir Laurence when he came to fetch his sister. Isabella was changing her shoes and

Antonia took the opportunity to slip down-stairs to exchange a few words with the gentleman.

'You will think me fanciful, perhaps,' she concluded.

'Not in the least. I am well aware that Bella does not want to leave Bath and I know why: she has set up a flirt here and it will spoil her fun to leave now.'

'How can you be so sure?'

'My sister is a minx,' he said bluntly. 'She positively thrives on assignations and secret meetings. She is also adept at giving her maid the slip. That is why I come to collect her from dancing lessons — although it is not my sole reason for coming here.' The tone did not change, but Antonia was unable to meet his hard gaze. She heard Isabella's footsteps on the landing above and was relieved to be spared the necessity of replying. Isabella pulled on her gloves as she came chattering down the stairs.

'I really do not know why you have to fetch me every day, Laurence. I am quite capable of walking home with Maria.'

Sir Laurence threw a quick glance at Antonia, drawing a responding twinkle from her own grey eyes.

'I know you are, child, but I needed the exercise. Goodbye, Miss Venn. Until Friday. I shall be here to collect you at nine o'clock.'

'Oh there is no need, sir. I can take a cab to Great Pulteney Street.'

'No, madam, I shall fetch you.'

Isabella giggled.

'You see how overbearing he is, Miss Venn? He must always have his own way.'

'Since it will be far more comfortable in a private carriage, I shall allow him to do so,' smiled Antonia. She held out her hand. 'Thank you, Sir Laurence. Until Friday.'

He raised her fingers to his lips.

'Nine o'clock, ma'am. Be ready.'

7

It seemed to Antonia that every member of her household turned out to see her leave for Brighton. Her trunk had already been collected from Queen Square and was even now on its way to Brighton under the watchful eye of the servants. Dawkin announced that Sir Laurence had arrived and after a final glance around the sitting-room. Antonia went out to meet him. She had purchased a new olive-green travelling dress for the occasion and she had chosen a matching bonnet ornamented by a curling ostrich feather, adding a touch of frivolity to her usually sober style. Miss Chittering was tearful, nervously repeating questions she had asked several times before as she followed Antonia into the hall.

'Pray do not worry, Beatrice.' Antonia hugged her. 'You will cope beautifully. I have every confidence in you.'

'I am so afraid I shall let you down.'

'Nonsense. It is only for a month or two after all, and if you have any problems you know my direction, you can write to me. Now, Beatrice, dry your tears. Here is Sir

Laurence waiting for me and he will not want to see this Friday face. Good morning, sir.' She glanced past him. 'Goodness, am I to be allowed to join you in your curricle? Your matched bays, too; I am honoured.'

Sir Laurence ran an approving eye over her as he helped her up into the carriage. His look was not lost on Antonia, who smiled inwardly.

'Only as far as Great Pulteney Street. Lady Burstock's travelling carriage awaits you there.' He climbed up beside her, gathering up the reins. 'Now, are you ready, Miss Venn, or must we wait while you go back for some vital item that you have missed?'

'No, sir, I am perfectly ready.'

He gave the word to his groom, who stood away from the horses' heads and scrambled up on to his place at the back of the curricle as it moved forward.

'I am used to driving my sister, you see, and she invariably forgets at least one thing.'

'For shame, sir. I think you are being too hard on Isabella.'

'We shall see, Miss Venn. Are all your own arrangements made? Will they manage without you?'

'Of course. Why should they not?'

'That companion of yours seemed about to fall into hysterics as you left.'

'Poor Beatrice. She is quite capable, but she does not believe it. I confess she has driven me to distraction with her worries.'

'I hope you will be able to forget your dancing school for a few weeks. You are very young to have such a burden on your shoulders.'

She turned her head to look at him. 'It cannot be so very different from your own estates, though on a much smaller scale.'

'In part, you are right. I am continually working to improve my land, investing what I can. But *I* inherited my problems. Miss Venn. My estates were in very poor shape when they passed to me. I did not choose to live that way.'

'Ah, but having chosen my independence, I am determined to make a success of it. I cannot go back now.'

'Do you regret it?'

'You have asked me that before.'

'And you evaded an answer.'

She tilted her head to one side to consider the question.

'No. I do not think I regret making my bid for freedom, only . . . it isn't freedom, is it? I am as surely locked into this new life as I was locked into the old one.'

'I would have thought you had sufficient

funds to set up household independently, if you so wished.'

'Then you have been misled, sir. My inheritance was scarcely enough to pay the lease on the house in Queen Square for the year.'

He stared at her. 'Then you were badly advised, my girl! That diamond was worth far more than that.'

It was Antonia's turn to stare. 'You — you mean the ring you gave me?'

'Yes, of course!' he replied impatiently. 'What else should I mean?'

She opened her mouth to reply, then shut it again. He thought she had sold the solitaire and was living on the proceeds. Antonia's mind went back to that cold and bustling yard of the coaching inn, remembering how a total stranger had pressed a ring into her hand, a gift that had meant so much to her at that time. How could he calmly assume that she had sold it at the first opportunity? She did not feel equal to the task of explaining herself, not in an open carriage with the groom sitting up behind. They had crossed Pulteney Bridge and were now travelling along Great Pulteney Street, where a large travelling carriage stood at Lady Burstock's door. She waited silently while he brought his team to a halt. As soon as his groom was holding their heads, Sir Laurence jumped down and came around the curricle to help her alight.

'Will you be escorting us, Sir Laurence, or do you intend to go on ahead and meet us at Brighton?'

'I shall follow you.'

'Slow work, with such a spirited team,' she said, giving the matched bays an appraising look.

'You know about horses, Miss Venn?'

'You forget, sir, my father considered himself something of an expert. He taught me to handle the ribbons although he would never allow me to drive his high-perch phaeton, but he did take me up in it sometimes on his occasional visits home. It never occurred to him that while he was showing off their paces I was sitting up beside him in a patched and faded gown.' She paused then summoned up a smile. 'It never mattered to me at the time, so I suppose it was not important.'

He looked as if he would speak, but Lady Burstock emerged from the house, and he walked forward to greet her.

'I have brought her safe and sound you see, Mama.'

Isabella, coming out of the house behind her mother, ran forward.

'I thought you would never come! You must sit beside me, Miss Venn and help to distract me from this horrible journey. Mama will be asleep within minutes and Laurence insists on driving himself.' She followed her mother into the carriage.

'Perhaps he does not wish to travel in a coach full of females,' murmured Antonia, waiting to embark.

He grinned at her. 'Indeed I can think of few fates worse than to share a closed carriage with my sister. She is an extremely poor traveller, you know.'

'Thank you, sir, I did *not* know.' She threw him a fulminating glance.

It was another ten minutes before they could drive away. Lady Burstock settled herself comfortably into one corner with her smelling salts in her hand but Isabella had to return twice to the house for items she suddenly discovered she had forgotten to pack. Eventually they were away, crossing Pulteney Bridge, then bowling along Walcot Street and out on to the London Road.

It proved a long and tedious journey and Antonia soon realized the truth of Sir Laurence's words. The sun shone down unceasingly on the carriage, making it very warm and they had not gone many miles before Isabella's chatter died away. She looked decidedly grey and the coach was forced to stop several times for her to alight and walk beside the hedgerows, breathing deeply to offset the nausea that threatened to overcome her. Sir Laurence took his sister up in the curricle for a few miles, but the benefits of the fresh air were no compensation for the hot sun which beat down, giving her a headache until she tearfully begged to be allowed to return to the coach.

Lady Burstock undertook the journey with her usual quiet fortitude, sitting back in the corner with her eyes closed, but she suffered just as much as Isabella, and Antonia could see the strain in her pale face. Sir Laurence had arranged for them to spend the night at a comfortable coaching inn, but the following day brought no relief from the blistering heat as they continued their journey.

★   ★   ★

When they finally arrived in Brighton, Antonia alone had the energy to appreciate the superiority of their position on Marine Parade. From her bedroom at the front of the house she looked out at the sea, sparkling in the evening sunlight. She threw up the sash window and breathed in the sea air, filling her lungs with its salty freshness. First thing in the morning, she vowed, she would walk along the promenade and perhaps investigate the bathing machines set out on the beach below. Looking at the pretty bracket clock she had set upon the mantelpiece, she realized there was scarcely an hour before dinner and she hurriedly allowed the maid to help her into a clean gown and re-pin her hair. She came downstairs to the drawing-room to find only Sir Laurence awaiting her.

'I am afraid both Mama and Isabella are too knocked up to join us, even though dinner has been set back.'

Antonia nodded. 'I expected as much. I went to see how Isabella did not an hour since and she had even then taken to her bed. And although Lady Burstock does not complain, it was clear she did not fare well on the journey.'

'If I had known it would be so hot we could have deferred — '

'You must not blame yourself, sir. As your mama said when we stopped *en route*, next week may be even hotter.'

'Yes, of course. How very reasonable you are, Miss Venn.'

She grimaced. 'And how unexciting. However, my aunt maintains that I can be as wayward as my poor papa upon occasion, and quite as obstinate.'

'And are you obstinate?' he asked, leading her into dinner.

'Disastrously so. My aunt says that once I have an idea in my head I will not be turned from it, however dire the consequences.'

'Such as running a dancing school.'

'I will not allow that to be considered an error. It is my bid for independence.'

He said nothing more but escorted her to a seat to the right of his own at the head of the table. Candles burned from a branched candlestick, scarcely necessary at first but as the meal progressed their glow augmented the fading daylight and kept the shadows at bay. They talked throughout the meal and Antonia was surprised at the ease with which she could converse with her host. Sir Laurence's manner was somewhat terse, but Antonia enjoyed his caustic wit and was in no way disturbed by his blunt speech. When the servants had removed the covers and placed a bowl of sweetmeats on the table, she ventured to enquire if *he* had ordered the table to be set so informally. Sir Laurence signalled to the footman to leave the wine on the table and then dismissed him.

'It is more convenient to sit thus, is it not? I did not want to be forever peering the length of the table to see you.'

'No indeed,' she murmured, much struck.

'And I can refill your glass myself,' he said, suiting the action to the words.

She wondered if he was flirting with her: it was her duty, she knew, to remove herself at this point and leave him to enjoy a solitary brandy, but the burgundy had weakened her resolve and since Sir Laurence showed no signs of wishing her to go, she accepted another glass of wine without demur.

'You room is satisfactory, Miss Venn?'

'Perfectly, sir, thank you.'

'I made sure you would like to look out over the promenade and the sea, but I fear it may be a little noisy for you?'

'By no means. I like the sound of the sea, it will soothe me to sleep.' She observed his raised brows. 'You look surprised. Do you think me one of those females who fears an open window at night? I have heard that the Prince considers the night air highly injurious to health, but I assure you I do not.'

'No, it is no more than I expect of you, Miss Venn.'

Her eyes twinkled. 'Surely, sir, you do not hold to His Highness's view? As a soldier there must have been many nights when you camped out under the stars.'

'Yes, of course, although I seem to recall it was raining almost every time it was necessary for us to bivouac in the open.

Damned uncomfortable.'

'And yet you miss that life?' She feared for a moment that she had offended him. Sir Laurence remained silent, staring into his wineglass. 'I am sorry . . .'

He waved one hand. 'No, don't apologize for your observation, Miss Venn. It is not entirely correct, however. I have no wish to return to the life of a soldier. God knows there is work enough here in England to keep me busy. But so many comrades and good friends are even now in Brussells, preparing to face the French.' He raised his glass in salute to the distant army. 'So many of them will lose their lives, Miss Venn, while I sit here facing nothing more dangerous than a stroll in the sea air.' He laughed bitterly and tossed off the wine, reaching for the bottle to refill his glass.

'Yet you have done your share, sir. No one could ask more.'

His mouth curled into a sneer. 'But *I* am still alive.'

'Would you have it otherwise, when Captain Norton and no doubt countless others worked so hard for your recovery?' She leaned forward, reaching out impulsively to grasp his hand. 'You have so much to offer, sir! You know as well as I that when peace comes those soldiers who do survive will be

196

paid off and they will need work. Without the help of landowners like yourself, what is to become of them?'

He stared at her, his brows drawn together above the flint-dark eyes, whose expression she could not decipher.

'Radical ideas, Miss Venn.'

She shrugged. 'Merely common sense, sir. A prosperous estate will support many more than a run-down property. My father's own small estate had to be sold off to pay his gambling debts — if it had come to me . . .'

'Would you have put your theories into practice?'

She looked at him. 'Of course, would not you?'

She realized her hand still covered his, but before she could withdraw, his fingers twisted beneath hers and caught her wrist.

'This is the second time you have chided me on my self-pity, Miss Venn.'

Her chin went up. 'And I will do so again, sir, when you fall into such a nonsensical melancholy.'

The sudden draught from the opening door caused the candles to flicker. Antonia sensed rather than saw Sir Laurence's irritation at the interruption. He released her hand and sat back in his chair. Lady

Burstock's abigail hovered nervously in the doorway.

'Well, what is it, woman?'

'If you please, sir, my lady sends her apologies for missing dinner and desires that you visit her before you retire, if it pleases you, sir.'

'Of course. Tell my lady I will be up directly.'

Antonia was aware of a faint feeling of disappointment. She looked up to find Sir Laurence watching her. The faint smile curving his lips drew an answering gleam from her.

She rose. 'What a chatterbox I am becoming. I had not realized the hour. I shall retire and leave you in peace. Goodnight, Sir Laurence.'

He raised his half-filled glass to her.

'Goodnight, Miss Venn, enjoy your night air.'

8

Once they were established, Sir Laurence left them to attend to his estates and the days settled into a comfortable routine. Lady Burstock's health improved with the rest and sea air and Isabella, although distracted at times, found enough to enjoy to sustain her spirits. Despite the absence of the Prince Regent and the shadow of war which hung over the country, there were sufficient families in Brighton to make a creditable showing at the Assemblies, where Isabella was an immediate success. Her fond mama happy to allow her spirited daughter to spread her wings a little before her come out in London later in the year and she was pleased to receive so many compliments on her daughter's pretty manners.

'It is a relief to know that she can behave herself in public,' Lady Burstock confided to Antonia as they sat together at one such Assembly, watching the dancers. 'There is nothing more unbecoming than a young lady who is too shy to utter a word or, even worse, who puts herself forward too much. Either way it brings censure upon her.'

'No danger of that,' Antonia assured her. 'Isabella conducts herself very properly, and judging by the admiring glances she is getting there will be no shortage of partners for her here.'

'Indeed not. It will help her to forget the swain she left languishing in Bath.'

★   ★   ★

Antonia watched Miss Burstock: the child looked happy enough dancing with a red-faced young man who seemed entranced by his partner. She found herself humming the tune, her foot tapping to the music. Catching Lady Burstock's eye she laughed self-consciously.

'I am very sorry, ma'am, my feet are positively *itching* to be on the dance floor.'

'Then you may be in luck,' murmured her companion. 'I perceive a gentleman bearing down upon us and I believe he has every intention of asking you to dance with him. Good evening, Sir Rigby.'

The gentleman executed a flourishing bow.

'Your servant, ma'am — Miss Venn.'

'Have you been in Brighton long?' enquired Lady Burstock.

'No, no, I arrived just yesterday, ma'am. But how is this, are you unescorted?'

'My son is attending to business at Oakford, Sir Rigby, although he plans to return to us as soon as may be. Is Rosamund with you? No? Isabella will be so disappointed.'

'This is but a fleeting visit, ma'am. I have left her with her aunts in the country. She will be sorry not to have come when I tell her you are here. Miss Venn, they are forming another set — will you give me the pleasure of standing up with me?'

Antonia hesitated only long enough to ascertain that Lady Burstock did not object and took her place beside Sir Rigby.

'I am in your debt sir,' she told him gaily, 'I was so longing to dance.'

'I am happy to be of service to you, Miss Venn. I shall quiz Oakford about this when I see him. Whisking you out of Bath in such a way, but what is the fellow thinking of to leave you alone in Brighton? Why, the young dog's wits have gone abegging. Serve him right if he came back to find I'd cut him out.'

'Sir Rigby, I am here as companion to Lady Burstock and her daughter,' she reminded him, a hint of reproach in her tone.

Unabashed, Sir Rigby gave a fat chuckle. 'Oh, of course, of course. I do not suggest otherwise, eh?' He squeezed her hand and she had to repress the desire to pull her fingers away. She tried to steer the conversation into safer waters.

'How is Miss Claremont?'

'Very well, very well indeed. Positively blooming. Of course she has a tendency to freckles but I have told her maid to keep using the lemon water. Perhaps you would care to walk out with me tomorrow morning, Miss Venn, and we can discuss the best treatments . . . '

Antonia laughingly declined but knew a moment's disquiet at the subtle difference in Sir Rigby's behaviour towards her. She did not like the innuendo in his tone and politely resisted his attempts to keep her on the floor for a second dance.

Isabella meanwhile was enjoying her local success. Under her mother's watchful eye she flirted harmlessly with the young men, comparing them all unfavourably to her beloved Charles. Naturally, she missed him and did not doubt for a moment that he would follow her to Brighton, but in the meantime she revelled in the adulation of the young gentlemen of Brighton and was overjoyed when her mama suggested holding a little evening party of their own.

'Nothing large or formal, you understand,' said Lady Burstock, 'just a snug little evening with friends.'

It was not to be expected that any young gentleman captivated by the incomparable Miss Burstock would want to miss such a party. Those lucky enough to claim family acquaintance with Lady Burstock duly received their invitations and several others urged their mamas to call without delay on Lady Burstock, who had the doubtful pleasure of finding that not one of her invitations was refused.

'Thus, we found ourselves in a most dreadful squeeze,' she declared, when the evening was over and the last of the guests had left her soirée.

'But it *was* the most wonderful success, Mama!' cried Isabella, her cheeks flushed with pleasure. She had enjoyed herself hugely, basking in the attentions of the young gentlemen vying for her favours. Her mother eyed her fondly.

'For you, perhaps, with all your beaux.'

'Dear Mama, did you not enjoy it? I made sure you would — and Antonia too.'

It had only taken a few days in Brighton for Isabella to establish first-name terms with her companion and Lady Burstock had soon followed suit. Now she looked a question at Antonia, who smiled.

'I certainly enjoyed myself, ma'am. Everyone so charming and determined to be

pleased. Their attentions were most flatter-
ing.'

'I do not know why you should be so
surprised, Antonia, for you are looking very
well,' said Isabella saucily, as she disappeared
up the stairs, 'I knew we were right to
persuade you to buy that orange sarcenet.'

'Bella is right, my dear, the colour is perfect
and the sea air has given you a most
becoming glow. Don't colour up, child, it is
no more than the truth.'

'Thank you, ma'am, but pray say no more
— you are putting me to the blush. I had best
follow Isabella's example and retire, with your
permission, before my head is quite turned by
all this praise.'

'Bless you, my dear, and thank you for
coming to Brighton with us.' Lady Burstock
leaned forward to kiss her cheek. 'Your
presence has been a tonic to me, and I know
Laurence feels happier with you here to help
me look after Isabella.'

Surprised and gratified, Antonia mumbled
her response and retired to her room, but it
was a long time before she could rest. Lady
Burstock's words kept running round in her
head. She was unreasonably pleased to think
that Sir Laurence considered her of use. She
carried her candle over to the tall mirror and
critically studied her reflection. Goodness,

she was looking positively brown. The daily promenades had brought colour to her cheeks and her soft honey-brown hair, brushed until it shone, hung in a sleek curtain over her shoulders.

'Well my girl,' she told her reflection, 'you will never achieve the head-turning beauty of Isabella, but you can still cut a shine.'

Admonishing herself for using such an unladylike term, Antonia climbed into bed, listening to the sound of the sea until it lulled her to sleep.

★ ★ ★

Isabella scowled over her breakfast. She had been in Brighton for two whole weeks and there was no word from Charles. Of course, she knew that it would be reprehensible of him to write to her clandestinely, yet she had hoped that he would find some way of getting a message to her. It would serve him right if she fell in love with someone else; after all there were plenty of pleasing young men in Brighton. She looked up as the footman entered with two letters on a tray and her heart rose when he presented one of these missives to Antonia. When she could no longer contain her curiosity she said, with studied indifference, 'Is your letter from Bath, Antonia?'

'Yes, from Beatrice. Unfortunately, she writes very much as she speaks and she has so crossed and recrossed the lines I can scarce read it.'

'I hope she is well?'

'I *think* so, it seems she has taken on another pupil — bravo, Beatrice. Oh, Charles has left Bath. And a good thing too. I am afraid it was very remiss of me not to send him home earlier.'

Miss Burstock derived small comfort from this, and turned instead to her mother, who was perusing her own letter, a single sheet covered in neat black writing.

'Is it from Laurence, Mama?'

'Mm . . . he sends his love and hopes you are behaving yourself. He says he will be back within a se'ennight, but he will be stopping in London first for more news of affairs on the Continent. He writes: *I think war is inevitable, although not for a few weeks yet, which will give Wellington time to bring in more forces from the Americas.*'

She stifled a sigh as she laid aside the letter. Isabella, observing her mama's low spirits, immediately tried to cheer her.

'Perhaps, Mama, you would care to walk to the church of St. Nicholas. You said we should make an effort to attend the services while we are in Brighton. St Nicholas is the parish church and its medieval architecture is considered very fine . . . '

Lady Burstock stared at her.

'Goodness, Isabella, are you now taking an interest in such things?'

'No, I learned it from one of my dancing partners at the Assembly,' she twinkled mischievously. 'However, I would be very happy to accompany you there, Mama, especially so since our way lies past the circulating library and I wish to change my book.'

A little over an hour later the ladies arrived at the church of St Nicholas. Lady Burstock assured her daughter gravely that the fine architecture had been worth the walk and that they would certainly attend the Sunday service. They started back along Church Street and had not gone far when a young man hailed the ladies. Isabella gave a small shriek.

'Harry!' She ran forward to meet the gentleman, her hands outstretched in welcome. Lady Burstock gave a small tut of exasperation.

'Isabella dear, pray remember we are on a public highway! Do I beg of you try for a little decorum. Good morning, Lord Henry. Please excuse my daughter's atrocious manners.'

Lord Henry Bressingham bowed, dismissing the apology with a smile.

'Servant, Lady Burstock, Bella. I didn't know you was in Brighton. Laurence with you?'

'No, he is at Oakford.' Isabella shook his arm impatiently. 'But what are you doing here? I thought you would be at Bressingham Park for the summer.'

The young man jumped back, pulling his arm free from Isabella's grip.

'Here, watch the coat, Bella — it's the very latest cut!' He smoothed the sleeve lovingly. 'Mama is still convinced that a spot of sea-bathing will do her good, so she insisted I escort her here, again.'

'Pray give my regards to your Mama, Harry. Tell her I shall call upon her.'

'And I am very sure she will want to see you, ma'am. Where are you staying?' Having ascertained that the ladies were on their way back to Marine Parade, Lord Henry immediately offered to escort them, an offer Lady Burstock readily accepted. The walk had been longer than she had anticipated and she was grateful for the support of his arm. She turned to Antonia.

'Miss Venn, allow me to present Lord Henry Bressingham to you. He is our neighbour at Burstock Hall and a very good friend.'

Lord Henry was a very fashionable young man, from the top of his curled and swept-back golden locks to the shining Hessians that gleamed upon his feet, but he greeted her with a good-natured smile.

'Delighted to meet you, Miss Venn. Is this your first visit to Brighton?'

'Yes, my lord, and I am enjoying it immensely.'

Lord Henry grimaced. 'Are you, by gad! Well I can tell you that when you have been here as many times as I have it is a different story.' He turned to Lady Burstock. 'Do you attend the Assembly tomorrow night, ma'am? I hope so, because I want to reserve a dance with Bella.'

That young lady giggled. 'Don't be absurd, Harry!'

'What! Are you telling me there ain't a flock of admirers waiting to partner you? I won't believe it.'

Miss Burstock's dark lashes dropped over her eyes. She said demurely, 'Everyone here is most kind, my lord.'

'Isabella, you are becoming a shocking flirt!' Lady Burstock frowned at her daughter, although there was a decided twinkle in her eyes.

'Oh fudge, Mama. Harry knows I am only funning,' replied her daughter, unabashed. She turned to Antonia. 'Laurence and I have known Harry for ever. He used to tease me unmercifully when I was still in the schoolroom.'

'For all that you have turned out quite tolerably,' he grinned.

'You do not deserve that I should dance with you.'

'But you will — and I beg that Miss Venn will honour me with a dance, too!'

* * *

With a partner assured for at least one dance, Antonia found herself looking forward to the Assembly: she took special pains over her toilet, coaxing her soft brown curls into a more elaborate style and choosing from her wardrobe a new gown of bronze satin edged with blond lace. It had remained unworn since her arrival in Brighton because she considered its low neckline unsuitable for a chaperon. However, on this occasion Lady Burstock would be present and she would not be called upon to fulfil that role. She felt a shiver of excitement as the silk slid over her limbs, emphasizing the ivory sheen of her neck and arms. The rich colour was reflected in her eyes, giving warmth to their usually cool grey depths. From her meagre selection of jewels she chose her mother's pearls and matching ear-drops, completing the picture with an embroidered shawl which she draped elegantly across her arms. As she made her way downstairs, she was gratified to receive a nod and smile of approval from Lady Burstock.

'Very pretty, my dear. The colour becomes you admirably.'

Antonia's hand crept to the low *décolletage*.

'Thank you — you do not think perhaps I should wear a kerchief . . . ?'

'By no means. You have a beautiful skin and the cut of the gown shows it to advantage. Enjoy yourself, my dear.'

★　★　★

Lord Henry Bressingham stood up with Isabella for the country dances while Lady Burstock and Antonia found seats at the end of the room, where they could watch the dancers. Antonia was amused to observe several young gentlemen casting envious glances at the young couple, obviously wishing they could take Lord Henry's place. Her attention was recalled by Lady Burstock, who informed her that Sir Rigby Claremont was making his way towards them. Miss Venn knew she should be pleased that her own attendance was not unnoticed, but she could not forget Sir Rigby's fulsome compliments and familiar style at their last meeting. She cast an imploring glance at Lady Burstock.

'Dear ma'am, I pray you will not abandon me.'

My lady looked amused but promised to remain with her. Almost before she had finished speaking Sir Rigby was upon them, making his low bow.

He suggested to Antonia that they should join the next set, but Lady Burstock intervened.

'I am afraid, Sir Rigby, that Antonia is already promised for the next dance — you know Lord Henry Bressingham, of course? He is presently dancing with my daughter.'

Sir Rigby's face fell.

'Ah yes — of course, of course.'

Antonia's ready sympathy was roused by his downcast mien.

'I am sorry, Sir Rigby, I *did* promise Lord Henry — yesterday, in fact.'

With a gusty sigh and another elaborate bow Sir Rigby ambled away. Lady Burstock watched him, amusement in her eyes.

'Poor man. He is very taken with you.'

'I wish he were not. In Bath I think he was restrained by the presence of his daughter, while here — but perhaps I refine too much upon trifles.'

'Perhaps, my dear, though I think you are right. You should not give him undue encouragement. Ah, here are Lord Henry and Isabella — well, my lord?'

Miss Burstock's face was alight with laughter.

'Oh Mama, would you believe it? Harry and I have not danced since I was in the schoolroom.'

'Such a time ago,' murmured her mother.

'She is vastly improved, ma'am, and I understand it is you, Miss Venn, that we must congratulate. Now, will you allow me the chance to compare the teacher with the pupil?'

Antonia gave him her hand. 'With pleasure, sir!'

The next dance was a lively gavotte and Sir Henry proved to be an energetic yet graceful partner. The fast tempo left little opportunity for speech and combined with the warmth of the rooms, it soon brought a glow to the dancers' cheeks. They remained on the dance-floor for the second gavotte but still the music ended all too soon for Antonia, who turned her sparkling eyes towards her partner as he led her back to her party.

'An excellent dance, my lord, thank you.'

'Thank *you*, Miss Venn. Isabella did not exaggerate your skills. Perhaps you will grant me another dance — that is if you are not promised for the rest of the evening?'

'Oh I can easily grant you another dance, sir, I am engaged to stand up with no one else,' she said frankly. 'It is the result of having so few acquaintances in Brighton, but I do not repine. I am happy to sit out with Lady Burstock and watch the younger ones.'

'As though you were in your dotage,' he declared. 'I will most certainly avail myself of this opportunity to lead you out again, Miss Venn. Pray say you will not refuse me.'

She laughingly agreed and once he had restored her to Lady Burstock, he lounged away.

'Such an amiable young man. Did I hear him correctly, you will dance with him again?'

'Yes, ma'am, that is, do you think I should not?'

'I do not see that it will do any harm, and he has the advantage of being an old family friend.'

'I think it is merely a cover for the fact that he wishes to dance with Isabella for at least half the evening,' Antonia guessed shrewdly, 'but if it keeps her mind away from her Bath liaison . . . '

'I pray it will do so. She is still a trifle distracted, but I know that with time she will forget this mysterious young man, as she has forgotten all the others.' She caught sight of a late arrival and exclaimed, 'Oh — heavens, Laurence!'

Following her glance, Antonia saw Sir Laurence crossing the room towards them. His tall figure and halting gait drew many eyes, but despite the dragging left leg, Antonia thought the powerful form beneath the black evening coat and silk knee breeches gave a suggestion of strength and energy that few men in the room could match. She was still glowing from the exertions of her dance with Lord Henry and the smiling face she turned towards Sir Laurence was positively radiant. His stern features relaxed into a smile.

'I thought I might find you here, Mama.' He kissed Lady Burstock's proffered cheek. 'Where is Bella — dancing, no doubt?'

'Yes, with Harry Bressingham. By the by, did you know he was coming to Brighton?'

'I saw him in Town last week. He said he would be escorting Lady Bressingham here.'

'Did you come direct from Town? You

should have sent us word; we would have waited for you.'

'I had intended to stay in London for a few days more, but everything seems quiet and I have left instructions at the Horse Guards to let me know if there is any news.'

'There is no word from Brussels?' put in Antonia.

'Not yet. Wellington has control now and I hear that more veterans are joining him daily. No one seems to think Bonaparte will strike before July. My compliments, Miss Venn. A very fetching gown.'

Antonia flushed. There had been scarcely a pause between his talk of impending war and the compliment, but it caused a tingle of pleasure to run through her.

'Th-thank you, sir.' She drew a deep breath, looking up at him shyly. 'The musicians are excellent, do you not think?'

'Are they? The dancers seem to appreciate them, at all events.' He looked at her, noting the heightened colour in her cheeks. 'Are you warm, Miss Venn, can I fetch you some lemonade, perhaps?'

'No-no, I have been dancing sir. I believe they are standing up for a waltz. Perhaps, perhaps you would like to try?' She was surprised at her own daring: Sir Laurence raised a brow but his look was surprised rather than disapproving.

Lady Burstock added her persuasion.

'Yes, go on, Laurence. Poor Antonia is desperate to dance.'

'So any partner will suffice?' he murmured.

Antonia saw the gleam in his eyes and responded in kind.

'I must be satisfied with any crumb, Sir Laurence.'

He laughed and she was emboldened to continue in a more serious tone.

'I would be honoured if you would ask me to dance, sir.'

With a nod he held out his arm to her and led her away. Antonia's spirits soared. She was aware of the surprised glances as they moved into the centre of the room.

'I fear you are to be disappointed, Miss Venn. This is the first time I have danced in public since I returned from the Peninsula.'

She squeezed his arm, anxious to reassure him. 'But I know how well you dance, sir.'

The slow, lilting music filled the room and the dancers began their stately progress. The dance-floor was not crowded, for the waltz was still not considered a suitable dance for very young ladies. Antonia put up her chin, well aware that numerous eyes were upon them. Sir Laurence's arm lay lightly across her back as he led her through the first, slow movement of the dance. Any shyness Antonia may have felt was forgotten in her concern for her companion. She gave him an encouraging smile: she knew her strength as a dancer, she felt at home with the steps and the music, and she concentrated on supporting her partner.

'You should dance more often, Sir Laurence, it is excellent exercise.'

His hand tightened on her fingers, the dark eyes glinting down at her.

'I will, an' you will be my partner!'

Isabella, coming up to stand beside Lady Burstock, gasped, 'Is that Laurence, Mama? Laurence *dancing*?'

Lady Burstock allowed herself a small triumphant smile.

'Yes, Isabella. It is.'

Lady Bressingham passed them on her way to the supperroom.

'My dear Lady Burstock, I do not know when I last saw Laurence looking so well. Who is his partner, do I know her?'

'A young guest who is spending the summer with us. The daughter of Philip Venn, do you remember him?'

'But of course! Darling Venn, we all had a soft spot for him, did we not?' She looked again at the dancers. 'So that is poor Venn's daughter — she looks well enough, but very ordinary compared to the ripe beauties one is used to seeing with your son since . . . ' She stopped, laughing a little self-consciously. 'But never mind that. I do not know what has become of Harry. If you should see him, my dear, please tell him I am gone in to supper.'

★ ★ ★

'Laurence, you sly thing. You told me that you never danced!' Isabella berated her brother soundly as he left the dance-floor with Antonia on his arm, 'I vow you shall not escape this evening without standing up with me for at least one dance.'

Sir Laurence appeared to be in an unusually mellow mood: he grinned at his sister.

'What, Bella? I did not think you lacked partners.'

'I don't, but I shall keep a dance free especially for you, *dear* brother! Antonia, how did you persuade him to it? Harry was as shocked as I when he saw you both — he is in the supper-room, by the by. Shall we go in, Mama? I am ready for supper — are you, Antonia?'

Glad of the distraction, Antonia assented readily. Her spirits were still soaring from the dance and she accompanied Lady Burstock and her party into the supper-room with the music still ringing in her head.

* * *

It was a very warm night and when they eventually returned to the ballroom the double doors leading out to the gardens had been thrown wide, allowing in a cooling breeze. Miss Burstock demanded her brother's attendance in the set that was forming for the next dance and Antonia, finding Lady Burstock engaged in conversation with another matron, found herself temporarily alone. It did not worry her: she was glad of the opportunity to relive every moment of her dance with Sir Laurence. She chose a seat by the open doors, where she had a clear view of the dancing. Antonia was thus engaged when a familiar voice recalled her attention.

'Ah, my dear Miss Venn — how fortunate for me to find you alone.'

She looked round to find Sir Rigby beaming at her. He sat down beside her, his corsets creaking as he lowered himself on to the chair. She was immediately aware of the scent of roses, with which he had liberally sprinkled himself that evening.

'You do not dance, my dear young lady? Perhaps you will allow me — '

'Thank you sir, but no. I have danced enough this evening and I am only too pleased to sit out.'

'Then you must let me keep you company. It would not do for such a pretty young thing to be alone, eh?' He leaned closer, the brandy fumes from his breath hot on her face.

Antonia began to fan herself vigorously, desperately searching for something to say.

'I do so enjoy watching the dance, Sir Rigby, do not you? So many beautiful gowns, and the sparkling lights, quite a spectacle.'

Her attempts to divert him did not succeed.

'I only care to watch when you are dancing, my dear. You cast all the rest into the shade.' The leering smile that accompanied these words sent a shudder through Antonia. She rose hurriedly.

'Excuse me, sir.'

'What is it, Miss Venn, are you ill?'

'No — yes. That is, I fear I am a little faint. It would be best to find Lady Burstock.'

Sir Rigby took her arm. 'No, no, my dear, what you need is a little fresh air. Come, let us step out into the garden for a moment — you will soon see that I am right.'

'No sir, I promise you I shall be well if only I can find my lady.' Her protests were overridden as he firmly propelled her towards the open door. Antonia felt unable to break away without an unseemly struggle. She looked round desperately for help, but Sir Rigby's bulky form screened her from the rest of the room and another couple of steps put her on the narrow terrace that overlooked the gardens.

'There, my dear, is that not a little cooler?'

She disengaged herself and stepped away from him.

'Yes it is, sir, I thank you — but — perhaps a glass of lemonade?'

'All in good time, Miss Venn. I cannot leave you until I am sure you will not faint.' He moved towards her and Antonia retreated, only to find her way blocked by the balustrade that bounded the terrace. The sickly sweet smell of rosewater threatened to choke her.

'I-I am feeling much better now, Sir Rigby, we should go back inside — '

'In a moment, my dear. First you must let me tell you how charming you are looking tonight. Oakford's a lucky dog, but you should consider, Miss Venn, I am a dozen times richer, think of that.'

She could think of nothing but his huge hand stealing round her waist. He had moved forward until the massive bulk of him was pressing against her. She put her hands on his chest, but he was too close now for her to hold him off.

'Please, Sir Rigby — '

'Just a little kiss then, my dear,' he muttered thickly. Don't be afraid, no one is going to notice and I can't resist you any longer. I have been very patient, you know.'

His mouth came closer and she turned her face away so that his kiss landed on her ear. His free hand crept up to her breast and she gave a small cry, desperately trying to push him away.

'Claremont!'

'What — what?' Sir Rigby turned to see who dared to address him so curtly and Antonia pushed past him. To her horror, she saw Sir Laurence and his sister standing in the doorway. With the lights of the ballroom behind them it was impossible to see their faces clearly, but Antonia was fully aware of her compromising situation. She tried to force her numbed brain to think of something to say, but it was Sir Laurence who spoke first.

'I believe you were right, Isabella, Miss Venn was overcome by the heat. Pray fetch her wrap, my dear; hurry now.' He waited until Miss Burstock had disappeared, then stepped further out on to the terrace. 'My dear Sir Rigby, I am sure Miss Venn no longer requires your services. We will bid you goodnight.'

'Damnation, Oakford, Miss Venn and I were having a-a little conversation, nothing more. She was feeling unwell and we stepped out here on to the terrace.' He gave a fat chuckle, winking at Sir Laurence. 'Why you cunning dog, you can't blame me for trying my luck, eh? Damme but you are the luckiest devil to have found such a plum — and to have her here, under Lady Burstock's own roof, too! Pity of it is I didn't make a bid earlier.'

'I would strongly advise you to hold your tongue, Claremont, if you know what's good for you.'

Sir Rigby puffed out his chest.

'Are you threatening me, sir?' He stared at Sir Laurence but something in that gentleman's implacable gaze caused him to look away and he said in a milder tone, 'Well, well, I know how it is with you young dogs. I'll leave you to your conquest. Perhaps, when you are grown tired of her . . .'

It seemed to Antonia that they had forgotten her presence but now, to her horror, she saw the tightening of Sir Laurence's jaw as he raised his fists. She cried out in alarm.

'No — please — remember where we are,

sir! A brawl could only distress Lady Burstock.'

Sir Laurence did not look at her but stared at Sir Rigby.

'Get out, Claremont, now, or you will find your age is no defence!'

Sir Rigby's normally ruddy countenance flushed even more crimson, but after the slightest hesitation he went without a word, leaving Antonia and Sir Laurence alone on the terrace. She dared not look at him, turning away to try to compose herself. She was shocked to find herself so upset by the encounter with Sir Rigby, but she was even more distressed that Sir Laurence had discovered them.

'An eventful evening,' he drawled. 'Tell me, Miss Venn, did you truly feel unwell, or was that merely a device to steal out here with that lecher?'

She clutched at the balustrade, trying to control her shivering.

'Do you really think I wanted this to happen?' she said, not looking round.

'No, perhaps not, but you were damned foolish to allow it. Yet why am I surprised? Why should I expect anything more of you.'

Antonia turned to stare at him. 'I beg your pardon?'

His lip curled. 'When I consider the

circumstances of our first meeting — perhaps that was only a charade — but you played it very well, my dear. Fooled me into thinking I could be the white knight, saving you with my generosity.'

Pale with fury Antonia struck him, her open palm catching him fully across the cheek.

'How dare you say such a thing to me!'

They stood silently, the lady's eyes dark with anger as she glared into his white face, the stare continuing until Isabella returned with the silk wrap and her anxious words broke the spell.

'Here we are, Antonia, let me put this about your shoulders. Poor dear, you are shaking. Let me take you back to Mama.'

'No, no, I am much better now, thank you. If only I can be quiet for a little while . . . '

Sir Laurence stepped forward and took her arm. 'You had best return to Mama, Isabella. Tell her I have taken Miss Venn home. I will return later to escort you back.'

'Oh, please — there is no need.'

'Pray do not argue, Miss Venn. You cannot wish to return to the ballroom.'

'No, sir, I do not.'

'Then we will slip out quietly through the gate at the end of the grounds. Isabella can take a message to the coachman to meet us there, or we can walk back to Marine Parade. It is but a few minutes' stroll, if you think you can manage that?'

Antonia could not argue.

'Thank you,' she spoke stiffly. 'You are very good.'

Once Isabella had left them, Sir Laurence escorted Antonia down the steps and through the darkened gardens to a small wicket gate in the wall that led out on to the street. It was a warm night, but Antonia was glad of her thin wrap, which she kept pulled tightly around her. Sir Laurence had tucked her hand into his arm and feeling her shiver, he glanced down.

'Cold, Miss Venn?'

'No, sir, furious — with you and with myself. If you doubted my integrity why did you allow me to come to Brighton as companion to your sister?'

'I have never doubted your . . . integrity, Miss Venn. My outburst was prompted by anger — when I saw you in the arms of another man.'

'You do not trust me, then.'

'Trust is something I have to learn, Antonia,' he muttered, continuing a moment later in a much stronger tone, 'but whatever were you thinking of to do such a thing?' She hung her head. 'I-I was *not* thinking. I could not break free.'

'The dance had just ended when Bella spotted you going outside. She said you were looking anxious and suggested we follow. I must say I was surprised at your choice of partner; you could do much better for yourself, you know.'

'Pray you, sir, I am in no mood for jesting. And — his comments — when you came outside.'

'That need not trouble you,' he said flatly.

Antonia felt her cheeks growing hot in the darkness.

'He-he thinks that I — that you — '

'Pray think no more of that, Miss Venn. Sir Rigby is a buffoon, but I shall make sure he does not bother you again.'

He spoke in the bored voice she had heard him use with others: it signified contempt. Antonia knew then how low she had sunk in his esteem. Tears welled in her eyes. It was not yet midnight and the clubs and Assemblies were still full. Antonia thought miserably that an hour since she would have dreamed of no greater pleasure than to be walking alone with Sir Laurence. Now all she wanted was to lock herself in her room and indulge in a long, comforting bout of tears.

★ ★ ★

The footman who admitted them to the house looked surprised to see them returning so early, but Sir Laurence escorted Antonia to the drawing-room and closed the door firmly upon his interested gaze.

'Would you like me to ring for your maid?' he asked her.

'No, thank you, I am quite recovered now.'

'Very well. I must get back. I suggest you go to bed, Miss Venn.'

'Yes. Thank you. Sir Laurence!'

He stopped at the door.

'I am sorry.'

His looked at her with his hard, uncompromising gaze.

'Yes. So too am I.'

9

Antonia left her room in some trepidation the following morning. She was reluctant to meet her hostess, but knowing that the trial must be faced sooner or later, she set her shoulders and entered the breakfast-room, hoping she did not look as nervous as she felt. She was relieved to find Lady Burstock alone there, and that lady's first words did much to put her at her ease.

'Antonia, my dear, I was afraid you might keep to your bed this morning. Isabella told me what occurred last night; how perfectly horrid for you.'

'It-it was, ma'am, and I am sorry to have embroiled you in such a sordid affair.'

'Nonsense, child. Laurence handled the whole thing so discreetly no one even noticed.'

Antonia flushed. 'I am afraid I have let him down, ma'am.'

'As to that, Laurence is forever rescuing Isabella from much worse scrapes than this.'

'But he brought me here to keep her out of them, not to add to his worries.'

Hearing the anguished note in Antonia's

voice, Lady Burstock leaned across the table to pat her hand.

'Then put this little incident out of your head, Antonia, and carry on with the task of looking after Isabella. So far your presence here has been invaluable to me, my dear. I know when Isabella is with you she is in safe hands.'

'Th-thank you, my lady, I will try not to let you down.'

'I am sure of it. Now, my dear, Laurence has already left the house, but he has promised to join us later this morning in the town. Isabella has heard of a new milliner in North Street — will you come with us?'

'Thank you, ma'am, but no. I have a letter to write to my aunt that should not be delayed any longer.'

Antonia was not sorry for an excuse to stay behind. Common sense told her that she was the injured party in the affair, but she could not forget Sir Laurence's cold, implacable look when he had left her. She sat at the small writing-desk in the drawing-room, trying to compose her letter to Mrs Haseley. She trimmed her pen and dipped it into the standish, but the ink had dried before she could think of what to write. Her thoughts kept returning to the Assembly: if only she had stayed with Lady Burstock, Sir Laurence might have danced with her a second time, and looked at her with warmth rather than that harsh, accusing stare. She shook her head, as if to dispel the image, dipped her pen into the ink again and forced herself to write. She had just finished the first sheet when a visitor was announced. Antonia jumped up to greet him.

'Charles!'

'Well, well, there is no need to cry all over me!' declared Mr Haseley, as his cousin threw her arms about him.

She stepped back, between tears and laughter.

'I beg your pardon. I have been feeling so sorry for myself and wishing desperately for someone to talk to. You are the answer to my prayers!'

He patted her arm, not a little embarrassed by this show of emotion from his usually calm cousin.

'What has happened to overset you, Cos? Has Lady Burstock behaved badly to you? Where is everyone, by the by?'

'They are all gone out, and no, I have been treated with nothing but kindness, except — oh Charles, I cannot tell you here: do you have time to walk with me?'

'Certainly. I have no plans for the morning. I have found myself lodgings in Brighton and have come to give you my direction.'

'You are staying here? What about your studies?'

'Oh I have decided not to go back until next term. I have lost too much time to make up now.'

Antonia was not convinced by his airy tone, but she did not pursue the matter, her own troubles overshadowing her concern for her cousin. Promising to be quick she ran upstairs to change into her walking dress and twenty minutes later they were strolling along the Esplanade. A heavy blanket of grey cloud covered the sky and a chill wind was blowing off the sea, causing Mr Haseley to pull up the fur collar of his redingote.

'I was just writing to your mama when you came in,' said Antonia. 'Have you a message from her, or mayhap she is in Brighton?'

'No, dash it! Papa cut up stiff about the studies I have missed and we came to cuffs as usual.'

'And does he know you are in Brighton? No, I thought not. Really, Charles, you should not disobey your father in this way.'

'Well, normally I would not, if . . . but never mind that. What of you, Cos? What has occurred to make you so unhappy?'

Antonia had intended to relate only the briefest outline of what had occurred the previous evening, but the temptation to pour out her story into his sympathetic ear was too great. Since Charles knew nothing of her first meeting in London with Sir Laurence, she did not relate that gentleman's accusations, and Mr Haseley was not inclined to think the evening so great a disaster, but Antonia was not to be comforted.

'Lady Burstock was all kindness this morning, but I felt myself quite sunk beyond reproach.'

'Well, I warned you to be careful of Claremont.'

'But he seemed so harmless in Bath.'

'Just shows how wrong you can be. Still, if Oakford has seen him off with his tail between his legs all the better.'

'But I wish it had not happened. We were getting on so well . . . Oh heavens, here he is!'

Mr Haseley looked up to see Lady Burstock and her daughter walking in their direction; between the ladies was a tall gentleman in a drab overcoat, the collar turned up against the chill wind.

'So that's Isabella's brother? By gad, he's dark. A regular blackamoor.'

'He is nothing of the kind,' retorted Antonia. 'His years in the Peninsula may have darkened his skin somewhat, but I consider it better than the fashionable pallor affected by so many gentlemen. Oh dear, they have seen us — there is no avoiding a meeting. Charles, pray be courteous.'

Antonia summoned up a smile as Lady Burstock and her children came up. She did not notice Isabella's conscious look and flushed cheek. One glance at Sir Laurence's stony face told her that his manner towards her had not changed since the previous evening and her heart sank even as the colour rose in her cheek. Lady Burstock greeted them kindly and lost no time in presenting Mr Haseley to her son. Charles bowed.

'How do you do, sir. I understand you were in the Peninsula — Dragoons, was it not? Prince of Wales' Own.' His eyes shone as Sir Laurence nodded his assent. 'By Jove, sir, I envy you that! It's my ambition, y'see, to be a cavalry officer — '

'Really?'

Sir Laurence's brief reply was not encouraging and Lady Burstock took pity on the young man, engaging him in conversation. Sir Laurence turned to Antonia.

'Your cousin is staying in Brighton?

'I believe so. He-he has told me very little of his plans.'

'Young men are always so secretive!' smiled Lady Burstock. 'Laurence was exactly the same when he was younger. You are about to contest that, my son, but it was so.'

Mr Haseley took advantage of Lady Burstock's lively exchange with her son to snatch a few words with Isabella and it took only a moment for that enterprising young lady to suggest an assignation at the circulating library for that very afternoon.

As the parties went on their way, Charles cast a look back over his shoulder.

'Sir Laurence is Isabella's guardian, I believe.'

'Yes. Lord Burstock left him in control of Bella's whole fortune.'

'Well, I must say he's a cold devil.'

'Oh no, he can be very kind, I assure you. It is just — I think he is still out with me.'

'Hmm, I can see you do not like to be in his bad books. He does not look like a man who takes kindly to being thwarted.' He realized his cousin was eyeing him anxiously and he laughed, squeezing her hand.

'Pray don't mind me rattling on, Cos! No doubt you would much prefer to hear how everyone is going on at home . . . '

* * *

Thursday dawned and with it the prospect of another Assembly. At breakfast, Isabella was naturally eager to discuss the evening and to know who would be going.

'I will wear the yellow again, I think, Mama, but I will need new ribbons for my hair — will you come with me this evening, Mama?'

'Do not look for me to accompany you,' remarked Sir Laurence, as he addressed a plate of cold meats. 'I am leaving for London directly I have finished my meal.'

She pouted.

'Oh must you? I made sure you would come.'

Lady Burstock laid down her fork.

'Do you plan to stay overnight, Laurence, or will you drive back today?'

'I had planned to put up at Grillon's tonight, but if you wish I can travel back.'

'No, we shall manage quite well without you, Laurence, although naturally we shall miss you this evening.'

'I have ordered Judd to bring the curricle round at eleven.' Sir Laurence rose. 'I had best collect my bag. Goodbye, Mama.' He dropped a light kiss upon her forehead. 'Take care of your mother while I am away, Bella.'

'Of course I will, Laurence! And you will be back tomorrow?'

'Yes, indeed. I must be back by dinnertime for I have invited Harry Bressingham to join us — did I not mention it?'

'No, Laurence, you did not.' Lady Burstock tried to look severe, drawing a smile from her son.

'My apologies, Mama. I met him last night at Freddie Collyer's card party. Lady Bressingham is gone to Winchester to attend Lady Pamela — she has produced an heir for Moran already, it seems.'

My lady looked at him, her eyes searching his face. Observing her anxiety, Sir Laurence smiled, albeit a little crookedly. He dropped a hand upon her shoulder.

'You need have no worries on that score, Mama. My interest in Lady Pamela is quite ended.'

'I am glad, my son.'

With a kiss for Isabella and a brief word of farewell to Antonia, he was gone, leaving his sister to gaze wide-eyed at her mother.

'Well, was he *really* in love with Pamela Bressingham, Mama?'

Lady Burstock reached for another piece of bread and butter.

'I never believed it to be serious, you know, but of course while Laurence was abroad he built up such a false image of her. He turned Pamela into a goddess, you see. It was inevitable that she would not stay upon that pedestal he had built for her.' She cast an apologetic glance at Antonia. 'I am sorry, my dear, we are talking of the past. It can be of no interest to you. Now, I had best see Cook and discuss what we are to set before Lord Henry tomorrow. There is the lamb, of course, and a tongue, but she must procure more fish and perhaps another cheese-cake . . . '

'And I will go in search of new ribbons, Mama. Antonia, will you go with me? Antonia, are you day-dreaming?'

Miss Venn smiled, rising from the table.

'I beg your pardon. Of course I will come with you. A little fresh air is just what I need to throw off this lethargy.'

Miss Burstock was soon engrossed in choosing ribbons from a rainbow-coloured assortment spread over the counter of a tiny shop in Church Street. A canary-yellow silk was chosen to match Isabella's sprig muslin with its tiny yellow roses, but a length of emerald green caught her eye. It was the perfect match for her new pelisse. She then would not leave the shop until she had bought a length of apricot ribbon, which she presented to Antonia.

'We can trim your cream satin with it,' she explained. 'Believe me, Antonia, I have a very good eye for colour — even Laurence owns it.'

Touched by this kindness, Antonia accompanied her young friend out on to Church Street, where they saw Lord Henry Bressingham coming towards them.

'Miss Burstock, Miss Venn, how do you do? Which way are you going? Marine Parade? Capital! I will escort you, if you do not object.'

'Not in the least,' replied Miss Burstock. 'You shall walk between us and give an arm to each, the pavement is quite wide enough.'

Having organized everything to her satisfaction, Miss Burstock walked along on Lord Henry's left arm, with Antonia on his right. Any awkwardness Antonia might have felt was dispelled by Lord Henry's grin as he held out his arm to her.

'We must do as we are bid, Miss Venn. But I have rarely received such a pleasant instruction, though I fear Miss Burstock is growing to be a most managing female.'

'Harry, I am not!' The young lady bridled, but upon seeing the mischief in his eyes she laughed. 'And you, sir, are becoming a shocking tease.'

He grinned, then turned to Antonia: 'I was sorry that we could not have our second dance at the assembly the other night, Miss Venn. Bella told me you were unwell — I trust you are now fully recovered?'

'Yes, thank you, sir. I am perfectly well.'

Isabella tugged at his sleeve.

'Harry, there is something I want to ask you. However, first I believe you are to be congratulated.'

'What? Oh, yes, Pamela's produced a boy. M'sister, Lady Moran,' he explained to Antonia. 'She's been lying in at Moran's country seat near Winchester.'

She nodded. 'Sir Laurence mentioned something of it this morning.'

'Yes, Harry, which is why I am *particularly* pleased that we have seen you. Mama says that Pamela and Laurence were wondrous great a few years ago, yet since he came back from the war he has rarely mentioned her. I know at first he was very ill, and then he was very busy looking after Mama's affairs after Papa died, but — from the things Mama has said I *know* something happened. When Pamela married Viscount Moran last year Mama expressly forbade me to mention it to Laurence, but today, he seemed quite unconcerned when he mentioned Pamela. I cannot understand it. Harry, pray won't you tell me? You know what occurred, do you not?'

Lord Henry's cheerful face grew unusually grave.

'Aye, I do.'

Isabella gave a little skip of delight. 'Oh famous! Pray tell us, Harry. Oh, I see why you are hesitating, you think it would be improper to speak of it before Antonia, but you must know that we consider her almost one of the family, Mama has said so.'

Antonia was moved to protest.

'Isabella, you must not press Lord Henry. Surely your brother or mama will tell you if they think you should know.'

Miss Burstock ignored her interruption: she turned her violet eyes upon the gentleman with such a melting look that she hoped he could not resist. 'Pray, Harry, can you not tell us? In confidence, of course. You may be assured it will go no further.'

'I've no doubt of Miss Venn's discretion, Bella, but I know what a chatterbox you can be!' he replied frankly.

Antonia knew she should command her young charge to press him no further, but she was shamefully aware that she too wanted to know more. She remained silent. His lordship shrugged.

'Well, I cannot see the harm in it. It was all over Town last season. Dozens of people know what happened and you will hear it when you go to London, so it is better coming from me, since I know the whole, rather than you should be given some

Banbury story with the truth twisted and altered out of all proportion. Let us turn here and walk through the Pavilion grounds, we are less likely to be overheard. But if you are going to skip along beside me like a hoyden, Bella, I shall say no more and take my leave of you now.'

Isabella immediately begged his pardon and promised to behave. Assured of her attention, Lord Henry walked on for a few moments, frowning slightly as he thought of what he was about to recount. Isabella squeezed his arm.

'Harry? will you not begin?'

'I was just deciding *where* to begin, it goes back such a dashed long time. You know, of course, that there was some talk of a match between Laurence and Pamela years ago. Pamela was still in the schoolroom and from what m'mother has said since, I believe it was merely idle chit-chat between the parents, but Laurence took it seriously and Pamela was ninny enough to think it the height of romance. Laurence joined the Dragoons as soon as he had finished his studies and we heard nothing more of him until the spring of '13, when he was brought back to England, badly wounded.'

Isabella shuddered. 'That was a dreadful time. I thought he would die, and I know

Mama thought so too, for a while, although she never said so to me and she would not give up. Papa arranged the very best care for Laurence. We had doctors living at the house for months.'

'There was no question of visiting Burstock Hall when Laurence was so ill but later, when my mother suggested we might make the journey, Pamela flatly refused to go.'

Lord Henry paused and when he spoke again it was slowly, choosing his words with care. 'My sister has never been able to cope with illness or injury. She-she has an abhorrence of the sick-room and is never the least use when anyone is ill, so it was quite understandable that she should not wish to see Laurence until he was well again. We were not aware *then* of the true situation.

'Laurence was not to know that while he had been away, Pamela had been enjoying herself in Town and rapidly becoming an acclaimed beauty. By the time he came back to England Mama was already talking of achieving a great match for m'sister and no one was surprised when Moran offered for her. Mama, of course, was overjoyed; not only is he a viscount, but he's also as rich as Croesus. The pity of it was, no one thought to write to Burstock Hall with the news. I had spent the best part the winter in Ireland

— we had decided to dispose of our estates there and I had been despatched to arrange the whole. The first I knew of any problem was a letter from Mama telling me to conclude the business as speedily as possible and be back in time for a grand ball she was planning. Mama was hurrying everything along because she did not want the betrothal to be overshadowed by the Peace Celebrations.'

Antonia was compelled to speak, to confirm the suspicion growing within her.

'And this was in the spring of '14?'

'Aye that's it. Following the worst dashed winter for years — Thames frozen and all that, you must remember it. Mama had Bressingham refurbished for the occasion. I can still see it now, the house decorated with yellow and white silk hangings and dashed yellow flowers everywhere, all to match Pamela's gold and white gown.'

'Oh, how exquisite,' breathed Isabella, entranced at the thought of such a spectacle. 'I wish I had been there.'

'I very much wish I had not,' he retorted. 'I arrived in Town just one day before the ball and it was only then I learned that neither Lady Burstock nor Laurence had been invited. Mama said at first it was because your papa had only recently died and

Laurence still not fully recovered, but I soon learned the whole. Pamela had confessed to Mama that she had entered into a secret engagement with Laurence and was too afraid to tell him she was to marry Moran. M'father had been off at some hunting lodge and had only just arrived, so the two women between them had decided that the best thing would be to say nothing until after the engagement, when Mama proposed writing to Lady Burstock to explain everything.' His face hardened. 'I should not speak ill of my family, Bella, but that was very wrong of them. However ill-considered it may have been for Laurence to enter into a secret engagement, Pamela should have informed him of her change of heart. I knew how he would react if he learned the truth by chance and I dashed off a note to him immediately, but it was too late.'

Antonia felt uncomfortably like an eavesdropper: she knew she had no right to hear the story Lord Henry was recounting but she could not bring herself to interrupt him. She found herself imagining the effect on Sir Laurence, struggling to regain his health, to learn that the woman he loved was about to marry another. She felt sickened by the cruel trick that had been played on him. Lord Henry was speaking again.

'Laurence arrived, mad as fire. Poor Moran had no idea what was happening. Have you ever met him, Bella? He is a year or two older than Laurence, but where your brother is tall and dark, Moran is fair and much stouter — and even his best friends would not call him needle-witted. Oakford flashed a ring in front of m'sister — a big solitaire that must have cost him a small fortune, and she almost fainted with desire. Laurence left at that point, but by then Moran was wondering aloud if Pamela was only marrying him for his money. Silly chit promptly fell into hysterics but Mama rallied to the occasion. She had Pamela carried out to an anteroom to recover and bid the orchestra strike up for another dance. She bullied the viscount and a number of others to make up a set to start things moving again. I made Mama write to Lady Burstock the next day to tell her the whole, and we were relieved when she responded to tell us that Laurence had arrived back safely and appeared quite philosophical about the whole episode. Miss Venn, what is it? Did you stumble?'

'Yes, yes, I am sorry, the flagway was uneven. Please, carry on with your story.'

'Laurence has never mentioned anything of this to me,' said Isabella thoughtfully. 'And Mama has only given me the merest hint. But when Laurence told us today that Pamela had provided Moran with an heir Mama looked at him in *such* a way, and he was at pains to assure her that — that his interest in her was at an end.'

'Well, I hope it is so,' said Lord Henry. He glanced at Antonia, walking silently on his right. 'Miss Venn, you are looking a little pale.'

'If I am silent it is because I am overset by all I have heard today. I am honoured by your confidences sir and you have my assurance that I shall not mention this to anyone.'

'No, nor I,' declared Isabella. 'But it is such a sad tale. If only they had been allowed to marry.'

'There is no reason why they should not have done so,' responded Lord Henry. 'My mother would have raised no objections to the match, if Pamela had been set on it. After all, Laurence's fortune may not be as great as Moran's, but he's not penniless.'

Isabella was not listening.

'I know just how it was!' she said, her eyes sparkling. 'Everyone saying they were too young, Pamela being dragged off to London to make a great match and Laurence going off to war to forget her. If only they had been stronger, they need never have been separated.'

'No, no that was not it at all,' declared the gentleman, between alarm and amusement, but she did not attend him: Miss Burstock's fertile imagination was racing ahead and she saw now a direct comparison between Lady Pamela's plight and her own situation. After their hurried meeting at the library, Charles had talked of joining up as soon as he was able and if he was allowed to do so, who could say that he too would not be horribly wounded, like Laurence, or even killed. The lessons were obvious to Isabella, it was just a matter of persuading Charles to her point of view.

'Pray remember that I have told you this in confidence, Bella,' said Lord Henry as they reached their house in Marine Parade. 'I told you because I wanted you to have the truth rather than the gossip you might hear in Town. But you must not repeat it.'

'No, no, Harry. I promise.'

Antonia held out her hand to him. 'I too, will not speak of it, my lord, but I am honoured that you trusted me.'

Taking her hand, he pressed it gratefully.

'I know that you have the best interests of the family at heart, Miss Venn.'

The two young ladies entered the house, each of them caught up in her own thoughts. Isabella went off to find her Mama, to make sure she had not forgotten her promise to escort her to the Assembly that evening, and Antonia thankfully shut herself in her room, her head reeling with all she had heard. Going over to her dressing-table, she hunted in one of the drawers for her prayer book. When she had found it she laid it on the table and opened it carefully at the marker, a pale-yellow rose pressed flat between the pages.

Third Movement:
Jetté

June 1815

10

Arriving late at the assembly rooms that evening, Mr Haseley found Miss Burstock in a mood of great excitement. Unfortunately, the public dance floor was not at all the place for an intimate discussion and she was obliged to wait until Mr Haseley could escort her in to supper to pour into his ears the sorry tale of Laurence and Lady Pamela. The version Charles heard from Miss Burstock was more than a little garbled and at the end of it he was obliged to ask his beloved why she thought it so important that he should share the story.

'After all, Bella, it's not something your brother would want you to be talking of.'

'Oh no, and I would not tell anyone except you, Charles. But don't you see it is exactly like our own case. *They* were not allowed to marry and look what occurred!'

'Well, what?'

She stared at him in amazement.

'She is married to a fat old viscount and Laurence very nearly lost his life!'

'But I don't see how that is anything like our case at all.'

'My dear Charles, if they had run off together, they would now be living happily instead of Laurence being so lonely and miserable.'

Since Charles had only met Sir Laurence once, briefly, he could not dispute this statement and he began to understand her meaning.

'Isabella, I do not think you realize just what is involved in running off together. You think it would be an exciting adventure, but — '

'No, no, I understand perfectly and it is not what I want to do, but what we *must* do. Mama and Laurence will never consent to our marriage, but once we have convinced them that we are serious, they will come round, I know it.'

'No, Bella.'

'But it is the only way.'

Mr Haseley was adamant.

'At least let me speak to your brother first. If, as you say, he has been disappointed in love perhaps he will look more favourably on our situation.'

Realizing he was not to be moved on this point, Isabella had to be content. Mr Haseley asked her when it would be best to call: she could not think that her brother would welcome a visit on his return from London:

his temper could be uncertain when he was tired. She promised to advise him of a suitable time, but since she was still convinced that his mission would fail, they parted on less than amicable terms.

Sir Laurence returned to Marine Parade shortly before dinner-time the following evening to find the ladies had already gone to their rooms to prepare for dinner. His appearance in the drawing-room thirty minutes later was greeted with unaffected pleasure by his mother and sister and when he turned to Antonia with a warm smile, she felt hopeful that the unfortunate incident with Sir Rigby might now be forgotten. As soon as Lord Henry arrived they went in to dinner, Lady Burstock eagerly questioning his lordship about his sister and her new baby. Antonia found herself watching Sir Laurence to see how he responded to the talk of Lady Pamela, but apart from commenting that he hoped the child would have its mother's looks, he showed little interest in the matter. In fact, he seemed in a remarkably good mood, and she was reminded of their very first dinner together in Marine Parade. He was determined to be pleased, laughing and joking with Lord Henry and gently teasing his sister. His remarks to Miss Venn were few, but she was conscious of his eyes upon her several times during the meal. After dinner, Lord Henry challenged Isabella to a game of backgammon, leaving the others to enjoy a friendly and not very serious game of ombre. This continued until the appearance of the tea tray, when the backgammon and cards were put aside and Antonia thought her pleasure in the evening complete when Sir Laurence handed her a cup of tea and sat down beside her. 'What is the news from London, sir?' she asked him.

'Nothing of import. A few skirmishes are reported, and French troop movements south of Brussels, but nothing substantial' He looked across the room. 'Isabella is in good spirits. I am glad to see her on such good terms with Harry.' He saw her questioning look and smiled. 'Don't worry, I am not match-making. Isabella is too young to be thinking of marriage, but when she does she could do worse than look to Harry Bressingham.'

'He is a very pleasant young man. Is — is his sister very like him?' she asked lightly, her curiosity overcoming discretion. She feared for a moment he would ask her why she wanted to know, but although he hesitated for a moment, he replied indifferently.

'She has the same fair hair, but Harry's countenance is more open and good-natured.

Lady Moran is considered by many to be beautiful. I thought so myself, once.' His dark eyes rested on her. 'Before you ask, Miss Venn, I will tell you: no, I do not still think so. I have had no interest in blondes for quite some time now.'

Antonia coloured hotly: how was she to take such a comment? Was he angry at her question? She risked looking at him and was relieved to see the smile had returned to his eyes. Despite herself she smiled back, relieved to know he had been teasing her. A moment later his attention was claimed by his sister and he moved away, leaving Antonia to finish her tea, and to go over again in her mind his comments to her.

★   ★   ★

The party broke up very early. Lady Burstock announced that she would be retiring, along with the young ladies, but she kindly invited Lord Henry to remain. Sir Laurence added his own invitation and when the ladies had left the room he walked over to the side table which held a number of decanters and glasses.

'Brandy, Harry?'

'Yes, thank you.'

Lord Henry stood before the mirror to

straighten his neck cloth.

'Very pleasant young woman, Miss Venn.' He shot a glance at his host. 'Intelligent, too, and not afraid to say what she thinks. Philip Venn's daughter, I think you said?'

'Aye. A gambler's daughter who runs a dancing school.'

'Does that matter?'

Sir Laurence tossed off his brandy.

'Dammit, Harry. She's poor as a church mouse. It has always been assumed that I would marry an heiress.' He grimaced. 'Since that debacle with Pamela I confess I haven't thought much about marrying anyone.'

'Until now?'

'She's under my skin, but marriage is out of the question.'

'She don't look like mistress material, Laurence old friend.'

'I know that, but Good God, Harry, an Oakford marry a dancing mistress? My father would turn in his grave. You didn't know him, did you? He died when I was a child. Very high in the in-step. Damned near ruined the estates to live in the manner he thought fitting for an Oakford. But I can hear him in my head even now — *marry a dancing mistress? As well offer for a whore* —'

Sir Laurence realized that Harry was not listening, but was looking over his shoulder towards the door, the habitual smile gone from his eyes. Sir Laurence swung round to see Antonia standing in the doorway, her face very white.

'I — excuse me — Lady Burstock asked me to fetch her book.'

Neither gentleman moved as she crossed the room to pick up a slim leather-bound volume from the sofa and hurry out of the room again. Sir Laurence groaned. Setting down his glass he ran out of the room after her.

'Antonia!' She had reached the stairs but stopped, her face averted. 'I am sorry — you should not have heard that.'

'Evidently.'

Still she did not look at him, but he could see that she was shaking. He put out a hand.

'Antonia, you do not understand — '

She turned her head at that, fixing him with stormy eyes.

'I understand perfectly, sir. You made yourself very clear.'

She tried to draw her hand away but his fingers closed over hers and held her firm. 'Antonia, let me explain, they were not my words!'

'Please remove your hand, sir,' she said icily. 'It is you who must understand that, unlike a-a whore, you cannot buy *me*!'

He released her. 'That is not what I meant — '

But she was gone, running up the stairs and out of sight. After standing, staring after her for a few moments, Sir Laurence walked slowly back into the drawing-room.

Lord Henry shook his head. 'I fear you've queered your pitch there, Laurence.'

'Damnation, Harry, why didn't you warn me?'

'Didn't see her, old friend, until it was too late.'

'How could I have been so — my God, what a coil! I would not hurt her for the world.'

'No, I daresay you would not.' Harry emptied his glass and set it down. He patted Sir Laurence on the shoulder. 'I'd best go. Cheer up, Laurence. Perhaps she will allow you to make your peace with her in the morning.'

But the next day Antonia took breakfast in her bedroom, pleading a headache. Sir Laurence was persuaded to take Isabella to see the Prince's Pavilion, despite his assertions that it would be swarming with workmen brought in to bring about more changes to the hapless building. With Isabella safely occupied, Lady Burstock coaxed Antonia to accompany her for a stroll along the promenade. Herself prone to migraines, Lady Burstock did not doubt that Antonia's pale cheeks were attributable to the headache and merely declared that she would feel better after a little sea air. The gentle exercise did indeed help to soothe Antonia's agitated spirits, although it did nothing to lift the depression that enveloped her. However, when they came upon Lady Bressingham and her son walking towards them Antonia was able to greet them with tolerable composure. The two older ladies immediately fell into conversation and Antonia was left to accept Lord Henry's escort, which she did with as much grace as she could muster.

'I'm glad to have this opportunity of a word with you, Miss Venn,' he began diffidently. 'Laurence was dashed upset about last evening, you know.'

'Indeed?'

It was not an encouraging response, but Lord Henry persevered.

'Aye. Those words you heard him utter — not his sentiments at all you know. With everyone expecting war, it's a very trying time for him, you see. He very much feels he should be there, but that wound of his prevents him. I know it does not excuse his behaviour,' he added quickly, reading her look, 'but he does not have that — that easy address that makes some men universally popular.'

She laughed bitterly. 'No indeed. He is one of the rudest men I know!'

'But he is sincere, Miss Venn, and I know he has a very true and deep regard for you.'

She turned her candid eyes upon him. 'You are an excellent ambassador for your friend, my lord, but it will not work.'

'No, no, I assure you, Miss Venn — '

'Pray say no more, my lord. The damage is done and even if I could forgive Sir Laurence, I can never forget his words.' She forced a smile. 'Pray do not look so downcast, sir. You have acquitted yourself nobly on your friend's behalf. Now let us talk of something else. Have you had word from Brussels?'

'Friends write of balls and society gossip, no hint of war, the very reason that everyone is gathering there.'

'Do you think it will come to that?'

'It is inevitable. The trouble is that the Allies have put together such a rag-tag army. Oakford is confident that with the Duke in command we can pull the thing off and I trust his judgement as a soldier far more than all these armchair generals in town who are spreading tales of doom and destruction. I think that at least with Wellington in command, we have a chance.'

'Oh sir, I pray you are right,' she said quietly.

★ ★ ★

Antonia avoided Sir Laurence for the rest of the day by keeping to her room and the following day, Saturday, followed much the same pattern, but Antonia knew that she would have to explain herself soon to her hostess. The only course open to her was to return to Bath, but she needed an excuse. She thought Lady Burstock might easily be persuaded that Miss Chittering could no longer manage without her and since Beatrice was a regular correspondent, she hoped it would not be too long before the post brought her word from Bath, and she could inform Lady Burstock that she must leave. On Sunday morning she sought some relief in a brisk walk with her cousin. Mr Haseley had come to the house in search of Isabella, but when Antonia informed him that everyone else had gone to church, he readily agreed to her request to accompany her along the Esplanade, for in Isabella's absence he desperately needed someone to talk to. Mr Haseley had that morning received a letter from his papa, informing him that he was to return to Oxford immediately or his allowance would be stopped. Antonia did not think her uncle's demand unreasonable.

'Why do you not return to Oxford, Charles? I know you wish to join up, but having promised you will not do so, surely you would be better to be occupied than kicking your heels here.'

'Oh you do not understand. Why should I waste my time studying, what good will that do me when I am a soldier, that's what I would like to know?' He wondered if he should tell her of his love for Isabella and decided he might safely work towards it. 'Besides, there are dozens of fellows younger than I am who are married and running their own houses.'

To his chagrin, she laughed.

'Oh Charles, that is too absurd. You are far too young to be considering marriage.'

'Of course I am not. You think that you know so much more of the world, but who was it warned you against Sir Rigby Claremont? And I was right, was I not?'

She flushed. 'Yes, Charles, on that occasion you were right, but that can scarcely make you fit to be a husband.'

'I don't see that at all. If only my father would make me a decent allowance, I could handle my own affairs quite satisfactorily.'

'Oh Charlie, please — do not say anything more. We are merely going over the same ground.' Antonia's head was pounding. She felt too tired to argue further with her cousin. Observing his injured expression she summoned up a smile. 'My dear Charles, I know you think you are up to every rig and row but believe me you are still very young. Do as you are bid. Go back to Oxford to please your papa. Then, when you have finished your studies, he will buy your commission.'

'But that is not what I — '

'No, Charles!' She stopped him sharply. 'I do not want to hear any more of your petty arguments. What good would it do? *I* cannot help you. You must go away and resolve this for yourself. Now escort me back, if you please. I am sorry I cannot ask you to step inside but I really do have the headache and I think I must lie down.'

Mr Haseley took a cool leave of his cousin and strode away from Marine Parade feeling that the world was very much against him. He had seen Isabella only once since the Assembly, when she had been walking near the Pavilion with her brother. There had been no chance for discussion, but one glance at Sir Laurence's grim countenance had informed him that that gentleman was in no mood to be charitable to young lovers.

Perhaps Isabella was right, he thought angrily: eloping might be the answer. At least then he could be his own master and if it took some time for their families to accept them so much the better; he would be able to prove how well he could manage without any help. A natural caution whispered to him that supporting himself and a wife might not be that easy, but he quashed his doubts. In any event, he was determined to make one last push to see Sir Laurence. Antonia had told him to deal with his own problems and he resolved that he would call on that gentleman on Monday, and would wait at the house until he had seen him.

★   ★   ★

'Oh — I am sorry. I thought you were out . . . ' Antonia stopped in the doorway to the drawing-room, but before she could retreat Sir Laurence spoke.

'That is quite obvious, Miss Venn. You would not otherwise have entered this room. Now you are here, I'd be grateful if you would spare me a moment of your time.'

Realizing it was more of a command than a request, Antonia closed the door and walked into the room.

'Please, sit down.'

Without looking at him, she sat down on a small sofa.

'You have been avoiding me, Antonia.'

'Yes, sir.'

'You don't deny it?'

'No, I don't deny it. I am waiting for an opportunity to return to Bath without giving rise to unwelcome speculation.'

'Will you not allow me to apologize?' Sitting down beside her, he reached for her hands.

Antonia jumped up as if she had been stung.

'I can never forgive you! If I could hurt *you* as much — '

'But what you heard was not — they were not my words,' he ground out. He came up to her, roughly gripping her shoulders. 'I would not hurt you, Antonia, I would never hurt you.'

His grip tightened and his mouth came down upon hers in a savage kiss. Antonia froze, at first from shock, then deliberately, as she resisted the stirring of desire within her and the impulse to return his kiss. When at last he let her go, her eyes blazed at him.

'Yes — that is how you treat servants, is it not?' she said, her voice scathing. 'You are contemptible; I despise you. You think me a very mercenary creature, unworthy to kiss the feet of an Oakford. Well, I can set right one misapprehension, sir. You think I sold your diamond to set up my dancing school. How wrong you are. It is still sitting in my strong-box in Bath. I arrived at my aunt's house at the same time as a letter telling me my mother had left me a small inheritance, in trust upon my attaining four-and-twenty. It was *that* I used to set up my dancing school. And you may be assured that as soon as I return to Bath your precious jewel will be sent back to you. Nothing could persuade me to remain under any obligation to you. I tell you for the last time that I will *never* forgive you, Sir Laurence, and if I avoid your company it is not because I am heartbroken, but because I find everything about you repugnant!'

For a moment they stared at each other, hard black eyes locked with stormy grey.

'Thank you, ma'am, you have made yourself abundantly clear. I will ensure that you do not have to suffer my company for too much longer before we can convey you back to Bath.'

She remained where she was, silent, while he turned on his heel and walked out, but once the door had closed behind him, Antonia's face crumpled and she threw herself on to the sofa, sobbing.

11

The following morning Sir Laurence set off early for London and with a fresh team he made good time, arriving in the City just as his man of business was finishing his lunch. Mr Edgar came forward to meet his client, brushing the crumbs from his black frock-coat.

'Sir Laurence, my dear sir. Have you eaten? Can I send out for something?'

'Thank you, no, Edgar, I am not hungry. You've heard the reports from Brussels? Is there anything new?'

'Nothing yet, sir. Only rumours of a massive defeat for the Allies. Nothing confirmed, of course, but many of my colleagues are selling out of the Funds for their clients.'

'I thought the jobbers had closed their books.'

Edgar polished his eyeglass with a large red silk handkerchief, the only indulgence of colour he allowed himself and a striking contrast to his black attire.

'There are ways, sir, if one knows how.'

Sir Laurence walked to the window.

Outside the summer sun was directly above the grey street, shining on the carriages that streamed through the thoroughfare. Everything looked quite ordinary, yet across the Channel thousands of soldiers were fighting, and dying, to protect these very people who seemed oblivious of the struggle. His soldier's training refused to let him believe that Wellington could lose.

'And do you?'

'Beg pardon, Sir Laurence?'

'Do you know how?'

Mr Edgar allowed himself a small smile. 'I think I can help you to sell out of the Funds, sir.'

'If you know how to sell then you will also know how to buy.'

The agent began to polish his eyeglass again, this time more vigorously.

'Sir Laurence? I'm sorry, I thought you said — '

'I did. I want to *buy*, not sell.' Sir Laurence turned from the window. 'Raise what capital you can for me and buy. This war's not over yet and I for one believe that the Duke will bring it off.'

Mr Edgar expostulated, argued and pleaded with his client but Sir Laurence was adamant. It took him some time to persuade that worthy gentleman that he was in earnest, but finally he left the City confident that his agent would do his best for him.

★ ★ ★

Dinner was over by the time Sir Laurence returned to Brighton that evening. The ladies were drinking tea in the drawing-room, and he was surprised to find Mr Haseley sitting with them.

Lady Burstock rose immediately to greet him.

'Laurence my dear, at last! How late you are.'

'My apologies, Mama. I stopped off at Horse Guards and the club in the hope of learning the latest reports.'

'And is there any news?'

'Nothing official. There are reports of defeat, but nothing to substantiate that. Informed opinion is still that Wellington will hold the day.'

He passed a hand across his eyes and, observing him from her seat by the window, Antonia realized how tired he looked. She said quietly, 'Have you eaten sir? Lady Burstock, shall I fetch up a meal . . . ?'

'No, thank you, I stopped to dine on the road,' said Sir Laurence. He cast an enquiring

271

glance at Mr Haseley, who had risen upon Sir Laurence's entrance and now stood uncomfortably beside his chair.

'Mr Haseley has been taking tea with us,' said Isabella brightly. 'He waited especially to see you and to hear your news.'

'Indeed? Then I am sorry there is not more to hear.'

Mr Haseley realized his host was preoccupied and mumbled something about taking his leave but Isabella shook her head at him.

'You cannot leave yet, Mr Haseley. I promised to show you my sketches of Brighton,' she said, glaring at him.

His mind still occupied by events in London, Sir Laurence bowed to the assembled company.

'If you will excuse me for a while, I have some work I would like to finish this evening.'

Isabella watched him leave and rose to place her teacup on the tray.

'This is your opportunity,' she hissed at Charles as she passed him. 'He will be in the study. Go now.'

'He has only just returned from Town, Bella. Are you sure?'

'Of course. Since you are determined to speak you had best do it now. *Go on!* Mama, dearest, can I fetch you more tea?'

Antonia, sitting quietly with an open book

on her lap, frowned as she observed this interchange. She was too far away to hear what was said but she saw Charles shrug his shoulders, then slip out of the room. An awful suspicion began to grow within her.

★   ★   ★

Charles found the study by the simple expedient of trying every door until he came to the right one. He found Sir Laurence sitting at his desk staring into space. A sheet of blank paper lay before him, but his pen was dry and unused at the side. A single lamp burned on the desk, augmenting the failing daylight. Charles coughed.

'Excuse me, Sir Laurence, might — might I have a word with you?'

Sir Laurence looked at him, frowning. Charles came further into the room. He tried to smile, but his lips felt too dry to stretch properly.

'You must be wondering just why I should intrude upon you, sir, and normally I would not dream of bothering you so late in the day, but, well, sir, it is a matter of the utmost importance.'

'Then hurry up and tell me what it is.'

Charles swallowed hard. This was not how he had imagined the scene at all. He stepped forward until he was in front of the desk.

'It-it's Isabella,' he blurted out. 'Sir we-um — that is, I want to marry her.'

'Do you, by God!'

'I know you will say I am very young, and that is true. I have not yet finished at Oxford, but my prospects are good,' Charles rushed on. 'My father owns a sizeable estate in Wiltshire, so I am not penniless.'

Sir Laurence was extremely tired. He had driven over a hundred miles, given his agent instructions that he could not be sure would not ruin him and all he wanted to do now was to sleep. He looked up at the eager young man hovering in front of him and bit back the withering retort that rose to his lips.

'Mr Haseley, it is very late. I do not think this is the right time to discuss this.'

'But there never *is* a right time!' Charles declared, Isabella's image haunting him.

'Perhaps, but there is certainly a wrong time,' retorted Sir Laurence. He rose, adding quietly, 'You are too young to be thinking of marriage, Mr Haseley, especially to my sister. I suggest you come back when you have finished your studies.'

'But that is another whole year!'

'Are you afraid she will not wait? Then that gives you your answer. However, if your attachment is genuine it will last another twelve months. I suggest you come back then.' He walked to the door and opened it. 'Goodnight, Mr Haseley.'

Charles stared at him. The hard eyes were not unkind, but it was obvious he would not be moved by further argument that night. Mr Haseley bowed and walked out. Isabella was waiting for him in the hall. As he approached she fell on him, demanding to know what had been said.

'He told me to come back in a year's time,' said Charles bitterly.

'What? He refused to let us marry?'

'No, not exactly. He said it is too soon.'

'So you have accepted that, and you are going to go away without arguing with him?'

'I don't think there is anything I *could* say to improve matters this evening,' he replied gloomily.

Isabella grabbed his hand.

'Then let us go in and face him together. He must see that I will not wait another year to marry — I want to be your wife now!'

'No, Isabella. You will only make things worse if you tackle him now. I can tell when a chap's all in and your brother has had a hard day. If you press him now he may forbid the banns altogether, then there would be nothing for it but to elope.'

She clung to him.

'Then let us do that! Oh Charles, I cannot live without you for another year. I could pawn my jewels, and once we are married I *know* Laurence will relent.'

'Oh do you? Well, I am not so sure. No, Isabella. I'll come back tomorrow to talk to him. After all, he did not have any objections to my suit, except my age.' He began to look more hopeful. 'In fact, I shouldn't be surprised if, after a good night's sleep, your brother agreed to a betrothal, at least.' He pinched her chin. 'Now you mustn't fret, my love. Everything will work out, you see if it doesn't.'

She looked up at him, tears sparkling like diamonds on the ends of her lashes.

'Oh Charles, what if he says no? What if he says I am never to see you again?'

'Then we will fly to the border, and hang the consequences!' he declared.

When Mr Haseley had gone Isabella went back into the drawing-room. Lady Burstock had finished her tea and was dozing fitfully on a sofa. Antonia smiled and patted a chair beside her.

'Come and sit over here, Bella, and tell me what you and Charles are about.'

Isabella flushed and tossed her head.

'Why nothing. I vow you are growing as suspicious as Laurence.' She felt Antonia's gaze upon her and relented, desperate to confide in someone. 'Oh very well — you have guessed it anyway, have you not? Charles and I are in love.'

'Oh heavens!'

Isabella pouted. 'You need not look so shocked. It is quite serious, you know. We have known each other for several weeks now.'

Antonia felt no desire to laugh.

'You met in Bath?'

Isabella nodded, her eyes shining. 'Is it not romantic? Charles would not have you blamed for our meeting, so we kept it a secret, only he met Mama, and because she is a great friend of *his* mama she invited him to dine with us. We also met at the Assemblies of course, where Mama allowed me to stand up with Charles, so I *know* she approves of him.'

'But not as a suitor, Isabella.'

Miss Burstock knelt before her, taking her hands between her own and shaking them, willing her to understand.

'But he is not like the other men I thought I loved,' she said ecstatically. 'Laurence cannot say that Charles is too old, or ineligible — '

'He could most certainly say that he is ineligible,' replied Antonia. 'Oh Isabella, can you not see the disparity between your fortunes?'

'Oh I do not care for that. I love him, Antonia, and he loves me.'

'Then I wish you happiness, my child.'

They looked up as Laurence came into the room and before Antonia could stop her, Isabella jumped up to greet him.

'Charles is coming back to see you tomorrow, Laurence. Please say you will be kind to him.'

'He would do better to stay away,' growled her brother. He shot a glance at Antonia. 'Did you put him up to this?'

'Pray do not be cross with Antonia. If Charles and I want to be married it is entirely our own affair.'

'Not until you are twenty-one, my girl.'

Isabella stared at him. 'You would not be so cruel.'

Sir Laurence threw himself down into a chair.

'No,' he said wearily, 'I have merely advised your lover to come back and see me in a year or so. Then I might consider his suit.'

'That is ridiculous.'

'No, *you* are ridiculous,' he snapped, his temper rising. 'Consider, Isabella. A young man I have met but once tells me he wants to marry you. It is obvious that you have been carrying on a clandestine affair with him in Bath. Does he expect me to fall on his neck and welcome him as the ideal suitor for my sister? And his fortune, so far beneath your own. Not that *that* would weigh with me, if I discovered you truly loved each other.'

'But we do!'

'Then prove it. I have already told him that if your attachment lasts I won't stand in your way.'

'Twelve whole months. Oh I hate you!'

It was not to be expected that Lady Burstock would sleep through this altercation. She woke up demanding to know what was happening and Isabella lost no time in pouring her woes into her mama's sympathetic ear.

Feeling very much in the way, Antonia excused herself and retired to her room, but not before she had heard Sir Laurence vowing to pack Isabella off to Oakford for the remainder of the summer. Miss Burstock's reply could only be guessed at, but she was in little doubt that such a spirited young lady would not accept this ruling without an argument and Antonia had no wish to be drawn further into the family's troubles. She undressed wearily and lay upon her bed, yet sleep eluded her. It was a warm night and the sound of the sea that had soothed her on other nights now seemed merely an irritation. Her unhappiness had settled into a dull but constant ache. She realized how foolish she had been to think that Sir Laurence could ever see her as anything more than a servant to be bought and commanded at will. She must return to Bath, but how to explain her decision to Lady Burstock and Isabella? Not for the world could she tell them the real reason: she could not expect that lady to believe her son would act in such an ungentlemanly fashion and even if she *could* make her believe it, she would not. Despite her words to Sir Laurence she had no wish to inflict pain on him or any member of his family. Her only hope was to receive a letter from Miss Chittering, then she could tell Lady Burstock that business required her immediate return. Tossing and turning, she dozed fitfully and was not sorry when the short summer night gave way to a grey dawn. An hour or so later she gave up trying to sleep and slipped quietly out of bed. The house was silent: she glanced at the bracket clock beside her bed. Five o'clock. The servants would soon be stirring. Antonia decided against summoning a sleepy-eyed maid to help her dress. She hunted amongst her gowns for the pale lemon sheath dress, which she slipped over her head and fastened easily with a narrow sash. The fresh cotton felt cool against her skin and she sat at her dressing-table, brushing out her hair.

She was just pinning up the final curls when she heard the front door opening. Her bedroom was directly above the door and she had grown used to the scrape of the heavy bolt being drawn back, but not usually so early in the morning. Antonia went to the window and glanced out. She could not see the top step without opening the window and leaning out, but there on the pavement were two bandboxes and, as she watched, a cloaked figure came down the steps to pick them up. There was no mistaking the capote bonnet with its emerald green ribbons, Antonia had been with Isabella when she had chosen them. Antonia snatched up her own straw bonnet and a shawl and ran out of the room. Only for a second did she consider raising the alarm. By the time she had roused Lady Burstock there was no telling where the child might be. She ran lightly down the stairs and quietly let herself out of the house. The cloaked figure was still in sight, hurrying along Marine Parade but hampered by the band-boxes. Antonia ran after her and was only fifty yards or so behind Isabella when she disappeared into a side street. Antonia pushed on, reaching the corner to see a travelling carriage waiting at the far end of the street. As Isabella hurried up, a young man jumped out of the carriage and Antonia had no difficulty in recognizing her cousin. He was looking anxious and in no way prepared for Miss Burstock's greeting: the young lady dropped the band-boxes and threw herself into his arms. Thus engaged, neither of the young lovers noticed Antonia running up to them.

'Charles, stop!'

At the sound of her voice the runaways jumped apart and looked round. The next second Mr Haseley was bundling Isabella into the coach.

'My luggage, Charles, quickly!' she cried, pointing to the abandoned boxes lying on the pavement.

Charles turned back for them and by the time he had handed the boxes to Isabella, Antonia had reached him. She grabbed his arm urgently.

'Charles, this is a terrible mistake. You must send Isabella home.'

'I can't do that, Cos. Everything is arranged.'

'You must see this is wrong,' she declared. 'Isabella, please step down and come back with me.'

Miss Burstock's anguished face appeared at the window.

'Oh Antonia, I can't. We would never be allowed to see each other again.'

'That is nonsense, child. Charles, you know this is wrong, she must come back with me.'

Mr Haseley hesitated. He was increasingly aware of the post-boys watching the scene with interest. He was beginning to regret having started this escapade but Isabella was here with him, and he desperately wanted her to stay. He disengaged himself from Antonia's grip and set his foot upon the step.

'I'm sorry, Cos, but it is too late. We are determined. You had best go back. Drive on.'

With a word to the post-boys he disappeared inside the coach, trying to pull the door behind him, but Antonia held it open.

'Charles, you must not do this!'

'Stand back, Antonia. Drive on, I say!'

The coach moved off, but instead of letting go, Antonia hung on to the door and as the carriage lurched forward she made a desperate jump and scrambled up into the coach.

'Charles! Are you mad?' cried Isabella, watching with horror from one corner as Mr Haseley helped his cousin on to the seat then reached out to pull up the steps and close the door.

'What could I do?' he demanded irritably.

'I could scarcely push her out of a moving carriage.'

'No, no, of course not, but we cannot take Antonia with us. We are *eloping*!'

'Do you mean to tell me you are really planning to go to Scotland?' demanded Antonia.

'But of course,' asserted Isabella.

Mr Haseley looked at his cousin, begging her to understand.

'Isabella is under age, Cos. We have no choice.'

'Charles, you do not know Sir Laurence's temper — there is every likelihood that he will kill you when he catches you.'

'Yes, well, I know he is likely to be very angry. However, I hope we will be many miles away by the time Isabella is missed.'

Antonia drew a breath. She turned to Isabella.

'You must know the distress this will cause your mama when she discovers you are gone! Consider, Bella, let Charles take you home now. We will smuggle you back inside and no one need be any the wiser.'

'I am sorry to cause Mama pain, naturally, but it will not be so bad, truly. She will understand why I had to do this. I have explained it all in my note.'

Mr Haseley stared at his beloved. 'You left a note?'

She returned his look defiantly. 'But of course! You do not think I would go without a word, leaving everyone to worry?'

Listening to this interchange Antonia felt that she was caught up in some farce, yet she was well aware that the consequences for these young people would be deadly serious. In vain she coaxed, cajoled and argued with them. At length she sank back against the worn and faded squabs of the coach.

'At least tell me when you planned this escapade?'

'I have been working on it all night!' retorted her cousin, a note of resentment creeping into his voice, 'I had a message from Bella at around midnight to say we must run away if we were not to be parted for ever. I was to have a carriage waiting in Grafton Street at six o'clock, or I would never see her again. What else could I do? I spent the night touring the coaching inns trying to find a carriage and a pretty penny it has cost me, I can tell you, because the lads on the box know there's something havey-cavey going on.'

Isabella smiled at him and patted his arm.

'I think you have managed things excellently, Charles. And tomorrow, when we are in London you may sell my jewellery, then we shall have plenty of money.'

Antonia put her head in her hands. They could not see how futile this would be. Sir Laurence would find them, she did not doubt that for a moment, the only question was how soon? She renewed her arguments but it was no use: Charles, suffering from a lack of sleep, was sullen and Isabella defiant. Even the thought of Laurence's anger did not move her.

'He has been angry with me before and it has passed. Besides, once we are married he will not want to cause a scandal, so he is bound to come round.'

Mr Haseley, who had been sulking in one corner of the coach, suddenly sat upright, his brow clearing.

'Do you know, my love, I have been thinking it over and I think that having Antonia with us will be no bad thing after all.' Observing the ladies' blank stares, he continued blithely, 'You see there can be nothing improper if Antonia accompanies us. She can act as your chaperon, Bella.'

'But I do not want a chaperon.'

'Very likely not, my love, but I cannot help thinking that your brother will be thankful for it and it will show him that we have observed the proprieties.'

'If you believe that, Charles, you are a bigger fool than I thought,' declared Miss Venn roundly. 'I have no intention of travelling to the border with you.'

'Yes, well, I don't see what else you *can* do, Cos! I cannot abandon you on the road, and we don't have enough funds to send you back to Brighton.'

Antonia bit back an angry retort. She tried to consider the situation calmly. She had no doubt that Sir Laurence would catch up with them, although she had no way of knowing how long that would be. Until then she could best serve him by remaining with these foolish children and delaying them as much as possible. She was surprised at the leisurely pace of their journey. Indeed, her cousin even remarked that they would raise far less comment if they did not push the horses. What Charles had not told her was that there was also the matter of finance to be considered. He had calculated that two horses were all he could afford if he was not to run out of money long before they reached Scotland.

12

It was not long before the heat of the fine summer's morning began to take its toll of Isabella. Antonia recognized the warning signs and as they were approaching Redhill she obliged her cousin to halt the coach at the next toll-gate, where she helped Isabella to alight from the coach and walked her slowly up and down the road in the shade of a large overhanging oak, until that young lady began to feel better. Mr Haseley waited by the carriage, curbing his impatience and striving to be civil to the aged gatekeeper, a sociable individual who welcomed this opportunity for a little company.

'Headin' for Lunnon, I shouldn't wonder,' remarked the attendant, running an experienced eye over the coach.

'What? Oh, yes — no. That is, we are visiting friends at — at Westerham. We shall be taking the Sevenoaks road from Redhill, of course. Do hurry, Cos. We shall take forever if we have to keep stopping like this.'

'I do feel a little better now, Antonia. Perhaps we should go back to the coach.'

Antonia put her hand on Isabella's brow,

delaying their journey as long as she dared.

'You are still a little feverish, child. A few more moments here in the shade will help.'

'She looks much better. Come along now — let us be moving — we cannot afford more delay.'

'Poor traveller is she, sir?' asked the ancient, leaning on the gate. 'The missus was just the same, God rest her soul. Couldn't bear to travel, 'cept it was by shank's nag, that's why we fetched up 'ere. 'Jem', she says to me, 'Jem me lad, I enjoys watching they coaches go by, but I ain't never gettin' in one again, not even when I cocks up me toes'. And so it was, sir, for when my poor missus finally quit this earth we carried 'er the three miles to Horley church on our shoulders — '

'Yes, very good of you, I'm sure,' Charles intervened hastily. 'Come along now, Bella, up into the coach. And you, Cos — ' He turned back to see Antonia discussing cures for travel sickness with the gatekeeper. Biting back his impatience he took her arm and led her to the waiting carriage. 'We really do not have time for all this, Antonia. And paying such attention to the old man makes it all the more likely that he will remember you.'

This was exactly what Antonia had in mind, but she meekly begged pardon and allowed him to help her into the coach.

'What a devil of a place to stop,' he muttered, when at last they were under way again. 'I really do not know what you were thinking of, Antonia, to be encouraging that curious old fellow. Heaven knows what you might have told him if I hadn't stopped you. Luckily I had the presence of mind to tell him we would be turning off at Redhill and heading east.'

'But why should you tell him that, when we are going to London?' asked Miss Burstock innocently.

'Because if we *are* being pursued we want to put them off the scent.' Mr Haseley settled back against the squabs and closed his eyes. 'Lord, I did not know this sort of thing could be so wearing.'

Miss Burstock continued to look pale, but she bore the continuing journey with fortitude and only begged him twice more to stop the coach. Towards noon they were approaching Purley and Antonia suggested they should find an inn where they could take luncheon. Miss Burstock shuddered.

'Oh no, I could not eat a thing.'

'Possibly not, Isabella, but I have not yet broken my fast and I have no doubt that Charles is quite famished.'

'Well, as a matter of fact I *am* hungry, but I had hoped that we might make London before we stop again.'

Antonia sighed. 'Very well, Charles, if that is what you wish, but I am feeling quite *faint* with hunger. I am not sure how much longer *I* can go on . . . '

He eyed her uneasily.

'Well, perhaps we could make a brief stop.' He leaned from the coach and carried on a brief conversation with the post-boys, after which he informed his companions that they would be stopping at the Lion, where they were assured of a very tolerable meal.

★   ★   ★

Purley was soon reached and the weary travellers found themselves driving under an ancient arch and into a cobbled yard. Mr Haseley jumped down to request a private parlour and luncheon from the landlord who had come out to meet them. One of the post-boys demanded that they too should receive some refreshment. Mr Haseley took exception to this, and a brief altercation followed until Isabella, climbing down from the coach, said crossly, 'Oh give them some money, Charles! Let us not be out here quarrelling.'

Mr Haseley looked as if he would dispute this, but Miss Burstock was already walking towards the door of the inn. Antonia, following her, enquired of the landlord how far they were from London.

'Well now, miss,' said that worthy, scratching his head, 'we must be a dozen miles or so from the capital. If that is your destination I would think you will be there in a couple of hours.'

'You must see a great deal of London-bound traffic,' she remarked.

'Aye, that we do, ma'am, this being one of the main roads to the city. I pride myself that my humble hostelry is as good as any you will find on this road.'

'It is a very fine inn,' said Antonia, looking round. 'No doubt it has been in existence for many years?'

'Why, yes, ma'am. I've been here for nigh on twenty years now, and my father before me. We do believe there's been an inn on this site since the Conquest, and that's a fact.'

'Antonia, pray let us go inside and order our meal. We do not want to waste the whole day.' Mr Haseley interrupted what promised to be a lengthy history to escort his cousin indoors.

The landlord went before and showed them into a private parlour. They were followed by a cheerful-looking woman in a snowy white apron, who promised to have luncheon on the table for them in a trice. Miss Burstock groaned at the mention of food and Antonia helped her to the settle in one corner of the room. Sitting her down, she tenderly removed Miss Burstock's bonnet and chafed her hands.

'There, Isabella. You will feel better directly if you sit quietly. Would you like some coffee, perhaps, or shall I fetch you a glass of water?'

Isabella groaned. 'I can swallow nothing. I feel so wretched!'

Mr Haseley hovered anxiously about her, not knowing how best to help his beloved.

'I think Antonia's right, my love. You must sit there quietly until you are feeling more the thing.'

At that moment the landlady returned carrying a tray laden with dishes, which she proceeded to set out on the table. Miss Burstock watched her, a look of revulsion on her face.

'Surely you do not intend to eat?' she demanded in failing accents.

'But of course,' declared Mr Haseley, holding a chair for Antonia before pulling up a seat for himself. 'You know I've had nothing to eat since dinner last night, and I am in a fair way to starving. I'll tell you what, Bella, I don't doubt you too might feel more the thing if you was to take a little food.'

Miss Burstock's answering groan aroused the landlady's sympathy.

'Oh, is the young lady feeling poorly? Perhaps miss would be better lying down. There's a spare room above stairs that you could have, sir, and welcome, if you think it would help.'

'Yes, I really do think I should feel better if I could lie down for a little while, Charles.'

Miss Venn was immediately out of her seat and helping Isabella to the stairs. She returned to the parlour a few moments later to report that Miss Burstock was resting. Mr Haseley, about to cut into a large steak pie, laid down his knife.

'You know, Cos, we're going to have the devil of a time getting to Scotland if Bella doesn't pick up.'

'My dear Charles, there is no possibility of you reaching Scotland,' replied his cousin wearily. 'Isabella's family will have raised the alarm by now and I should not be at all surprised if you are overtaken before nightfall.'

He shook his head at her.

'Don't see that at all,' he responded between mouthfuls of pie. 'Once we are in London there's every chance to lose ourselves. We will avoid the main coaching inns, find a snug little place to spend the night and be away again before anyone is the wiser.'

'Oh Charles, don't be such a fool. Turn back now; there's still time. Sir Laurence may be angry, but — '

'No, it's too late, don't you see? We are committed. And Bella would not turn back even if *I* wished to, which I don't, of course.' His young face clouded. 'You see, I love her to distraction, Cos. I will do anything to keep her with me.'

His eyes pleaded with her to understand and with a sigh Antonia sat down at the table. It was useless to argue. Instead she turned her attention to the food spread out on the table and helped herself to a few slices of ham. She found that she was very hungry, and enjoyed her meal far more than she had anticipated. The landlady brought in a pot of coffee and by the time their host returned to clear the table Mr Haseley at least was feeling much more optimistic. The entry of Miss Burstock, looking refreshed from her rest, added to his good humour and although she declared she was not at all hungry, she agreed to Miss Venn's request to take a cup of coffee and some bread and butter. Realizing that they had lost a couple of hours, Mr Haseley pulled out his pocket watch and frowned at it. The day was slipping away from them and he could scarcely contain his impatience while

Isabella finished her scant meal. She was still swallowing the last of her coffee when he sent the landlord away with orders to have the coach at the door without delay. Antonia touched his arm.

'If you would spare me just a few moments, Charles? I left in such a hurry this morning, I would like to go upstairs to wash my face before we set off again.'

'What? Oh very well, but be quick about it.'

Antonia went upstairs to the chamber so recently vacated by Isabella. The landlady had thoughtfully provided a jug of warm water and she used it to wash her face and hands. Glancing in the small mirror that hung on the wall, she was shocked at her appearance. The curls she had pinned up so roughly that morning had been sadly flattened by her bonnet. She pulled out the pins and set about tidying her hair, thinking it was another chance to delay the runaways. The sound of a carriage clattering into the courtyard took her running to the window: with a sigh of relief she recognized the matched bays harnessed to the curricle even before she had sight of the driver.

'Oh thank goodness.'

Looking down from the upstairs window, Antonia watched as Sir Laurence tossed the reins to his groom and jumped down from the carriage. He paused briefly to speak to the innkeeper, then disappeared into the building. His face was hidden from her by his curly brimmed beaver, but she could imagine his anger and was immediately anxious for her cousin's safety. Hurriedly pinning up the last of her curls, Antonia ran downstairs to the private parlour.

She entered a few moments after Sir Laurence, and took in the whole scene in an instant: Charles was in the far corner of the room, holding Isabella, who was sobbing quietly, while Sir Laurence stood just inside the room with his back to her. Hearing the door open he looked round, his impatient glance turning to amazement when he saw Antonia.

'What the devil are you going here?'

'I came with them. I — '

'*You what?*' His eyes, angry before, positively blazed with fury yet his voice, when he spoke again, was icy calm. 'So, you have found your way to be revenged upon me.' He drew off his gloves, keeping his eyes fixed on her face. 'No doubt you thought this the ideal opportunity. Marry your cousin to an heiress and serve me an ill turn into the bargain. Did you really think you would get all the way to the border, or was it your plan merely to ruin my sister?'

'Sir, you misunderstand. I have been with Isabella the whole time — '

'How could I have been so mistaken in you?' he ground out. 'You ingratiated yourself with my mother, won Isabella's trust — my congratulations, Miss Venn, you are a fortune-hunter par excellence, and you almost carried it off.'

Antonia stared at him. At first she flushed to the roots of her hair as she grasped the meaning of his words, then she grew pale with rage. Her eyes glittered angrily.

'Well, sir, what an excellent way to repay you for your arrogance. La, what fun we have had!'

His face darkened as he struggled with his temper. She thought for a moment he would strike her and she put up her chin, challenging him. Instead he swung round to face Mr Haseley, who was still comforting Isabella.

'Take your hands off my sister!'

Mr Haseley gently disengaged himself from Isabella's grasp. He said stiffly, 'Sir, if you wish to name your friends — '

'Don't be a fool, boy! You know I can't call out a pup like you. Get out of here, before I throw you out.'

'I cannot go without an explana — '

With one swift movement Sir Laurence

caught him by the throat and pinned him to the wall. In vain Mr Haseley's fingers clawed at the strong grip.

'Be damned to your explanations, you insolent whelp! I ought to thrash you to within an inch of your life.'

'Laurence, no, I pray you, let him go, *let him go!*' screamed Isabella.

Her brother paid her no heed. Antonia, her arms around Isabella, said scornfully, 'Shame on you, sir. He is only a boy, let him go.'

For a tense moment Sir Laurence continued to hold the young man, his face dark with rage, then he thrust him away.

'Get out. Take your hired coach and get out of here.'

Charles coughed and rubbed his tender throat. His brain seethed with a mixture of hurt, rage and remorse. He drew himself up and forced himself to look directly at Sir Laurence, his own blue eyes meeting the cold hard gaze.

'Sir, I shall call on you in due course.'

'Be damned to you — get out!'

Antonia added her own persuasion. 'Charles, there is nothing for you to do here, you had best go.'

Charles hesitated, then bowed with as much dignity as he could muster and, with a final glance at Isabella, he left the room.

'Come, Isabella, I am taking you home.'

'No. I will not go with you.'

'Don't give me any of your histrionics, girl.'

'Antonia, you must go with me.'

'I beg your pardon, Isabella, but *nothing* would induce me to travel with your brother,' said Antonia, her voice vibrant with anger.

'Then I will not go,' cried Miss Burstock, a note of hysteria in her voice.

Her brother looked at her. When at last he spoke, his voice was dangerously quiet.

'Isabella, I am tired. Please do not make this more difficult. I promise you I shall have no hesitation in boxing your ears if I have to.'

Isabella flounced down on to the settle, looking mutinous.

'Oh, you are abominable!' She turned a tearful face towards Miss Venn. 'Please Antonia, do not abandon me now.'

Glancing out of the window, Antonia caught a glimpse of her cousin disappearing in the hired coach. The fury that had overtaken her a few moments earlier had subsided and common sense began to reassert itself. She said stiffly, 'Having no other means of travelling, and no money with me, it seems I have little choice but to return with you.'

'You are still in my mother's employ,' retorted Sir Laurence icily, 'so you can make yourself useful by attending my sister on the journey. After that you may consider your contract terminated.'

'Assuredly, sir, nothing would suit me more!'

They did not speak again. Ignoring the interested stares of the landlord and his wife, Antonia helped the sobbing Isabella into the curricle, where she sat crushed between the two rigidly correct figures. If she felt ill on the journey back to Brighton Miss Burstock did not mention it. The curricle lurched and swayed as Sir Laurence kept his team moving swiftly towards the coast and his groom, with uncharacteristic tact, forbore to criticize his excessive speed and merely stared woodenly at the road.

★   ★   ★

The travellers reached Brighton in the early evening. Lady Burstock was looking out for them and was waiting in the hall as Sir Laurence escorted his charge into the house. With a cry Isabella tumbled into her mama's open arms. Antonia, left to climb down from the curricle unaided, followed them into the drawing-room. Lady Burstock led Isabella to a small sofa where they sat down together, my lady's arms remaining firmly wrapped around her daughter. She looked pale and drawn, but there was a faint smile in her eyes as she removed Isabella's bonnet and smoothed the black curls that tumbled about her shoulders. Antonia walked to the window, where she stood silently watching the family. She was aware that Sir Laurence's dragging step was more pronounced and his face was grey, the lines of strain deeply etched around his eyes. Lady Burstock was looking searchingly at him.

'Was it a hard journey, my dear?'

'Not as bad as I expected. I thought they would be much further ahead. I caught up with them at Purley.' He rubbed his tired eyes. 'They had some hare-brained scheme of getting to Scotland, pawning Bella's jewels on the way. Heaven knows how far they expected to get.'

'Oh Mama, I am so sorry, I am so sorry! I never meant to make you unhappy — I just wanted to be with Charles but it has all gone so wrong. I have been *such* a wretch.'

'You deserve to be flogged for the trouble you have caused,' declared her brother brutally.

'Hush, Laurence.' Lady Burstock frowned at him and continued to soothe her daughter. 'It is all right, darling. You have been very foolish, but it is over now.'

'It has been such a *wretched* day — everything went wrong, even at the start.'

'You should be thankful you have escaped so lightly,' growled Sir Laurence, dropping wearily into a chair. 'Young Haseley is nothing more than a damned fortune-hunter.'

'He is not!' cried Isabella, in defence of her beloved. She turned her tear-stained face towards Lady Burstock. 'Mama, please believe me. He wanted to speak to you so many times, even in Bath but . . . but it was I who said you would not listen. And I was right, for look what happened when he *did* come to see Laurence. You laughed at him.' She stared accusingly at her brother.

'And what else should I do when a penniless whelp comes begging for your hand? Little did I know then that he had a conspirator within this very house. Yes, Mama, Miss Venn has connived at their attachment, and even sought to aid them.'

Isabella, gulping back a sob, fixed her bewildered eyes upon him.

'Aye, you may stare, miss. Her quiet manner was all an act to marry you off to her worthless cousin,' he said bitterly. 'I've no doubt she carried his letters to you, told you how much he loved you; then, the final irony, she came along to protect your virtue on the long drive north. A cunning scheme, but the vixen reckoned without me.'

Antonia paled. At the back of her mind she knew Sir Laurence was tired, possibly even in pain from his injured leg, but his scathing attack cut her deeply. She turned to Lady Burstock.

'It was not like that at all, ma'am,' she said quietly. 'I knew nothing of their attachment until last night. And then this morning, when I chanced to see Isabella leaving the house, I — I followed her.'

'But you cannot deny that they met in Bath,' snapped Sir Laurence.

She locked her hands together to stop them shaking. 'No, I do not deny that.'

Isabella stared at her brother. 'You cannot think that Antonia *approved* of our elopement, Laurence? She was most strongly against it. She kept telling us how wrong it was, and that Charles should turn about immediately and take me home.'

'If Miss Venn was so keen to prevent this elopement, why did she not come to me?' demanded Sir Laurence.

Isabella bit her lip. 'She would have done so, I am sure, if we had not kidnapped her. It was Charles who thought it would be a good idea if she came with us, you see, to act as a chaperon.'

'Oh my God!'

'I do not understand, Bella,' Lady Burstock looked bemused. 'Pray, explain yourself.' Miss Burstock wiped her eyes with her handkerchief.

'Antonia wanted us to turn back, but we would not, *I* would not,' she added truthfully. 'Charles and I thought that once we were far enough from Brighton she would relent and agree to act as my chaperon. She had no money or luggage, you see, because she left the house this morning with no plans for a journey, so . . . so she had no choice but to stay with us. Oh Mama, she was so very angry, saying how much pain I would be causing you and that Laurence would not rest until he had found us — '

'She was right there!' interjected Sir Laurence.

Isabella buried her face in her mother's skirts.

'Oh Mama, it was never my wish to hurt you, but I love Charles so very much, and I knew you and Laurence would never let us marry and . . . and Charles is army mad, just as Laurence was, and I could not bear for him to go away and be killed!'

Lady Burstock smiled. 'I think you are exaggerating, Bella.'

'But I am not!' declared Miss Burstock vehemently. 'Don't you see? If Charles and I do *not* marry he will join the army to fight in this horrid war and he will be wounded or . . . or killed and our lives will be blighted for ever, just like Laurence's!'

Her brother's black brows snapped together. 'What the devil does that mean?'

Isabella wiped her eyes. 'If you had been allowed to marry P-Pamela Bressingham you would not have gone back to the P-Peninsula and suffered that dreadful injury . . . '

'My dear child, I was far too young to know what I was about.'

'That is what everyone has told you,' she cried, 'but you loved her, did you not? You carried her locket with you for years!'

'Who told you that?'

'H-Harry Bressingham. He told us there had been a secret engagement and . . . and if you had been allowed to marry then you would not have gone back to P-Portugal or been wounded — and, of course, Pamela would never have married Viscount Moran and left you heartbroken.'

'You think I have been nursing a broken heart all these years?' He gave a wry smile. 'I promise you I have not.'

'But you were still in love with her last spring, when you went to Bressingham Hall.'

'It would appear Harry has been very busy

with my affairs,' he remarked drily.

'You must not blame him, Laurence, I made him tell — in fact he said it was best we heard the story from him, rather than some garbled version.'

'We?'

'Antonia was there, but I knew she would not tell a soul.'

Lady Burstock watched her son anxiously, her heart aching at the sight of his tired face. Meeting her eyes, he read the question in them and shook his head.

'Be assured, Mama, I have no interest in Lady Pamela. I think it had died even before I learned of her engagement. My actions on that occasion sprang more from wounded pride than a broken heart.'

'I thought as much, my son. In fact I have thought for some time that your interest lay in quite another direction.'

Sir Laurence shrugged and turned away, but the look in his eyes told Lady Burstock all she needed to know. She smiled at Antonia. 'I think we owe Miss Venn our gratitude for her efforts.'

'I did what I could to avoid a scandal, ma'am, but you can have no further use for me here. There is a coach to London in the morning.' She turned to Sir Laurence. 'Perhaps, sir, you will furnish me with a reckoning of how much I owe you, for my accommodation, and transport — '

'Don't be so damned silly!'

Her eyes flashed. She drew herself up to her full height.

'I was always reluctant to take this position, and after what has occurred there is nothing that would induce me to remain in your debt!' She walked towards the door.

'Antonia — wait.'

She turned. 'I never gave you leave to use my name!' she told him witheringly. Her gaze shifted to Lady Burstock and she continued in a milder tone, 'I will be leaving early tomorrow, so I take my leave of you now, ma'am. Thank you for your kindness to me and pray believe that I would never willingly hurt you or any member of your family. You at least have never treated me like a servant.'

'I know that, my child. But will you not reconsider?'

'No, my lady, it is impossible. Goodbye, ma'am, Isabella, goodbye.'

13

An air of depression hung over Lady Burstock's establishment like a tangible cloud. It was not to be expected that the servants would remain in ignorance of the previous day's excitement even though they were not in possession of all the facts. It was accepted that Sir Laurence's tiger knew the full story, but he was so damnably close-lipped that there was nothing to be gained in that direction. However, Miss Burstock's maid was a little more forthcoming and it was soon generally known below stairs that Isabella had tried to run away, only to be brought back by Sir Laurence and Miss Venn. That lady's departure at the crack of dawn had given rise to further speculation, but since she had been held in esteem by the servants who had come in contact with her, the most popular view was that she had decided she could no longer stay in such a disreputable household, packed her bags and left.

Lady Burstock coaxed Isabella from her bedchamber, but she could not settle to anything and wandered listlessly about the morning-room under the watchful eye of her mother, who was quietly employed with her embroidery. When Sir Laurence entered with the London newspapers, Isabella ignored his greeting and flounced to the sofa, where she sat down and began to flick idly through the pages of the *Ladies Magazine*. Sir Laurence regarded her for a moment, but made no comment. Lady Burstock put aside her embroidery frame.

'Is there news, Laurence?'

He handed her one of the papers.

'Reports of a retreat towards Brussels. And talk of evacuating the town, but it is conjecture, several days old, too. I must go to London if I am to learn more.'

'Must you go? You look tired, my son. Can your journey not wait another day?'

He stood before the empty fireplace, staring unseeingly into the cold hearth.

'No, Mama. I have lost a day already. I had a report yesterday that we were beaten at — where was it? — Quatre Bras. Had I not been otherwise engaged . . . ' He glanced at Isabella, who flushed guiltily. 'If I had gone to Town yesterday I might have salvaged something. I was so sure of Wellington that I instructed Edgar to buy into the Funds that everyone else seemed so eager to sell. However, if Bonaparte *has* been victorious'

— his hand, resting on the mantel shelf, clenched itself into a fist — 'if we have lost, I must rescue what I can.' He smiled at my lady's worried face. 'Pray do not look so concerned, Mama. I have not lost everything. It is merely a setback and my plans to improve Oakford must wait a little longer.' Any reply was forestalled by the entrance of a footman bearing a visiting card, which he presented to Sir Laurence. He picked it up, frowning at the inscription. 'Oh damnation — what the devil does he want now?'

Lady Burstock looked up. 'What is it, my dear?'

'Haseley!'

'Charles!' Isabella was on her feet in an instant, eyes shining.

'Sit down, Isabella, he is come to see me, not you.' The sparkle left her eyes and noting her dampened spirits he continued in a milder tone, 'Patience, child. Your heart will mend in time. Now, I had best see what the damned young fool wants . . . '

⋆ ⋆ ⋆

To Mr Haseley, left to kick his heels in the drawing-room, the waiting seemed interminable. He tugged at his cravat, which felt

uncomfortably tight. The ignominious con-
clusion of his flight with Isabella had left him
burning with anger and remorse. Sir Laurence's refusal to call him out cut deeply into
his youthful pride. A sleepless night had given
him the opportunity to review his conduct of
the past few months. An honest young man,
Mr Haseley had to admit that he had been at
fault in his dealings with Isabella. He had
allowed himself to forget propriety and to
conduct an illicit romance with Miss
Burstock. It was wrong of them, but as a
gentleman and one so much older than his
dear Isabella, he should not have allowed the
situation to continue. He could have spoken
to Lady Burstock at any time, and with
hindsight he knew now that that course of
action would have been far more honourable
than the secretive way he had behaved. As a
man of honour he knew he must make his
apology to Sir Laurence.

Besides, there were the bandboxes. He had
been in such a temper when he left Purley
that he had travelled some miles before he
realized that Isabella's luggage was still on the
floor of the coach. They must be returned, of
course, and he had decided against sending
them with a servant, preferring to use the
opportunity to speak to Sir Laurence.
Unfortunately, the task that had seemed so

straightforward in the privacy of his rooms now appeared fraught with difficulty. He thought Sir Laurence might refuse to see him and order him out of the house. This worry at least was soon dispelled, when Sir Laurence entered the drawing-room. His demeanour was not welcoming, the black brows drawn together and his mouth looking decidedly grim. When he spoke, his greeting was less than cordial.

'Well, sir?'

Mr Haseley swallowed.

'I-I have come to return Miss Burstock's luggage. It was left in the carriage yesterday. You may assure Isab — Miss Burstock that the bandboxes have not been opened.'

'Thank you. I will inform her.'

The tone was dismissive, but Mr Haseley was not to be put off.

'I-I would also like to offer you my apology.'

'The devil you would!'

'Our actions yesterday were foolish, sir, but we were carried away by our affection for each other.' He observed Sir Laurence's look of disbelief and declared, 'It is true! You cannot think that anything other than the deepest passion would make your sister undertake such a ruinous course of action.'

'On the contrary,' retorted Miss Burstock's

fond brother, 'I believe she would do it for the sheer excitement.'

'No, no, Sir Laurence. Isabella was distraught at the thought of hurting you and Lady Burstock. She is very young, of course, and . . . and that is why I felt I must come to offer you my apology. I should not have allowed it. Indeed, the blame for the whole episode is mine.'

Some of the harshness had left Sir Laurence's face and he regarded his guest now with sardonic amusement.

'Do you mean this elopement was your idea? I had rather thought it would be Bella's mad-cap scheme!'

Mr Haseley could not deny it, but he blurted out, 'I should have stopped her!'

'Yes, you should.'

The young man drew a long breath.

'Sir Laurence, if you wish now to demand satisfaction, I admit I was wrong.'

'I have already told you a gentleman does not call out a boy scarce out of short-coats, even if he is a fortune-hunter.'

'That I never was, sir. I love Isabella for herself.'

'And what, pray did you intend to live on once you were married?'

'I don't know,' came the frank reply. 'I was hoping that Papa might still buy me a commission — ' He was interrupted by Sir Laurence, who threw back his head and laughed out loud at that.

'Oh my God. I cannot see Bella following the drum.'

'No, she was not at all happy with the idea but she said she would try it, if it would make me happy.'

Sir Laurence regarded him with interest.

'She said that, did she? She would not last a month.'

The young man did not reply. They seemed to have strayed some way from the purpose of his visit, which had been to offer a stiff apology for his outrageous conduct.

'Well, is that it?' demanded Sir Laurence. 'Have you said all you came to say to me?'

'Yes, sir. Except, yesterday you laid the blame at my cousin's door. She knew nothing of our plans.'

'So I understand.'

'She was dead-set against the elopement, and looking back, I can see now that she tried to slow us down at every turn. At the time I thought she was being devilish attentive to Bella, who is a poor traveller — but you already know that, sir. No, she insisted we stop when Bella was feeling poorly, and at Purley, she encouraged her to lie down and rest, rather than push on to London.'

'I suppose she knew I would catch up with you at some stage.'

'But it beats me how you found us so quickly, sir.'

'Mainly because Bella left a note.'

'Oh, yes, the note.' Mr Haseley shook his head. 'Damme if I know why women feel it necessary to write and tell people everything!'

Sir Laurence had taken out his snuffbox and flicked up the lid. He said grimly, 'You should thank God she *did* leave one, young man. If I had not discovered you the same day, I would have been obliged to kill you.'

Charles swallowed. 'I suppose you think me a blackguard.'

'No, merely a foolish youth who has allowed himself to be carried away by a pretty face. Don't look so downcast, boy. You are not the first young man to have made a fool of himself over a woman.' Sir Laurence helped himself to a pinch of snuff. 'What do you do now?'

'I am leaving for Wiltshire today. I suppose I must finish my studies.'

'What about a commission?'

Charles shrugged, a frown clouding his fair brow.

'M'father insists that I finish at Oxford first, although when he learns of this episode . . .'

Sir Laurence put away his snuffbox and walked over to the writing-desk, where he took up a visiting card and scribbled a note on the back.

'Here. Give this to your father. If he would like to write to me when he thinks you are ready, I will put him in touch with my own regiment, the 12th Light Dragoons ... I should think that would suit you?'

Mr Haseley blinked and stared at him, the colour flooding to his cheeks then ebbing away again as he took the card.

'S-suit me! Aye, aye it would! Th-thank you, sir! But ... but why? After all that has happened!'

Sir Laurence shrugged. He walked to the door.

'Your actions were those of a foolish and headstrong young puppy, but it took courage to come here and face me today. Besides,' he added, his eyes glinting, 'this might give you something to think of other than my minx of a sister.'

'Yes, I mean — th-thank you, sir!' stammered Mr Haseley, clutching the card tightly in his hand. 'I-I don't know what else to say.'

'Then say nothing. Go home and make your peace with your parents, then if you seriously wish to pay court to Bella you had best come and stay with us at Oakford and do the thing properly, though I warn you that Bella is likely to lose all interest in you if she thinks I will not oppose the match.'

Mr Haseley, feeling that the world had suddenly gone mad, could only stare at his host and mutter a few inarticulate words as Sir Laurence rang for a footman to show him out.

★　★　★

Once Mr Haseley had left the house, Sir Laurence returned to the morning-room, where Isabella immediately pounced upon him.

'Well, what has happened — Laurence, you have not hurt him?'

'Hurt him? No, not at all. Why should you think that?'

His sister eyed him doubtfully. 'But yesterday you said — '

'He came to return your bandboxes, Bella, nothing more. I have had them taken up to your room.'

'Then — he is gone?'

'Yes. I believe he is leaving Brighton today.'

'You — you did not quarrel with him?'

'Quarrel? No, I believe it was a most civilized meeting. He offered me an apology, which I accepted, and that was the end of the matter.' Two pairs of dark eyes were fixed on him in wonder and he continued smoothly, 'Young Haseley is a pleasant enough young man. I have no doubt that in a few years he will make a very fine soldier.'

Miss Burstock gave a little shriek.

'Laurence, you did not encourage him to join up? Oh good heavens, he will be killed.'

'Do not be so foolish, Bella. He will not obtain his commission this year at least, though if this dashed affair goes ill with us we shall need a good many more soldiers.'

Lady Burstock waved her hand towards the newspaper she had been reading.

'The reports are not good, my dear.'

'No, but they are unreliable. I am going to London to find out more accurate news, if I can.' He looked at his sister. 'Thanks to young Haseley's visit I am going to be damnably late and shall not be able to return this evening — can I trust you to look after Mama?'

Isabella flushed.

'I shall not fail you, Laurence,' she said quietly. 'You have my word upon it.'

★ ★ ★

Sir Laurence set off for London in a sombre mood. His groom was perched up behind him in the curricle, but Judd knew his master too well to disturb him with idle chatter and maintained a stony silence for the greater part of the journey. Sir Laurence kept his eyes on the road, but his thoughts ran over the events of the previous day: anger still burned within him but it was directed mainly at himself. Mr Haseley's visit that morning had dispelled any lingering doubts he had of that young man. He was very young and damnably foolish, but he was no fortune-hunter. One had to admire him for coming to apologize as he did, and for defending his cousin. Laurence frowned: he did not need young Haseley to tell him how wrong he had been. His hands tightened on the reins, causing the bays to check. He corrected immediately, and when the horses had settled back into their stride his thoughts were soon drawn back to that last meeting with Antonia. He had treated her abominably, accusing her of conspiring against him — his damned temper! Even now he could see the way his harsh words had driven the smile from her eyes, destroying that serenity he had come to value so much.

'Damnation, what a fool I've been!' he muttered, his hands again tugging at the reins and causing the soft-mouthed bays to break their step, bringing a stern admonition from his tiger.

'Don't fret, Judd,' he growled, 'it was merely a loss of concentration.'

'Aye, well, that's not at all like you, master,' retorted that worthy, shaking his head, 'I've never known you to lose your touch, even when you was cup-sodden.'

'And I've not lost my touch now, damn you.'

The groom sank once more into silence, only his occasional frowning glance at his master betraying any anxiety. He was forced to remonstrate again when they reached Kennington where, instead of bearing left at the turnpike, Sir Laurence carried straight on.

'Sir, you've missed the turning. Surely you'll be wanting to go through Lambeth to Westminster Bridge.'

'Not tonight, Judd. I shall cross at London Bridge — I want to stop in Gracechurch Street before we go into Town.'

Judd looked perplexed, but his years of service had taught him the futility of arguing with his master and instead he folded his arms and sat back in a disapproving silence which Sir Laurence completely failed to notice.

★ ★ ★

The Spread Eagle was as busy as ever and there was nothing unusual in the sight of a solitary young female waiting for the Bath mail. Miss Venn handed her luggage to the landlord and asked him how long it would be before the mail departed. The landlord consulted his watch.

'Oh, an hour yet, miss. Perhaps you would like to step inside and take some refreshment while you wait?'

'Yes, thank you. A little coffee and bread and butter would be welcome.'

He showed her to the parlour before going off to fetch her coffee. There were only four travellers in the room beside herself: an anxious-looking woman and her daughter, a kindly-faced parson and a rotund gentleman with a fine pair of whiskers and ruddy complexion, but after a glance in her direction as she sat down and a faint nod from the parson, they all ignored her, a situation that suited Antonia's mood per-fectly. She had spent four hours in the coach from Brighton and felt a weariness not altogether resulting from the journey. All she wanted now was to be in Bath, in her own home. She took off her bonnet and placed it on the table beside her. Leaning back, she closed her eyes: her head was pounding and the constant noise from the yard beyond the open window jarred her nerves.

'Your coffee, miss.' The serving-maid hovered anxiously before her with a small tray. 'I'll just put it all down here on the table beside you. There. Is that all, miss, or can I fetch you anything more?'

'Thank you. That is all.'

Antonia had not broken her fast that day and was feeling a little light-headed. She thankfully nibbled at the bread and butter, which made her feel a little better. Then, holding the cup between both her hands, she sipped the hot liquid, lost in her own thoughts.

'Ah, there you are!'

At the sound of the familiar voice she took too large a sip and choked. Looking up, she saw Sir Laurence, the capes of his drab-coloured driving coat spilling from his shoulders and almost filling the doorway.

'Perhaps, Miss Venn, you would allow me a few moments in private?'

Aware of the interested stares of her fellow passengers, Antonia decided it would be best to acquiesce. She put down her cup and walked silently out of the room. He escorted her across the passage to a smaller, private parlour.

'Is this necessary, Sir Laurence?' she asked

coldly. 'There is nothing more you need to say to me.'

'Oh but there is.' He closed the door behind him but did not advance into the room. 'I have to apologize for my behaviour yesterday. My accusations, the intemperate language I used towards you, it was unforgivable.' He paused. 'I was angry when I set out to overtake the runaways but when I discovered *you* were with them — ! I should have listened to you, but my curst temper — I have wronged you, Antonia. All the way to London I could think of nothing else. That is why I have broken my journey to find you, to beg you to forgive me.'

The hope that had been rising within her breast sank again. So he had not come to London solely to find her. She felt bitterly disappointed and took refuge in anger.

'Of course I can forgive you, sir. It is now forgotten. As a matter of fact, I was just thinking how fortunate it is that you have arrived, for I have been reckoning up in my head how much it is that I owe you for my lodging in Brighton.'

'It is not important.'

'And we must not forget my food as well,' She opened her reticule and began to search in it. 'I have only ten guineas on me at present, Sir Laurence, but if you will take that

I will forward you the balance as soon as I reach Bath.'

'I will not take your money, woman!'

'I have no wish to be your debtor, sir.'

'You are not.'

'Then I bid you good day. Pray now, let me pass. The mail will be leaving soon and I do not wish to lose my place.'

He made no attempt to move away from the door.

'Antonia, one thing more.'

'Sir, you have made your sentiments most plain. I am well aware how much you despise me.'

The black brows snapped together.

'Despise you? You have accused me of that before, but it is not so, it could never be. If I have appeared distant it has been because of my circumstances, not yours. My estates are heavily encumbered, my inheritance was already wasted when I came to it.'

As if that would matter to me! she cried inwardly.

He continued, 'I know I can restore my fortunes, given time, but presently I cannot be considered a wealthy man.'

Antonia's mouth felt dry. This was her chance. She must tell him she did not care for his wealth. Her heart hammered painfully against her ribs as she forced herself to speak.

'Sir, your fortune is of no consequence to me.' The words sounded cold, unfeeling, not at all as she had intended. She closed her eyes in despair.

'No, of course not.' He sighed. 'What a fool I have been.'

Outside the window the horses were being harnessed to the mail coach. The driver, tankard in one hand, was watching the proceedings with a critical eye.

'The mail is ready to leave,' she said.

'No doubt you are looking forward to returning to Bath.'

'Of course. There is nothing else for me.' She waited, hoping he would contradict her, but he said nothing. He did not appear to have heard her.

'I remember most of it now,' he muttered. 'Our first meeting. You said then you thought I might be an angel.' He laughed harshly. 'How mistaken you were. More likely you think of me now as a devil come to plague you.'

Through the door she could hear the landlord calling to the passengers to embark. There were only a few minutes left. She put up her chin and looked into that stern dark face that was now so dear to her.

'Better perhaps if we had never met,' she challenged him. He stood silently, not looking at her. Antonia stepped forward, holding out her hand. 'Goodbye, Sir Laurence.'

Remembering their first parting, she wondered if he would repeat his action and kiss her. Perhaps then he would declare that he would not let her go back to Bath, that she must return with him to Brighton. She waited hopefully, but after a long moment he merely bowed and stepped aside, ignoring her outstretched fingers.

'Goodbye, Miss Venn.'

Her heart sank. Hot tears pricked her eyelids but she would not let them fall. With her head high, she walked out to the waiting coach, disconcerting the bewhiskered gentleman who stood aside for her to precede him by muttering, 'Foolish man! Stupid, stupid man!'

★ ★ ★

Sir Laurence climbed back into his curricle and followed the Bath mail out of the yard. His hands snatched at the reins and one of the bays shied nervously, but observing his master's stony countenance, Judd forbore to comment. Sir Laurence brought them through the City streets without mishap and the concentration required to guide the spirited team through the heavy traffic did

327

much to restore his temper, although his mood did not lighten. When they reached the offices of Glossop, Dinting and Edgar, Sir Laurence left his tiger to walk the horses while he went inside. His visit proved very short. Mr Edgar was gone out to see a client, his clerk could not say where or how long he would be but perhaps his lordship would care to wait. Sir Laurence did not care to wait but left a message for Mr Edgar, with instructions that he could be reached at Grillon's Hotel. Judd noted that the frown was engraved even deeper on his master's countenance when he returned to his curricle. He drove to Grillon's where he instructed Judd to stable the horses, curtly informing his loyal servant that he would not be required again that evening. Judd eyed his master with some disapproval, but he knew better than to question his orders, especially when the black mood was upon him, so he took himself off to indulge in a glass or two of blue ruin at the local gin-house.

★ ★ ★

Sir Laurence took a solitary dinner in the hotel. There was no message from his man of business and it was in a mood of deep depression that he set off in the fading light of the June evening for Brooks's in St. James's Street. As he had expected, the talk was all of war, although there was an air of unreality as the members laid bets on a victory for Napoleon with an insouciance that Sir Laurence found repellent. An acquaintance hailed him jovially, offering him odds against Wellington's winning the day. Sir Laurence managed a grim little smile.

'You'd catch cold at that, my friend. I have already wagered my last groat on Wellington. My pockets are well and truly to let.'

As he came out of the card-room he found himself face to face with Sir Rigby Claremont. Remembering their last meeting, Sir Laurence gave him the merest nod, but the older man scarcely noticed his hauteur.

'Bad business this, eh Oakford? The Allies have lost and are even now fleeing Brussels, I hear.'

Sir Laurence stared hard at him. 'Oh? Who told you that?'

'Had it from Grayshott, who heard it from one of his friends in the City.'

Sir Laurence relaxed. 'Another rumour, in fact.'

'Aye, but there's no smoke without fire, my boy. I think we're really in the suds this time. I always thought we were relying far too much on Wellington. But there it is . . . will you not join me in a bottle, sir? We could mayhap drown our sorrows — what say you, m'boy?'

'No, thank you, Sir Rigby. I-er — I have an engagement.'

'Just as you like, my dear sir. I'll wish you good evening.'

Sir Laurence watched him walk away then consulted his watch: eleven o'clock. The night was young yet but despite his depression he had no desire to drink himself into oblivion or try his luck in the card-room. He left the club and stepped out into the street, where the darkness was alleviated by the lighted windows and flaring torches on each side of the wide road. He set off along the street, so lost in his own thoughts that he did not notice the tall figure in the black frock-coat standing in a doorway, enjoying a cigarillo. The gentleman watched Sir Laurence as he approached and hailed him. At first Sir Laurence did not appear to hear him, but upon being called a second time he started and looked up.

'I beg your pardon, Nathan, I did not see you there. My thoughts were elsewhere.'

'So it would appear.' The gentleman gently exhaled a cloud of grey smoke. 'Leg paining you, Oakford?'

'No, I can't claim that as my excuse.' Sir Laurence paused, tapping his cane upon the pavement. 'If you want to know, Nathan, I was thinking what a damnable coil this is. Every report I've heard tells me Wellington is beaten. Yet I was so sure he would win that I told my man to buy into the Funds when everyone was rushing to sell. Today he could not be contacted, so I have had no chance to salvage anything. Added to that — well, let us just say that I'm about as low as I've ever been.'

'That's not like you, my friend.' The sharp black eyes were fixed on Sir Laurence. Not thinking of doing anything foolish, are you, Laurence?'

'What? Oh, end it all, you mean? Good God, no.' He sighed. 'I confess the idea crossed my mind about eighteen months ago, but someone I . . . *once* . . . knew reminded me of my duty, told me how fortunate I was to have my life, when so many had lost theirs.' Sir Laurence laughed, but without humour. 'Ironic that the same person should now be part of this damned coil!' he glanced up at the tall figure in the doorway. 'What of you, Nathan? You are said to have the finest contacts in Europe, what have *you* heard?'

Mr Rothschild laughed gently. He flicked the remains of his cigarillo into the street and laid a friendly hand upon Sir Laurence's shoulder.

'Go home, my friend. Go home and don't give up hope just yet.' He sauntered away, leaving Sir Lawrence to continue his solitary walk along St James's.

The busy thoroughfare seemed unusually quiet, but the lull ended when a dusty chaise and four thundered into view from Piccadilly. The horses were sweating and foam-flecked as they raced along St. James's Street. Sir Laurence instinctively stopped to watch as the coach hurtled towards him. It was followed by a small cavalcade of riders and carriages and behind them a ragged crowd, cheering and shouting. Sir Laurence stared as the coach swept past, two carved and gilded figures hung on poles protruding from its windows. French eagles, captured French eagles! He stepped back to let the mob surge past him, following the coach on to St. James's Square. Windows were thrown up along the street and figures were tumbling out of the houses to join in the celebrations.

'Wellington's done it,' muttered Sir Laurence, leaning back against the wall. 'He's beaten Bonaparte!'

Finale

December 1815

14

The rain coursed down the window of the little sitting-room and dripped disconsolately onto the sill. Sitting at her desk, Antonia's eyes were fixed on the window but she was lost in reverie and saw nothing of the dreary scene. There was a light scratching at the door and Dawkin entered with a lighted taper.

'I thought we should light the candles, madam, seeing as the rain has made it so dark.' Receiving no reply he came into the room, setting the taper to each of the candles and finally taking up the poker and raking the fire until he had coaxed it into a cheerful blaze. 'Miss Chittering is returned, ma'am, and says to tell you that she will be with you directly.' He coughed gently. 'Shall I fetch in the tea tray?'

'What? Oh — oh yes, if you would, Dawkin. Thank you.'

She still did not turn from the window and the butler withdrew. As he walked to the kitchens Dawkin gave a faint sigh. The mistress had changed, she had lost her sparkle. Ever since she had come back from

Brighton he had noticed a difference in the house. She would no longer dance across the hall (which he had deplored, of course) or sing as she went about the house. He missed that more than he cared to admit. Perhaps she was wishful to return to her Society life. After all, it was where she belonged. He had never approved of a young woman setting up her own establishment, it was unnatural. Yet although he had deplored the old master's decision to lease the property, there was no denying that the dancing school had brought the old house alive during the past year.

When Miss Chittering came in she found Antonia sitting by a cheerful fire.

'La, my dear Antonia, what a day. So cold and damp — we were all chilled to the bone at the church.'

'Come and warm yourself by the fire, Beatrice. How went the funeral?'

'Oh my dear, so affecting.' Miss Chittering sank into a chair and stretched her hands to the flames. 'It was a very simple service and Miss Cowan invited us back to her lodgings for a cold collation. Poor woman, She will miss her sister most dreadfully. Of course, there were very few of us there. It was a dismal scene, what with the rain and the chill wind, but Miss Cowan bore it all with such dignity. I vow my heart went out to her;

heaven knows how she will occupy herself now. I did wonder — ' She broke off, casting a speculative look at Miss Venn. 'I wondered whether we might be able to find a little work for her? You will recall she came in to play for me while you were away. Miss Cowan was used to be a teacher, you know, before she set up home with her widowed sister, but with Mrs Norton gone she will have so little to do.'

Antonia sighed and spread her hands.

'Oh Beatrice, if I could — but you know as well as I that we are only just making enough to cover our costs and I cannot afford to pay another person.'

'Oh my dearest, I know it. But perhaps if I could invite her to come along and help occasionally, not for the money, you see, but the occupation. It would do her so much good to have something to do! Her lodging is secure, for I heard Sir Laurence telling her that he would continue to support her.'

Antonia looked up.

'Sir Laurence? Sir Laurence was at the funeral?'

'Why yes, dear. Did I not say? He was at the church when I arrived and accompanied Miss Cowan back to her lodging. From something that was said, I do believe it was he who arranged and paid for the funeral. He has always been so kind to Mrs Norton and her sister.'

Antonia stared into the fire, her fingers pleating and unpleating her handkerchief in her lap.

'Did — how was he?'

'Oh he was very well. There was no sign of the injury to his leg and I heard him assuring Miss Cowan that it rarely bothered him now. He courteously exchanged a few words with me. Dearest Isabella's first season was a success — but of course you know that because she wrote to you herself, did she not? Oh, here is Dawkin with the tea tray. Just what we need on such a dreary day. Thank you, Dawkin. Shall I make it, dear? Now, what was I saying? Oh yes. Isabella, dear child. I understand she and her mama are going to Burstock Hall for Christmas, where Sir Laurence is planning to join them when he has concluded his business in Bath.'

Antonia had told Beatrice nothing of the events leading up to her quitting Brighton and it was with some trepidation that she asked if Sir Laurence had mentioned her name. She tried to sound casual and was grateful that her companion's attention was at that moment given to pouring the tea.

'No, Antonia, I don't think he did. But we spoke for such a short time, you see, and we were discussing poor Miss Cowan's plight. He seemed to feel very much as I do that she would be better for a little employment.'

'Beatrice! You did not suggest to him that we might be able to help her?'

Miss Chittering coloured and began rearranging the tea cups.

'No, no — that is, not exactly.' She handed a cup to Antonia. 'It is merely that I was telling him how much happier *I* had been since coming to Bath to help you and he agreed that something similar might suit poor Miss Cowan. But you must not think he *expects* us to help her,' she added quickly, observing Antonia's look of dismay. 'I had already told him how quiet we have been. Of course we did not expect Miss Burstock to return to Bath, did we, my love? Nor Miss Claremont, of course, because they were both going to Town. But even with the new pupils we have gained, our classes have not grown as we would have liked.'

'Oh heavens, you told him all that?' cried Antonia, jumping up.

'Why yes, my love. There seemed no harm — '

'Oh how I wish you had not told him anything at all!' She found Miss Chittering gazing at her with a mixture of hurt and bewilderment in her eyes and said more gently, 'I would not for the world have him think we are struggling, Beatrice.'

'Well, I am sorry if you do not like it, Antonia, but it was only idle chatter, and there is no harm done, after all . . . '

'No, of course you are right.' Antonia sighed and resumed her seat. 'It does not matter, for I do not suppose we shall ever see him again.' After a brief pause she forced a smile. 'Let us think instead of a much more pleasurable event. My Aunt Haseley arrives here tomorrow. I have given Mrs Widdecombe instructions to prepare the rooms, but perhaps you would check the arrangements for me before she arrives, Beatrice?'

'Of course, my love. Leave it to me! Dear Mrs Haseley, I am so looking forward to seeing her again. And dear Master Charles is coming with her, is he not? I wonder what he has found to amuse him since he left us?'

Antonia met her companion's innocent gaze with a bland smile, but made a mental note to warn Charles to say nothing of Brighton.

★   ★   ★

Antonia was busily engaged with a dancing class when her aunt and cousin arrived the next day. As soon as the lesson was over she

340

hurried to meet them in the drawing-room and was immediately enveloped in a warm embrace by her aunt.

'My dear child, let me look at you. Poor love, you are so pale.'

'Now don't fuss, Aunt, I pray you. If you remember I wrote to tell you I had been laid low with influenza and it has left me a little hagged, nothing more. Charles.' She turned to greet her cousin, holding out her hands to him and staring in admiration as she took in his scarlet regimentals. 'So you have your commission. Well done, my dear.'

He coloured slightly and laughed. 'Thank you, yes. Do you like it? I am now a member of the Prince of Wales' Own! I never really expected anything so grand, but Sir Laurence came to see Papa and explained that he would give me an introduction.'

'He said *what*?'

'Yes, is it not above anything great, Antonia?' declared Mrs Haseley. 'Despite that awful episode in Brighton — and Charles has told me all about that, my love — Sir Laurence made it very clear that he wanted to help Charles. He even offered to buy his commission but my dear Jonas would not entertain such an idea and said that it was a poor thing if he could not afford to fund his own son, but, of course, with Sir Laurence's letters of introduction everything has gone so smoothly.'

'Aye, 'twas mighty good of him, especially when you consider — ' Charles stopped. 'But enough of that. Have you heard from Sir Laurence, Cos?'

She shook her head, saying brightly, 'No. There is no reason why I should do so. I believe he was in Bath yesterday for a funeral, but I have not seen him, and have no expectation of doing so. But let us talk of you, Charles, do you not regret giving up your studies?'

He grinned. 'Not at all. I am off to London in the morning to join the regiment, but I wanted to see you first, to show you my uniform,' he added ingenuously.

'And you look very well in it, Cousin,' she told him, laughing.

'The London coach leaves in the morning from the White Hart. Mama is coming to see me off — I would very much like you to come too, Antonia.'

'I am sorry, my dear, but it is impossible.'

'No doubt you have dancing lessons to conduct,' suggested Mrs Haseley.

'I do, Aunt, but that is not the reason.' Antonia took a seat on the sofa beside her aunt. 'I have another appointment tomorrow morning. You see, some weeks ago I received a letter from the agent informing me that the old gentleman who owns the building wishes to sell when the lease expires at the end of the month and offering me the first option to buy. Unfortunately, that is out of the question, and I had to tell him so. I have this morning received another letter saying that a buyer has been found and he wishes to call on me at ten o'clock tomorrow morning to discuss the future arrangements.'

'Well, that sounds hopeful,' remarked Mrs Haseley. 'At least it would appear that the new owner does not want to turn you out of doors.'

'Perhaps not, but we have the property at a very good rent and if he wishes to increase it, I cannot see that we will be able to stay.' She sighed. 'The worst of it is, Aunt, that I am no longer sure it is what I want to do. The past few weeks I have found it increasingly difficult to maintain an interest.'

Mrs Haseley took her hands.

'Then, my dear, give it up and come home with me. We would be so happy to have you back with us.'

'Thank you, dearest of aunts, but what of the pupils, and what of Beatrice?'

'Oh, there are other dancing schools, my love, and as for Miss Chittering — I've no doubt we can find room for her.'

'Oh that is kind of you, Aunt, but it is not that. Here, you see, Beatrice feels *valuable*. You will be amazed at how happy she is, organizing the younger pupils, keeping the books, virtually running the school. In fact, she leaves me very little to do. I could not take that away from her. No, I must face our new landlord and try if I can persuade him to let us continue on the same terms as before.'

★ ★ ★

A clear sky the following morning heralded a bright winter's day and Antonia rose early to take her leave of her cousin. She stood on the doorstep with Miss Chittering, waving until Charles and his mama were out of sight. Miss Chittering took out her handkerchief and dabbed at her eyes.

'Oh, the dear boy! How handsome he looks in his uniform.'

'Indeed, and so proud. I do hope he will be happy now. Let us hope the army can give some direction to his energies.'

'Oh no doubt of it. But, my dear, come in out of this cold wind. I would not for the world have you contract another chill. We should prepare for the lesson. The girls will be here any moment, you know.'

'I'm afraid you must take the lesson for me

today, Beatrice. I am sorry to ask it of you.'

'No, no, I remember now that our new landlord is calling here, is he not? Now you run along and collect your thoughts, Antonia, and you must not worry about the dancing class. It is no problem for me, I assure you. In fact, I enjoy taking the classes. I never thought I would do so, it seemed so daunting at first, but now, well, I have grown quite used to it. Do you know the name of your visitor? No, well, I do hope he will prove accommodating. We have been so happy here, have we not? And the school *is* a success, even though we shall never be rich. The accounts balance every month and we have made so many friends; I really do think this has been the happiest time of my life.'

'My dear Beatrice, there is not the slightest need to cry. I shall do my best to persuade him to let us remain here at the same advantageous rates.' Her eyes gleamed for a moment. 'That is why I dressed so carefully today in my very best gown, even adding this lace cap to give me a little extra sobriety. I hope he appreciates my efforts.' Miss Chittering's anxious frown did not lift and Antonia put her arms about her. 'My dear, you must not worry. I have no doubt the new owner is a reasonable man and we shall soon come to some amicable arrangement.' Antonia sounded far more confident that she felt, but her words had the desired effect, for Miss Chittering wiped her eyes and went off upstairs to prepare for the first lesson, while Antonia was left to await her visitor. She sat at her desk, going over her accounts once more, double-checking the calculations of what she could afford to pay.

Dawkin scratched on the door. 'Sir Laurence Oakford, ma'am.'

She started up, glancing at the clock. It wanted but five minutes to ten o'clock. What if her new landlord should arrive and find her alone with a man? She was about to instruct Dawkin to say she was not at home when she heard an impatient step outside the door and the next moment Sir Laurence was before her.

★   ★   ★

It was some time before Antonia could command her voice. She had thought often of this moment. She looked at him, taking in every detail. His powerful frame looked even bigger than she remembered, but there was less strain around his eyes. He looked relaxed, assured of his welcome. The thought irritated her.

'I am sure, sir, I do not know what right you have to walk in uninvited,' she told him, as Dawkin withdrew.

'Does that mean I am not welcome?'

'Yes — no! That is, it is not convenient — '

'And what in damnation have you put on your head?'

'Sir?'

'When did you take to wearing a cap? It makes you look decidedly matronly.'

'That is the intention,' she retorted. 'Oh, I wish you would go. I-I am expecting a visitor. The new owner of this house.'

'And you think he would object to my presence?'

'I hardly think it will help my cause.'

Sir Laurence merely grinned at her. 'Then I promise to slip out through the servants' door the moment he arrives.'

She could not prevent a smile. 'Just think of the gossip *that* would occasion.' She sat down, inviting him to do the same: the temptation to keep him with her too great to be resisted. 'I sent your ring to you at Burstock. I hope you received it safely.'

'The diamond? Yes, thank you. But it was unnecessary.'

She put up her chin, stifling a sigh. She owed him nothing now.

'How are Lady Burstock and Isabella?'

'Well, thank you. I am joining them at Burstock this Christmas.'

'Yes, so I understand. You attended Mrs Norton's funeral, I believe?'

He nodded. 'A sad affair, but the poor woman is out of her misery now, although her sister will miss her.'

Remembering Miss Chittering's remarks, Antonia was loath to dwell on the subject. 'Your sister enjoyed her first season?'

'Very much. It was a great success.'

'Naturally. She could not fail to be a hit.'

'She has come from Town with her head full of compliments — there were several suitors for her hand, but she is too young to be thinking of marriage.'

His words brought back unpleasant memories of Brighton and she said hurriedly, 'And your estates, you were planning improvements.'

'Yes. My faith in Wellington was handsomely repaid. You know, I think, that I asked Edgar to buy into the Funds when everyone else was selling out? It was a risk, but once news came through that we had beaten Napoleon the value of my investments soared. It has allowed me to bring forward my plans. Oakford is being refurbished and I am restocking the park with deer. I wish you might see it.'

Aware of the compliment being paid to her, Antonia sought for something to say to cover her confusion.

'And your friend? The colonel who owned the house in Brighton?'

'Monkton? He returned safely, thank God.' After a moment he continued, 'I have also set up a manufactory on my estate in Cheshire, making furniture. Nothing fancy, you understand, just plain, honest goods. There is wood there in abundance, and water power. I have a good man in charge, experienced. He thinks we might even be running at a profit within two years. I employ mainly military men, ex-soldiers; God knows there's enough of 'em, poor devils!'

'I am so glad you are doing something to help them.'

'You once told me it was my duty to do so.'

Antonia coloured. 'I hope I was never so impolite.'

'Is it bad manners to stop a person wallowing in self-pity? I assure you I was very grateful.'

His words warmed her.

'I, too, am grateful, Sir Laurence. I understand you were instrumental in obtaining a commission for my cousin Charles.'

He stood up abruptly and walked to the window.

'Haseley has already thanked me sufficiently on that head. You need not consider yourself beholden to me.'

She hung her head: there had been a small hope that he had acted to obtain her good opinion, but apparently she had been wrong. Sir Laurence was still speaking, his gaze fixed on the rain-streaked window.

'No, I did not come here for your gratitude. When we last met in London, I think we were both . . . overset. I had hoped since then, you might have come to think a little more favourably of me. When I received your ring — '

'The solitaire was never mine to keep. I had never considered it so. And my — my anger has long since died, Sir Laurence. Your apology at our last meeting was sincere and I should have accepted it, had I not been so angry.'

'And with good reason! I had insulted you — heaven knows how often since then I have wished so many things unsaid — but perhaps you would have forgiven more readily if you had known that they were the words of a man in torment.'

Antonia jumped up.

'Pray sir, say no more. I do understand in some measure what you were suffering! Your anxiety over the battle, your sister's behaviour.'

He turned to face her.

'But you have missed the major reason for my distress. I had discovered — to my surprise — that I was very much in love.'

Antonia stopped. She pressed her hands to her hot cheeks. Sir Laurence moved closer.

'I handled it very ill, did I not?' he said, reaching up to take her hands. 'I was so stupidly jealous and I had so little to offer you. Then, when I had treated you so abominably, I thought I had lost all hope of gaining your affection.'

Antonia could not raise her eyes but she said, with difficulty, 'You already had that, sir, if only you had realized it.'

There was a silence. Sir Laurence remained before her, clasping her hands between his own long fingers until Antonia, unable to resist, dared to look up: the ardent glow in his dark eyes made her catch her breath. The next moment he had swept her into his arms and was kissing her ruthlessly. At last he raised his head, but his arms remained tightly around her. Antonia was content to stay there, her head resting on his shoulder. Gazing up into his face she watched the smile turn to a frown.

'Must you wear that damned thing on your head?'

'I beg your pardon?'

'That cap. You have beautiful hair. It should not be hidden by a piece of lace.'

'Oh heavens!' She struggled to free herself from his arms. 'I had almost forgot. He will be here at any moment!'

'Who?'

'The person who has bought the house. That is the reason I am wearing the cap. To make me look more responsible.' She laughed. 'Do you think that is ridiculous? It is, I know, but, to be serious, I *must* make a good impression if I am to keep the house.'

He observed her agitation with amusement.

'Why should you? You can tell him you no longer need the house, that you are going to marry me!'

'Oh no — I can't — '

'What!'

'No, no, of course I will marry you, if you should ask me,' she added, with a momentary gleam of humour. 'But what am I to do about the dancing school? If I close it, what is to become of Beatrice? She has been so happy here, I cannot send her back to live in lonely poverty.' She took a hasty turn about the room, an anguished look upon her face. She said dejectedly, 'Perhaps, perhaps I should not consider marriage . . . '

The amusement left Sir Laurence's eyes.

'Now that, madam, I cannot allow. You will be my wife if I have to carry you to the altar!'

She came to him immediately, her own eyes glowing.

'Yes, I really think you would do that. But — '

'If you are worrying about your companion, do you think she is capable of running the school? With a little help, of course. Perhaps Miss Cowan might consider joining her.'

She stared at him.

'You have already discussed this with Beatrice!'

'Well, not in detail,' he assured her soothingly, 'but to set up these two ladies comfortably in their own establishment would seem an ideal solution.'

'Yes, oh, but what if he will not accept the same terms? The school cannot possibly afford more.'

'You need not worry about that, my love.'

'But I do. I cannot have you funding this venture. I was determined from the outset that I would be self-sufficient in this, so I must ask you to leave, my love, and I will negotiate this myself.' She glanced at the clock. 'Heavens, it is nearly eleven. Why is he so late?'

'Antonia — '

'Oh, what on earth does he mean, keeping me waiting this way?'

'Perhaps, my dear, I should give you this.' Sir Laurence reached inside his coat and pulled out a large paper, folded and tied with a red silk ribbon, secured with a wax seal. 'It is in the nature of ... er ... a wedding present.'

Slowly she broke the seal and opened the document.

'But it is the deeds to a house. *This* house — I don't understand.'

Sir Laurence smiled at her. 'When you returned the ring, my man of business was at Burstock, so I gave it to him to sell and when I heard that a certain house in Queen Square was available ...'

'You — *you* bought my house?'

'Yes.'

'But why?'

'I wanted to ensure no one could take away your independence. I did not know how you would receive me; I was quite prepared for you to dismiss me summarily from your life and if that had been so, the house would have been put into trust, the terms set at the present rate for as long as you required it.

Now, however, I hope that you will accept it. It is yours to do with, as you wish.'

'Do you mean that — that I may continue my dancing school here?'

'If you so desire.'

She hugged the document to her, looking around the room as she tried to come to terms with this revelation. After a long moment she fixed her grey eyes anxiously upon his face.

'Do you truly believe that Beatrice and Miss Cowan could make a success of it?'

'Do you?'

She considered.

'Yes,' she said slowly, 'yes I do. Oh Laurence, can this really be true?'

'Assuredly so, my love.' He watched her as she walked to the window, gazing out into the square.

'I was so sure that this was what I wanted, to be independent, to have control over my life.'

'I will not take that from you, Antonia. I want you to work with me, as a partner, to help me with my plans for the manufactory. I hope next year to be able to provide better housing for the men and their families, perhaps to set up more manufactories, to help as many ex-soldiers as I can — God knows no one else seems to care. I could give you a month or so in London every year, but most of my time would be spent on the estates, overseeing the improvements.' He paused. 'I am not offering you a life of unalloyed luxury, my love: I will expect you to work with me, not be holding court in Town for dozens of admirers — '

'I would never want that!'

He smiled. 'I never thought you would. So — will you be my partner, Antonia? Will you marry me?'

She bit her lip, rapidly blinking away the tears that had suddenly filled her eyes.

'Oh yes,' she whispered. 'Gladly, my love!'

From upstairs came the strains of a pavanne as Miss Chittering continued with the dancing lesson. Sir Laurence held out his hand to Antonia. She took it, returning the pressure of his fingers as he smiled down at her.

'Will you dance, my lady?'

'With you, sir, aye. For the rest of my life.'

We do hope that you have enjoyed reading this large print book.

Did you know that all of our titles are available for purchase?

We publish a wide range of high quality large print books including:
Romances, Mysteries, Classics
General Fiction
Non Fiction and Westerns

Special interest titles available in large print are:
The Little Oxford Dictionary
Music Book
Song Book
Hymn Book
Service Book

Also available from us courtesy of Oxford University Press:
Young Readers' Dictionary
(large print edition)
Young Readers' Thesaurus
(large print edition)

For further information or a free brochure, please contact us at:
Ulverscroft Large Print Books Ltd.,
The Green, Bradgate Road, Anstey,
Leicester, LE7 7FU, England.
Tel: (00 44) 0116 236 4325
Fax: (00 44) 0116 234 0205

Other titles published by
The House of Ulverscroft:

A LADY AT MIDNIGHT

Melinda Hammond

When Amelia Langridge accepts an invitation to stay in London as companion to Camilla Strickland, it is to enjoy herself before settling down as the wife of dependable Edmund Crannock. Camilla's intention is to capture a rich husband, and her mother is happy to allow Amelia to remain in the background. Camilla attracts the attention of Earl Rossleigh, but the earl is intent on a much more dangerous quarry, and it is Amelia who finds herself caught up in his tangled affairs ... A merry dance through the Georgian world of duels, sparkling romance and adventure.

THE HIGHCLOUGH LADY

Melinda Hammond

Governess Verity Shore longs for a little adventure, but when Rafe Bannerman arrives to carry her off to Highclough she soon discovers that life can be a little too exciting! An estate on the edge of the wild Yorkshire Moors, Highclough is Verity's inheritance, but the land is coveted, not only by her handsome cousin Luke but also by Rafe. With her very life in danger, whom can she trust?

AUTUMN BRIDE

Melinda Hammond

When Major Lagallan suggests to Miss Caroline Hetton that she should marry his young brother, she can hardly believe her good fortune, and at first sight Vivyan Lagallan seems to be the perfect bridegroom; young, charming and exceedingly handsome. Yet upon closer acquaintance, Caroline is disturbed by his wild restless spirit, and discovers that he has a taste for excitement that eventually endangers not only his life, but hers, too.